STONE COLD
Liar

Also by Noire

The Misadventures of Mink LaRue Series
Natural Born Liar
Sexy Little Liar
Dirty Rotten Liar
Red Hot Liar

Lifestyles of the Rich and Shameless (with Kiki Swinson)

Maneater (with Mary B. Morrison)

STONE COLD Liar

The Misadventures of Mink LaRue

NOIRE

KENSINGTON PUBLISHING CORP.
www.kensingtonbooks.com

DAFINA BOOKS are published by

Kensington Publishing Corp.
119 West 40th Street
New York, NY 10018

ISBN-13: 978-1-61773-495-3
ISBN-10: 1-61773-495-0
First Kensington Trade Paperback Printing: September 2015

eISBN-13: 978-1-61773-496-0
eISBN-10: 1-61773-496-9
First Kensington Electronic Edition: September 2015

10 9 8 7 6 5 4 3 2 1

Printed in the United States of America

This latest misadventure of Mink LaRue is dedicated to the readers who have been hanging with me for the whole damn ride! Through the ups and the downs, the triumphs and the trials, you've waited anxiously for each book to drop and loved my stories and my characters from the beginning to the end. I've given you different flows and different flavors, and nothing less than absolute quality writing in every single book, and you've rewarded me with your loyalty and your hunger for more. I keep saying it over and over again and I'll never get tired of telling you: I've got the best readers in the whole damn game because y'all #DemandQuality every time you jump on this urban erotic train. Chooo Chooo! Muahh :))) I lub y'all!

Acknowledgments

I give my thanks and love to God for blessing me with an original voice and a creative mind during a time when readers are fed up with stories in the market that are beginning to all sound the same. When my name is on the cover there is never any doubt that my works are pure, original creations from my own fire pen, which is what every reader wants and deserves to receive when they buy a book. Big thanks are going out to Nisaa, who has been through so much over the last two years but still finds time to put up with her silly sissy and continue to be my best friend. Thank you to my Boo, who I now know that I just can't live without, and the beautiful little mini-me that we created from our love. Black, Reem, Man, Missy, Ree, Jay, and my entire UET team, I thank you for ten solid years of support and for all the little things you do behind the scenes to help make what I do a big success. Big ups to my Urban Erotic Tales Book Club fam, and all my loyal readers and friends. I see you, Reem Raw, on that Empire State of Minez! and I encourage all my readers to check out the fire in his pen! Now do what you came to do! Let's get at con-mami Mink LaRue!

Muah:)))
Noire

WARNING!

This here ain't no romance
It's an Urban Erotic Tale,
Dy-Nasty's on lockdown and she's begging for some bail!
Selah's on a mission to get back her wedding ring,
While someone shot poor Viceroy and nobody saw a thing!
Mink is getting stalked by her psycho killer ex,
While Barron's getting played by Miss GiGi Molinex!
Blackmails, kidnaps, dirty schemes, the Dominions are under fire,
Let's see who spins the biggest tale in this stone cold crew of liars!

CHAPTER 1

Just when I thought my slick Harlem hustle was a wrap and it was time to worm my way back into the rotten core of the Big Apple, life hit the pause button and put the track on rewind so I could back my grind up and get it pumping all over again! No pain, no *mothafuckin'* gain was the song floating around in my head as me and Big Suge got buck-naked and alligator-wrestled around in his big ol' bed.

"Yeah, right there, Big Poppa!" I moaned as he licked my cinnamon nipples then flipped me over so he could hit it up from the back. He slapped my right ass-cheek with his big old bronco-busting hands and hot sparks shot straight through my coochie as my booty jiggled in his palm.

Suge was packin' man-meat by the truckload and I arched my back and presented him with my very best gift. He slid his thick fingers from my clit up to my spine, then aimed the head of his monster dick at my spot and got to digging me out like he was on his way to China.

We fucked like two long-lost lovers who hadn't seen each other in years, and there was way more than just some regular sex going on between us in that bed.

"Fuck was you going?" Suge growled as he gripped my ass and dug me out like we were in a big bang contest. "You was tryna leave me, Mink? Huh? You was fuckin' tryna leave me?"

"Hell no!" I screeched, arching my back and clenching my booty cheeks as he bucked his hips and deep-drilled the hell outta me. Run back to New York and leave all this Southern-style black snake back in Texas? Sheeiit. My legs were gapped open wide, ass pointing at the ceiling as slobber ran outta my mouth and dripped from my chin. "I wasn't going no damn where!" I babbled like a mothafucka. "I swear to God I wasn't!"

Suge amped shit up about ten notches as he rammed his big dick up in my guts hard enough to make my throat sore.

"Oooh, goddamn!" I shrieked, spreading my legs wider and taking that meat like a natural pro. "Goddamn, goddamn, goddamn!"

"This is it right here," Suge grunted behind me as he bucked his hips and got all up in my na-na. "Work that booty, baby!"

Fifteen minutes later I had nutted twice and was purring like a kitten as I slobbered all over Suge's arm. I felt real damn lucky to be in his bed and back on his good side because some kinda way in the midst of all my schemes and ganks, shit had gone wrong, wrong, *wrong* for me down in the Great State of Texas and my boo-thang Suge had gotten *sick* of my ass!

I mean he had shut me and my drama all the way down when I got in my feelings and started acting real ill in front of one of his ex-girlfriends.

You ain't stupid but you jealous as fuck and you're insecure too, and when you fuckin' with a nigga like me that's even worse.

He had that shit right too because for the first time in my life Mink Minaj was *jealous!* That's right. Me, Harlem's number one stunna was salty over some other chick and walking around with my ass on my shoulders! I couldn't stand watching her thirsty ass throw them moves down on my boo, so I had decided to cut my losses and put a padlock on my heart.

I had been on my way to the airport planning to get the hell outta Dodge, and I'd asked the limo driver to slide me over to Suge's crib so I could say one last good-bye. Suge had stood in his doorway looking like a big scoop of chocolate chip ice cream and eyeballing me as warm Texas rain beat down in buckets between us.

I can't even lie, my lil hoodrat heart-string had snapped in half when he backed up and closed his door in my face, and I had just told my driver to leave when the door opened again and Big Suge walked outside in that thunderstorm and scooped me up from the back of the fancy whip. And now we were upstairs chillin' like a mothafucka after having the kind of wild makeup sex that could set the sheets on fire and burn the whole damn house down.

It was hard to believe that so much had changed in my life in such a short period of time. Me and my girl Bowlegged Bunni Baines had come to Texas looking to turn a quick dollar and we had ended up knee-deep in a family full of billionaires. With dollar signs in our eyes, us two lil Harlem pole scrippers had messed around and found ourselves getting caught up in one crazy misadventure after the next, and we had worked our shady game until our pockets were full and swole.

But life as a hood-rich oil socialite wasn't crackin' up to be everything that I needed it to be. Between my hating-ass adopted brother Barron, my ratchet-ass identical twin, Dy-Nasty, and trying to come to terms with the fact that my mama had fed me a big-ass lie for my entire life, I got blindsided and smacked with a dose of reality that took me right down to the mat. And when my uncle-bae boo Suge got fed and blasted me outta the water for talking shit to his banana-shaped Asian ex-girlfriend who had a big-shot lawyer's degree, I was ready to blow my top.

It was all too much, even for a tough ghetto slicksta like me, and when it was all said and done Mizz Mink was left in

her feelings and looking stupid in the face. Without telling a
soul, I had decided that it was time to bounce up outta the
dirty South and head back into more familiar beat-ass terri-
tory, so I called my welfare-queen ghetto-fabulous Granny up
in Harlem to tell her I was coming home! But before I could
get the words outta my mouth good, her trifling ass was hitting
me up for some cash.

"Look, I got a real important bill to pay, Mink. Be a good
girl and send your old Granny a couple of dollars before you
get on that airplane, okay darling?"

"But I'm getting up outta here tonight, Granny. I'll pay the
bill for you as soon as I get home, okay? The plane ride is only
a few hours long."

"But what if it crash?"

Bill my ass. Granny was slick as motor oil and she was a
big-ass liar too. If I sent her some money I knew she was just
gonna shop it up and drink it up, but I got on the computer
and went ahead and sent her some ends anyway.

"Mink!" Granny had called me thirty minutes later from
Western Union. "Two thousand dollars? Where you get all this
money from, baby?" she wanted to know. "You ain't down
south slangin' no dope, now is you?"

Uh-uh. I wasn't about to tell nan'one of those lying-ass
LaRues that I had lucked up on a million-dollar fortune.
Them trifling yellow fuckas woulda rolled up on the mansion
ready to tie the whole family up and shake us down. Instead, I
lied and told Granny that I had hit the number for a nice hunk
of change, and that I had just felt like sliding a couple of racks
to her.

Still in my feelings, I had told Granny to go ahead and tear
Aunt Bibby off a few dollars too. Not too much, just a few. I
was still kinda salty with my aunt for not telling me the truth
about the lie I'd been living sooner, but I was also grateful that
she confirmed that not every damn thing Mama had told me
was a lie. I might not'a been Jude Jackson's real daughter, but I

would always be Moe LaRue's child, and even though I would never forget how Mama had driven me into the cold-ass Hudson River and tried to kill me, I still loved her. Faults and all.

Besides, I was raised to be the loyal type, and even though Aunt Bibby said I was stupid for doing it, I had bought Jude Jackson a beautiful headstone for her grave that simply said, "Mama."

Truth be told, I would prolly never understand why I had been abandoned by my real mother, but now that I had been through a lil something with a man myself, I could see how a weak-minded woman could let a dude knock her off her square. But life has a way of pulling its own little ganks on you. And now, as I laid in Suge's bed sweaty and fucked out, I put all thoughts of Granny, Mama, and everybody else outta my mind. The only thing I had on the brain right now was taking me a lil nap, then waking up next to my man and going in for round number two so Suge could come at me again and bang my lights out.

Completely out!

CHAPTER 2

Election night had the whole city buzzing, and even though all the votes hadn't been tallied yet, Rodney Ruddman's cocky ass was sitting in his office at the Omni Hotel doing lines and feeling just like a winner.

As with the other candidates, this wasn't a money thing for him at all. Hell naw. Ruddman was the CEO of the multi-billion-dollar corporation Ruddman Energy. He was an oil baller and had plenty of cash, but what he was lusting for was the vast amount of power and control he would have at his fingertips if he won the race for chairman of the Texas Railroad Commission. Putting his name on that position would give him the ability to make suckers like Viceroy Dominion get down on his crusty knees and kiss his fucking ring. Or face his fucking wrath.

Ruddman had dressed up nicely for the occasion tonight by stuffing his bulging stomach into a black and white tuxedo made from the finest fabric that money could buy. His shoes had been specially made for his wide, flat feet, and the uber-expensive watch on his wrist was one of only three like it in the whole world.

He ran his hand over his face, wiping away traces of white powder from his nose as he prepared to return downstairs to the media room where an election-watch party was being held in his honor by his donors and supporters. He had slipped away and come upstairs alone to get his head right, and it wouldn't be long before his staff noticed his absence and came looking for him. Ruddman glanced at the wide-screen television screen that sat before him. Right now the race was a tie between him and that bastard Viceroy Dominion, but with several precincts still out he genuinely felt like he could pull in the win.

Ruddman clicked off the television then leaned over the small silver tray on his desk and snorted his last line of white powder. As much as he would have liked to kick back and enjoy the thrill of his victory by himself, it was time to go downstairs and rejoin his campaign team. He wiped at his nose again, then reached inside a drawer and retrieved a crystal decanter, then poured himself a stiff one in his favorite glass, sipping from it as he walked toward the foyer. Feeling lifted and humming a tune, he had just stepped out of his office when a young thug wearing a black hooded sweatshirt slammed a fist in his chest and drove him backward as he bum-rushed the shit outta him.

"Fuck you going, old man? Get your black ass back in there!" the young thug barked, muscling Ruddman backward and shoving him against the reception desk.

"What in the world?" Ruddman muttered as he tumbled backward in panic. "What the hell is going on here?"

The young thug slid his hood off his head revealing his face, and at the same time he reached around and withdrew a glistening silver pistol from the small of his back.

"Surprise, surprise, you lying muthafucka!" Zeke Washington growled as he aimed a chrome Smith and Wesson gat straight at Ruddman's thick neck.

"Zeke? What the hell are you doing, son?" Ruddman

barked in disbelief as he raised his short T-rex arms in the air. "You come your ass in here pulling a goddamn gun on me after the way I looked out for you? I thought we had a deal?"

"*We* had a deal, but *your* ass lied!" Zeke snarled.

"What the hell did I lie about?" Ruddman sounded like a cowardly lion who was about to shit up his five-thousand-dollar tuxedo.

"I know all about you and your slick fuckin' deals, Ruddman. You was quick to drop a dime on Viceroy's shit, but according to dat shiesty nigga Wally Su you was sliding him some big lettuce leafs under the table to forge legal documents too!"

"I was not!" Ruddman bellowed, swelling up all indignant and shit.

"Bullshit!" Zeke barked on him. "I seen copies of the old checks, my nigga! They came from your company and had your fuckin' signature on 'em! Fuck with me and I'll have them shits sent to the goddamn newspapers! You was down for the whole ride, you fat muthafucka! Them same bitches who took my father down are the ones who helped you get filthy fuckin' rich too!"

"So *what?*" Ruddman barked, feeling himself. "Every goddamn body was scraping and scrambling back then! This is a dog-eat-dog business, it's just that your father couldn't bite hard enough or chew fast enough! But I told you how to get his money back! If you had just did what the fuck I said then you and your mother could be sitting pretty right now because I gave you an instruction manual on what to do!"

Zeke gun-checked him. "You told me that Viceroy wasn't gonna live long enough to see this fuckin' election, and not only is that muthafucka still here, he's about to fuckin' win it! You was way off base with this whole damn setup! That bastard don't care that I got my father's papers! His ass ain't scared to go to court! That grimy fucka told me he was gonna give me an important job with his company and then tried to stick me in the goddamn mailroom!"

Ruddman frowned. The mailroom was exactly where he would have put the kid too.

"Look, Zeke, what the fuck are you *really* doing here?" Ruddman asked quietly, a cunning and deadly glint emanating from his beady eyes. "If you're going to rat me out over those old bribes to Wally Su, then why haven't you taken your story to the airwaves and sold it to the highest bidder yet? And if you have a problem with how Viceroy ass-fucked your daddy, then why aren't you over at his place waving a gun up under his goddamn nose?"

"Oh, don't worry my nigga," Zeke barked. "I came to blast a hole in your grill first, but Viceroy's black ass is on deck next!"

"But why do you want to shoot me? Yeah, I admit it. I knew what was going down back then and I made a lot of money behind it. But what the fuck did I do to *you?*"

"Don't play stupid, nigga. All this shit was your fault from the gate," Zeke accused. "You came at me like this shit was a sure-shot and I was gonna get paid. You was just tryna use me so you could get some play off Viceroy, but you fucked up, homey! I ain't my daddy. Don't nobody ride my dick for free! You shoulda known better than to underestimate a hungry nigga with dust in his pockets and nothing to lose."

"But—"

"Shut the fuck up and turn on a TV up in this bitch," Zeke snapped.

Ruddman led the boy back to his office and did as he was told. The local news was predicting that almost fifty percent of the precincts were reporting and the race was still a dead heat.

"Don't worry, Zeke, this situation will take care of itself," Ruddman said. "You don't wanna do anything drastic that you'll end up regretting later on. Believe me, I wanna smash Viceroy just as bad as you do."

"Nah, nigga," Zeke cocked his pistol as a wave of anger rushed over his heart. "That's where you're wrong. Your fam wasn't jerked out of millions of dollars and an oil empire, muh'fucka. *Minez* was. You didn't have to watch other people living the life that was meant for you. *I* did. You just can't make bullshit promises to a nigga like me and then don't keep them! I don't give a fuck which one of y'all rich bastards wins this election. All I'm tryna do is even the score for my daddy, and as far as I'm concerned, both of y'all grimy muthafuckas gotta go!"

CHAPTER 3

It was a warm breezy night, but GiGi Molinex had put the top down on the oil-black Maserati anyway. The radio was blasting Katy Perry's "Last Friday Night," and GiGi was murdering that shit, singing off-key at the top of her lungs as she sped down the highway with the wind whipping through her fiery-red hair.

On her right, her chocolate-bunny boo-thang Barron was chilling beside her in the passenger seat of his own whip. He looked shook in the face and tight in the ass, but GiGi kept right on singing because she didn't give a damn. After a whirl-wind romance where she had worked her way into his head and lured him into her honey trap with her superior sex game, the ebony and ivory love birds were sneaking out of Texas together and riding off to parts unknown. Or at least unknown to one of them.

"You okay?" she yelled at him above the music and the sound of the wind.

He nodded grimly and GiGi smiled inside. This jungle-fever-having mark had been all in her face and hanging off her bra strap for weeks, and now that their little Texas two-step was about to become a permanent hustle his mug was twisted like he was having second thoughts. GiGi jerked the steering to the right and peeled off into an exit lane and shot up the ramp. Her tires squealed as she braked at a traffic light, and Barron seized the moment to break his silence.

"Yo," he said, turning down the music as he faced her. "Exactly what type of party are we going to again?"

GiGi almost sneered, but she caught herself and plastered on her winning smile. *This shook motherfucker,* she thought bitterly. She wasn't feeling that bitch-tremble in his voice and that uncertain look on his face was not cute either. In fact it was ugly as hell and it made him look soft and weak.

"What do you mean what type of party?" she said brightly in her best chipper-little-white-girl voice. "It's a party-party, but does it even matter? Let's just hang out and have a little fun tonight!"

Barron shrugged. "I'm down to hang out, but I'm just saying. It must be a pretty decent spread if it's on this side of town."

GiGi giggled inside. This idiot-ass multi-billionaire was about to get nice and fucked up. Barron was a gold-digging white woman's dream, and after laying her smooth pussy game down on him it hadn't taken much convincing to get him to turn his back on his family and align himself with her. With his father pissing him off left and right and making him feel like a dumbnut, convincing Barron to blow Dallas and ride shotgun across the state line with her had been a pretty small feat.

"Of course it's a nice spread. I told you I'm taking you to meet one of my good friends, and all of my friends are prosperous," GiGi responded as she pumped the gas pedal and revved the engine. "Tess throws the most epic parties in the state of Texas, and tonight is going to be major."

"Well, you know the election is being held tonight," Barron said quietly. "Since I can't be at the watch party with the rest of my family I wanna try to catch the coverage on television. My pops seems to think he has a good shot at winning this thing."

"*Tah!*" GiGi flicked her manicured hand at him and rolled her eyes as she turned the music up again and hit the gas. "Goodness gracious. For once can you forget about your *father*, Barron? I mean, I'm getting sick of hearing about that ancient old dude. Didn't you tell me you wanted to blow this shitty gig and be your own man? That's why we agreed to take this journey together in the first place, remember? Besides, you're tired of your father treating you like a little flunky, aren't you? He doesn't appreciate you! It's time for you to start living your life for yourself, Barron, and the first step is to get turnt up at Tess's party tonight. Just look at it like a farewell bash. We're about to say *adios* to all your old drama and *hola!* to a life that's exciting and new!"

GiGi was laying her smooth-tongue hustle down on him nice and thick, but she could still see the worry-wheels turning around and around in Barron's head. She sucked her teeth in disgust. This motherfucker was a mama's boy down to the bone. He loved his family and carried their problems on his shoulders. But fortunately he loved him some white pussy too, so while he was sitting there swimming all in his feelings, it was GiGi's prediction that it would just take a little more coaxing to make him come around and do whatever she wanted.

"Yeah, I guess you're right," Barron finally said as she rounded the corner and nosed the whip down a private, tree-lined driveway. There were Porsches, Bentleys, Mercedes, and Puegots, and GiGi parked his whip among them haphazardly, blocking a few in.

"Yeah," Barron said, loosening up. "Fuck it, baby. I'm done with all that old drama. I'm young and I'm doing my thing. I'll be a'ight. Fuck it."

"That's right, baby!" GiGi agreed as she smiled and reached over to caress the rock-hard muscle in his upper thigh. "Just kick back and let your afro grow out for the night, okay? You work very hard and you deserve it. Trust me, this party is going to be *so* turnt up! Forget watching some boring election on television. If your father wins, then he wins. If he loses, he loses. Either way, you can read about that shit in the newspaper tomorrow."

GiGi was grinning as she reached over and placed her hand on Barron's belt buckle. She slid her palm down to the lump in his crotch and felt his dick leap like a bolt of lightning had shot through it. Her fingers were soft and deft and she had no shame at all as she got him unbuckled and zipped down, and freed his warm, erect bone from the confines of his white drawers.

"Yo, ain't you gonna put the top up first?" Barron moaned as she gripped his meat and pumped it expertly in her small fist.

"Hell no," GiGi said coyly. "I believe in free love and I don't have a damn thing to hide." She giggled as she leaned over and lowered her wet lips toward the crown of his bone. She gave it two hot licks and then paused and asked, "Are you sure you don't want to go someplace and find a television to watch?"

"Nah," Barron moaned, palming the back of her head and pushing her face lower as he leaned back and got ready to enjoy him some nice wet brain. "I'm straight, baby. Fuck that TV."

"Good," GiGi said, diving down with her mouth wide open and ready to suck the meat off his stiff chocolate bone. "Because the only thing you need to be thinking about watching tonight is *me.*"

Ten minutes later GiGi had blown Barron into heaven and emptied his nutsack by giving him some of the best neck pussy he had ever received. She had scooped his warm nuts into her palm and bathed them lovingly with her soft pink tongue while jacking the shaft of his dick in a grip so tight it almost hurt. Barron had screeched like a bitch when he blew his load into the confines of her steaming hot mouth, and his whole body trembled as GiGi slurped the crown of his dick and milked every last drop of liquid sugar from his balls like she was sucking from a straw. By the time she came up for air and licked her red, swollen lips, the party crowd had thickened outside the huge house and the driveway was packed full of even more expensive cars.

Loud music could be heard blasting from inside the house and a few drunk dudes had come outside to laugh hysterically and talk silly white-boy shit in the front courtyard. GiGi and Barron exited their whip and she took his hand as they walked straight up in the spot and were greeted by a wild-ass scene.

White folks were packed in the joint wall-to-wall, dancing, jumping around like idiots, and slurping brew out of large wooden kegs. It reminded Barron of a wild frat party, but in a huge, expensive crib.

GiGi flitted around air-kissing the cheeks of people that she knew, and Barron hung right at her side as they maneuvered through the crowd. After getting elbowed and bumped and jostled by a bunch of sweaty blond freaks, GiGi finally found Tess, the hostess of the party, and introduced her to Barron.

"Hey B-Dawg, nice to meet you," Tess said as her eyeballs rolled around in her head and she showed her teeth. The girl was fucked up and she didn't mind admitting it.

"Look, I'm rolling hard right now but I don't mind sharing, so please help yourselves to whatever you want. There's plenty of liquor, molly, weed, horse, and ecstasy floating around. Dig in and get busy with whatever floats your boat."

GiGi and Tess made a quick business transaction and GiGi stuffed a small package down in her purse. Barron wasn't feeling all the hardcore street-drugs, but he played it loose because he didn't want to ruin the party for GiGi. He still hadn't recovered from that crazy-horrible night at his own frat party when some stupid muthafucka had slipped some hot shit in his drink and got him all fucked up. As hard as he tried, he couldn't shake the flashbacks or the memory of those photos that somebody had snapped of his lips all up on some stray nigga's dick, or that fuggly-ass mugshot he had taken with his eyebrows shaved off and his lashes all mascaraed up and lipstick plastered all over his mouth. Nah, fuck all that. These white fiends could keep their mind-altering psychotic drugs. Barron was gonna stick to beer and a little bit of weed tonight.

GiGi snuck a quick glance at Barron out the corner of her eye. She was the type of chick who knew men. She could read their asses like a book, and right now her instincts were telling her that Barron was going to be a problem. Unless she got something on him and got him where she wanted him first.

Smiling, she led him to a sitting area off the kitchen area, which was less crowded and a lot less noisy. Ignoring the par-tygoers in the room, they got comfortable on a soft leather couch and GiGi pulled two paper plane joints out of her purse and set them on a low coffee table. To the unsuspecting eye the joints looked identical. But GiGi knew very well that one was packed with sticky green, and the other contained some highly potent weed that had been laced with a nice amount of PCP.

"I know the last few weeks have been really tough for you," GiGi said soothingly as she scooted closer to Barron and crawled into his lap. "And even after that bomb blow job I gave you, I can tell you're still just a little bit antsy."

"Here," she said, smiling brightly as she passed him the laced joint. "Hit this baby up and kick back with me. We'll chill in here for a while, then get out there on the dance floor and work off some tension whenever you feel up to it. And really, if you're not having any fun in, say, thirty minutes or so, then we don't have to stay. We can go someplace else and celebrate our freedom. Let's just play it by ear, okay?"

Barron smiled at his boo and lit up the rollie. Him and GiGi made small talk and laughed at a couple of cats who were playing beer pong loudly in the corner. They were clearly flagged and didn't care who was winning. They were just down-ing beer for the fuck of it. It didn't take long for Barron to feel the effects of the PCP. Beads of sweat popped out on his fore-head and he unbuttoned the neck of his polo shirt.

"Are you okay?" GiGi asked as she fanned him with her hand. "You ready to go work up a little sweat on the dance floor?"

"Yeah," Barron responded slowly as he wiped the back of his hand over his forehead. "I'm high as fuck and I need to move around a little bit. Let's do it."

The music was bumping as GiGi walked behind Barron and watched him stumble toward the main room. A sea of spaced-out faces and half-naked bodies soaked in sweat were dancing to M.G.K. and Barron jumped right in the mix and closed his eyes and started nodding his head vigorously to the beat. GiGi giggled under her breath as she continued to watch him. He was getting amped as fuck as the powerful drugs coursed through his bloodstream and played with his mind. It wasn't long before Barron was gripped in a dusty haze. He had worked up a full sweat and he started flinging his arms and wildly twisting in circles. GiGi giggled as she stepped back a little and grooved from a distance. Barron was looking crazy as hell, dancing off-beat, completely in a zone of his own. His movements became so bizarre that others in the crowd began to take notice. Then Barron started to sing, drawing more and more attention to himself. People were clapping for him and laughing like crazy, and Barron seemed to love the attention, but then he fucked around and got a little too reckless.

"Whoa!" a young white chick with sky-blue hair ex-claimed loudly. "This guy is wavy! Shit! He's taking all his clothes off . . . did someone hire a stripper?"

Barron was on full tilt as he ripped off his shirt, pulled down his pants, and stripped down to his tighty whiteys. His tongue hung loosely from his mouth as he rolled his stomach and popped his hips. With the sound of the roaring crowd amping him up, he danced like he was trying to shake a demon out of his ass. Through all of this, GiGi just stood back and watched. She was waiting for the crowd to turn against him and get completely weirded out by his dark skin and swiveling hips. She whipped out her cell phone so she could videotape him scaring the shit outta all the pretty little white girls so she could use it against him later, but the exact opposite was happening. Instead of being turned off by his tomfoolery, these fucking idiots were promoting it.

The crowd got even louder as they cheered Barron on. A bunch of silly white dudes surrounded him and started trying to jack his moves. Some blond sorority-type girls cut in trying to get some too, wiggling their hips and giggling out loud as they ran their pale fingers over his pumped-up chocolate flesh, and GiGi got pissed. These young bitches were thirsty as hell, and quite a few of the guys were too. They were staring at Barron's crotch and enjoying his mega dick-print and the way his hefty man-meat jiggled.

"Hey GiGi!" Tess made her way over to the edge of the crowd. "Your friend is freaking awesome! He looks completely hammered, but fuck it we're all hammered."

That was the last straw and GiGi rolled her eyes. She stormed over and pulled Barron out of the moshpit of partygoers and snatched up his clothes. The crowd was still cheering him on as she yanked him through the room and stomped outside to the car. Her little scheme hadn't gone down quite the way she had planned, but she wasn't fazed at all. She was a professional at this hustle, and a chick like her always had a little something slick under her hat. Besides, Barron was hers for life now and she was sure there'd be more than enough opportunities in the future to fuck him up, and fuck him up good.

CHAPTER 4

The election results were soon to be announced, and back at the Dominion Mansion Journey Haggar, chief of security, had the premises on lock and all his ducks lined up in a row. Viceroy Dominion was a real paranoid dude, and he changed his door cylinders and switched up his elaborate security systems on the regular. He liked to rotate his security staff out among various companies every two years too, but Journey Haggar was the exception. He had been on the job for six years now and he wasn't about to leave anytime soon.

Journey had earned himself a permanent position when he'd argued Viceroy down for skimping on the staff and working the hell outta them for measly pay. He had told the big boss right to his face that penny-pinching on security was a sure way to get his shit stole, and he warned him about hiring low-level guards who had larceny in their eyes and nothing to lose.

At first Viceroy had bucked at the back talk from a lowly employee, but later that night in his office, over some yak and some smokes, he'd admitted to Journey that he liked the fact that he wasn't no ass kisser. Viceroy told the young buck that he had mad respect for him for working his way up outta the gutter the same way that he had done back in Houston.

Hearing those kinda words coming outta a rich man's mouth had meant the world to Journey. He was a hood-head body-builder who was young and outspoken, and he had been an ex-gang leader from Port Arthur before joining the military for a stint. Viceroy was well aware of Journey's background, yet he had hired him anyway. And in Journey's eyes, Viceroy Domin-ion had saved his life by giving him a chance, and in turn he had grown fiercely loyal to the Dominion family.

"Ga' head inside and do a thorough security check and make sure all the cameras and monitors are on point," Journey directed his two subordinates that were on duty for the night. "I'll take the perimeter for the next hour, but I want you to radio in with me every twenty minutes, got it?"

The two guards went inside to do as they were instructed and Journey checked the gun on his hip and then hopped on the four-wheeler and proceeded to cruise the property. Noth-ing too crazy ever really popped off at the mansion but Journey was always ready for the slightest sign of static because both the streets and the military had taught him to stay on guard.

He took his time scouring the property as he rode around the estate for a few, and then he turned around and headed on back. He was coming up on the tool sheds near the far side of the house when something out of the ordinary caught his eye. At first he thought it was the shadow of a tree swaying in the wind, and then he noticed the door swinging back and forth on the last shed, the one where the maintenance workers kept their tools.

Lazy fuckers. They'd done a lotta work reseeding the grass after the recent barbeque, so he figured one of the workers had simply forgotten to turn the lock. Journey hopped off the four-wheeler and went to close the latch, and that's when he realized that the lock had been completely broken off.

Right away Journey's street senses started tingling, but before he could uncheck his heat a shadow rose up and he was gripped up from behind in a dope-fiend headlock.

Journey immediately grabbed at the forearm that was clenched around his neck and to his surprise that shit didn't feel all that strong. He squatted down on his powerful legs, reached back and grabbed the intruder by the back of his shirt, and then used his superior strength to flip the guy completely over his head.

Thunk!

Journey slammed the dude down hard on his back and started going to work. His rock-hard fists smashed into the man's face unmercifully as he growled, "You musta thought I was a pussy nigga, huh?" he talked mad shit as he wilded out on the guy. "You cased up the wrong fuckin' crib, muthafucka! I'ma break ya face for you, you piece of shit!"

The guy on the receiving end of Journey's brutality was squirming and doing his best to deflect the blows. Journey reached for his piece to gun-check him, and that's when a hulking figure ran up and caught him on the blindside.

WHACK!

The impact of the punch knocked Journey right on his ass. In an instant he was on the reciprocating end of the beating as the big guy drilled him with a series of brutal punches and kicks. Of course the other dude had to get him some get-back, and before he knew it Journey was getting jumped viciously as the intruders tore off into his ass and dragged him inside the storage shed.

"Bitch-ass nigga!" One of the men barked as he kicked Journey square in his face. The force of the blow made him see stars and he damn near passed out.

Journey rolled around on the floor of the dark shed trying to shield his head and protect himself, but he was getting fucked up. He rolled over to his right and felt for his gun, but as soon as he managed to grab hold of it one of the guys noticed.

"Oh shit, yo! He got a strap . . . get to the house, yo! He got a strap!"

Journey cocked his gat and started shooting blindly in the dark. He heard the sound of feet scattering but he continued to shoot until he was out of rounds. The gunblasts had been deafening inside the small shed, and as soon as he stopped shooting there was nothing but dead silence.

Journey pulled himself to his feet with the empty burner clenched in his hand, then stumbled outside with his ribs aching and warm blood pouring from a gash in his forehead. Wiping the blood from his eyes, he scanned the area as best as he could, and then abandoning the four-wheeler, he hauled ass around to the front of the mansion. Moments later he busted through the service door and damn near collapsed as the other two guards came to his aid.

"Yo! What happened, Journey?" They picked him up by his arms and his ankles and carried him into the living room. "What the fuck happened?"

"I got jumped," Journey groaned as the pain in his ribs intensified. "Two dudes . . . couldn't see 'em that good . . . black, though. Sound the fuckin' alarm. Call Mr. Dominion and then do a sweep through every room up in this bitch. Code nine, muthafuckas! Them bastards was tryna get up in the house!"

CHAPTER 5

Gutta sped down the Dallas highway with his heart pumping triple-time. Him and Shy had just tried to infiltrate the Dominion mansion and almost fucked around and got popped in the process.

"Yo, son! Slow the fuck down!" Shy said, gripping the dashboard with one hand as he hurried up and tried to put on his seat belt. "We ain't tryna get pulled over, nigga, they probably done already called the police on us, bruh!"

Gutta took it easy on the gas pedal and barely paid any attention to the blood that was smeared all over his hands and shirt. They had fucked up big-time and he was so fucking mad he could hardly think straight. That security guard had almost tagged both of them. They had been giving his thick ass a real good ass-whipping until they fucked around and let him get hold of his heat. Gutta and Shy had been stuck like fuck. They were packin' burners too, but they had left their tools in the whip and agreed not to fire off no rounds and make no noise because they didn't wanna draw no attention. So much for that plan.

"Yo, that stupid-ass guard came along and fucked everything up, man!" Gutta bitched as his breathing started to slow to an even pace. "That's why I told you to make sure you hemmed the nigga up nice and tight, muthafucka! You let dude flip you right on yo narrow ass!"

"Man, whatever," Shy said, waving him off. "That nigga was strong as hell, I ain't gon' front. When he got me down you shoulda domed him! This coulda been some real smooth stick-up action but you was too busy worrying about tagging Mink! Man, fuck all that sneaking in and being quiet shit! We shoulda smoked that play-cop from the rip and just ran up in the goddamn joint. You know how we do, kick in the door waving the four-four!"

Gutta shook his head at Shy's stupidity. The Dominion joint wasn't some fuckin' pissy project apartment where you could just bum-rush the door and lay everybody down. It was a multi-million-dollar estate that probably had a swat team on standby. Gutta was pissed, but he also understood just how lucky him and Shy truly were. As mad as he was for not getting up in that crib and finding that bitch Mink and stealing her loot, being booked into a Texas jail and prosecuted to the fullest extent, or possibly catching a bullet in the dome and clocking out on the floor of a tool shed woulda been much, much worse.

They drove for about fifteen miles before Gutta felt safe enough to pull over at a gas station. Looking around cautiously, they switched and ditched their bloody clothes for some brand-new gear that they had stashed in the trunk.

"A'ight, we fucked that part of the program up. So what's the next move, big bro?" Shy asked as he rolled up a swisher sweet full of some good crypto weed. He packed that shit in real tight because his nerves were fuckin' frazzled. "We gone head back to the hotel now?"

"Naw, that little chickenhead Pilar invited us to her crib for dinner," Gutta said. "I was gonna say fuck it and leave the bitch hanging, but since the lick went sour we might as well roll up on her and let her fix us some good home-cooked food."

They GPS'd their way to the chick's huge crib, and when they banged on the door Pilar opened it without even asking who it was. Her hair was frizzled and she looked tired and washed out, but she greeted her thugged-out nigga Gutta with a big smile anyway.

"Damn!" Shy said looking at her like she was a crazy-ass fool as she stepped back to let them inside. "It's like that out here in the 'burbs, baby? Black folks just snatch open they doors in the middle of the night without checking the scene?"

"Hey, honey," Pilar gave Gutta a nice big kiss. "How you doing, Shy? Please, come on in. What took y'all so long?"

Gutta and Shy were led through the foyer of Pilar's elegant home and seated in a beautiful dining area.

"I nodded off watching the election coverage," Pilar said, rubbing her eyes, "but to tell the truth I thought y'all had fronted on me and wasn't gonna come so I put the food away hours ago. The steaks are probably dry as hell and harder than bricks right now, but I'll try to tenderize them a little bit when I'm heating them up."

Pilar switched her plump booty into the kitchen to heat up the food and left Gutta and Shy sitting alone in the dining room.

"Ay," Gutta growled as he stood up and paced the floor. "I'm pissed the fuck off, yo. We gotta get next to that stankin' bitch Mink and get us some ends, yo, real talk. I'm losing my goddamn patience with this country shit down here. I swear to God when I find Mink I'ma kidnap that hoe, and after her people pay up on the fuckin' ransom money I'ma rip her grimy head off."

Shy nodded in agreement. They definitely had to roll up on that bitch and do her ass. They had come way down here to

handle their business, and while Texas was chill and the hun-
nies were cute, he was ready to get his cash and get back to
Harlem to spend it.

Shy glanced around and took in all the elegant paintings,
appliances, and furniture that was in the house and nodded.
The pad was laced the fuck out. It probably wasn't as big as
Mink's crib had looked from the outside, but you could tell
whoever owned it was caked up. They had all kinds of finery
up in this bitch. Persian rugs and Basquiat paintings even com-
plemented the solid-gold chandeliers.

"Yo, Gutta," Shy asked quietly. "How many acres of cow
grass you think this crib is sitting on?"

"I'ono," Gutta said, still in his feelings about the botched
chance to steal Mink and puff out his pockets. "Probably ten
to fifteen or some shit like that. Who knows. Maybe a hundred."

"Ay, this shit is mad nice, nigga," Shy said as his eyes went
on deep roam. "I mean, I know you got a score to settle with
Mink and all that shit, but the bigger goal is to come up on
some real paper while we down here, ain't it?"

"Of course, nigga," Gutta said as he side-eyed his boy.
"Money over bitches every day of the week. What the fuck
you tryna say?"

"I'm sayin'," Shy whispered looking toward the kitchen,
"what the fuck do we need with Mink when we got this other
rich bitch *right here?*"

"What?"

"Yo, Pilar's family got a couple dollars on them too, my
nigga. Look around! You see where we sitting at? You seen
them Bentleys and shit parked out front? Somebody up in this
muthafucka is *paid,* bro! Fuck Mink! Let's snatch this bitch
right here up and cash out, you feel me?"

Gutta's eyes got big as hell, and just then Pilar yelled from
the kitchen.

"Dinner's ready, fellas! I'll bring it out in just a minute." She giggled. "I hope y'all are real hungry because this steak is tough as hell!"

Gutta looked at Shy and they both smiled at the same time.

You damn right we hungry and we 'bout to eat too!

They gave each other some dap then got up and crept toward the kitchen.

CHAPTER 6

Now that me and Big Suge had gotten us an understanding again, life was all good in my hood. He had walked outta his bedroom butt-naked, swinging dick and throwing muscles all over the place as he went downstairs to fix us something to eat, and I was stretched out in his big old bed grinning my ass off and feeling Gucci like a mothafucka. My man had put a sweet Texas long stroke down on my ass that had my legs feeling like they were paralyzed, and when his phone rang on the nightstand I was barely able to reach over and answer that shit.

Ringgggg . . . Ringgggg.

My after-sex zone was so deep that I was slobbering like hell, and I grabbed at the phone then sat up and swallowed a mouthful of drool.

"H-h-hello?"

"Excuse me, I don't mean to bother you, but I'm trying to reach Mr. Dominion."

"W-who is this?"

"My name is Thomas Topaz. I work on the night security detail for Journey Haggar, and I need to inform Mr. Dominion that we just had a serious security incident at the Dominion Estate."

"Oh yeah?" I said, stretching lazily. "What kinda incident you talking about?"

"An attempted robbery. Somebody just tried to rob his house."

"Oh shit!" I rolled over and came up on my knees butt-ass naked. "Get the hell outta here! Somebody tried to put a lick down on us? Are you *serious?*"

"I'm dead serious," dude said quietly. "Our chief security officer took a beat down and he told me to call Mr. Dominion to inform him that someone may have tried to breach the house. However, it's election night and he's not answering his phone, so my next instructions were to call his brother."

"Oh *shit!*" I said again as I glanced at the clock on the dresser. I'd been so busy getting my guts dug out that I had forgotten all about the goddamn election! "Umm, hold up," I said, snatching the sheet from the bed and wrapping it around my naked booty. Finally some goddamn excitement was happening up in that damn mansion and my ass was missing out on it! I felt my adrenaline surge. A robbery? A beat-down? This was some New York type a' shit and I couldn't wait to sound the alarm.

"Suge!" I ran over to the door and hollered downstairs. "Suge! Some fool just tried to rob the fuckin' mansion, boo! Crank up the goddamn truck baby and let's roll out!"

CHAPTER 7

Gutta didn't like making major changes to his plans on such short notice because it left too much room for shit to go wrong. But this was a come-up that he just couldn't let slide by. He had been using Pilar to get closer to his true target from the gate, but the failed mission at the mansion, and Shy's brilliant new suggestion, had just changed the game dramatically. Hell yeah. Fuck chasing Mink. He was gonna snatch this bitch right here and let the money come to him.

Creeping up behind Pilar, Gutta wrapped his big hands around her tight waist as she was arranging the last bit of soul food on the plates for him and Shy.

"Damn that shit smells good, baby," Gutta whispered in her ear as he grinded his meat into her from behind. "You trying to make a nigga fall in love, huh?"

"This is how I get down for my bae," Pilar said with a smile as she poked her ass out and pushed her pillow-soft cheeks deep into Gutta's crotch. "A bad bitch like me knows exactly how to treat a man."

"Oh yeah?" Gutta growled, "Well too bad, bitch," his voice

dropped into a cold snarl. "Cause I ain't ya bae, and this here shit is about to get real!"

Gutta's hands moved quicker than lightning from Pilar's waist to her neck as he gripped her flesh tightly, cutting off her air and putting her in the sleeper hold. His strong biceps flexed as he lifted her, bucking like crazy, off her feet. Her small body flailed around as she kicked the plates of food off the counter, making a big-ass mess as she fought in vain for her next breath. The struggle was brief and futile as Gutta grimaced and held tight and Pilar slipped into the blackness of unconsciousness.

"That's right, baby. Take a nice little nap," Gutta said as he eased up the pressure trying not to break her pretty little neck in the process. "You ain't as fine as that conniving bitch Mink, but you'll do a'ight for now."

"Now that's what the fuck I'm talking 'bout," Shy said from behind his partner as he stepped up and lit up a cigar. "Keep this bitch in la-la land while I go ransack the crib real quick, yo. I know these rich niggas got some A-1 expensive shit up in this pad. We just hit the muthafuckin' jackpot, my nigga, so let's ante up on whatever the fuck they got in here and then get ghost, my G."

"Yo! Don't you touch a muthafuckin' thing up in here, you idiot," Gutta growled as he glared at Shy with murder in his eyes. "We didn't come for no petty-ass kick-door robbery, nigga! This the *kidnap* game, remember? That means this shit is *federal*. This bitch comes from a family that got hella bread, and it don't get much more high-profile than that! If we don't play our cards all the fuckin' way right then be prepared to do eighty-five percent of the hundred years they gon' smack our black asses with in the federal pen, ya dig?"

Shy backed down. "A'ight, big bruh you right," he said, shaking his head at his own stupidity. Gutta *was* right. This was the big-boy level they were playing on, and Shy knew them alphabet boys only liked to play for keeps. "Fuck the lick then. Let's just raise the hell up outta here, man."

"Wrong answer again," Gutta said as he scooped up Pilar's limp body in his arms and carried her over to the couch. "First you're gonna go find something I can use to put over her eyes as a blindfold. Then we gonna wipe down anything we might have touched in this muthafucka before we head out. We don't need no fingerprints left behind that these bitch-ass cops can trace back to us."

"That's real shit, bro-sky," Shy said as he looked down at Pilar, who was slobbering from the side of her mouth like she was taking a good-ass nap. "She really is a bad little chick, bro. But these silverspoon-fed hoes is all the same at the end of the day. They greedy as fuck and act like they shit don't stink."

"Yeah, she is a pretty one," Gutta agreed as he looked at her. "But fuck all that, after we get this ransom money and dead that bitch Mink, we can buy a thousand hoes who look ten times better than this one. Now let's get this shit put in motion and dip the fuck outta here cause we ain't got all day. Let's pick up this grub real quick and then clean this kitchen up and get everything back in order. I want it to look like we were never even here."

"But what if the bitch wakes up?" Shy asked.

Gutta shrugged. "If the bitch wakes up I'll choke her ass back out again."

Surrounded by her husband's campaign staffers and sipping champagne, Selah was busy skinning and grinning and cheesing and pleasing when all hell broke loose at the Ritz Hotel. Gunshots sounded in the outside foyer and pure madness washed over the election-watch party as staffers and supporters freaked the fuck out at the sight of Viceroy's body sprawled on the floor with bright red blood staining his chest.

"Oh my *Godddddd!* He's been shot!" a waitress had

screamed in a high-pitched voice. "He's been shot! My God, Mr. Dominion has been shot!"

Selah had dropped her glass of champagne and damn near fainted. Not even the sight of Viceroy looking mangled and burnt to a crisp after that oil rig explosion could have prepared her for what she saw when she ran out into that foyer and saw her man laid out on the floor like a corpse.

All the breath had left her body, and her feet felt rooted in place as several staffers cursed and rushed to Viceroy's side, while others ran around in circles screaming their asses off and fumbling with their cell phones trying to dial 911.

Time moved in matrix slow-mo as the paramedics arrived and got Viceroy up on a stretcher. He was unconscious and his face was ashen and gray from shock and blood loss. Selah had been whisked away with him as they rushed him downstairs in a private elevator and out of the hotel, and right now she was riding with him in the back of the ambulance, holding tightly to a railing as the sirens wailed and the driver followed a police escort toward the nearest emergency room.

"Viceroy!" Selah threw her head back and shrieked. She clutched her midsection and trembled like a leaf as the thought of losing her man sent shock waves of grief roaring through her body. "Viceroy don't *gooooo!* Please don't leave me! Baby, hold on. Hold *on!*

Viceroy lay on the stretcher with an oxygen mask over his face as a paramedic worked on him furiously. His white tuxedo shirt had been ripped away and his whole chest was bloody and exposed. Selah moaned in fear. Her man looked like he was holding on by a thread, and her lips began moving furiously in a silent and desperate prayer.

It took forever and a day to reach the hospital, and by the time they arrived Viceroy was still passed clean out. A team of emergency personnel were waiting to spring into action the moment the ambulance stopped and its doors flew opened. The workers were deft and experienced as they removed Viceroy's unconscious body from the vehicle and rushed his stretcher toward the open doors.

"Please," Selah begged the medical team as she tumbled out the door behind her man. "Save him!" she screeched at the top of her lungs. Good or bad, for better or for worse, she had spent more than twenty-five years with this man and she wasn't ready to lose him yet. "Dear sweet God up in Heaven, *save him!*"

CHAPTER 8

Rodney Ruddman was mad as fuck as he stood in his office staring down the barrel of a loaded gat as he pleaded for his life with the young thug, Zeke Washington.

"Look my man, Viceroy Dominion is the one who lied like a muthafucka and cheated your father out of a fortune! So why the hell are you over here fucking with me?"

"Kill all that goddamn noise! You must think shit is sweet, huh?" Zeke growled. "You ain't no better than Viceroy. Both of y'all bitches are just the same. Y'all rich niggas been shittin' on us poor folks for years! Making money and profiting off the blood, sweat, and tears that hood people like my daddy scratched and slaved for. Well, today is payback day, nigga!"

"Payback? Fool is you crazy? I *worked* for mine! I don't owe nobody shit!"

"Like I said, my father sweated blood and tears. I want what's mine!"

"And like I said, why the hell are you fucking with me and not Dominion?"

Suddenly Zeke grinned. "Don't worry, old man. I ain't the

type to discriminate. After I clap yo old ass that nigga Viceroy can kiss his ass good-bye too."

Just then a "BREAKING NEWS" alert sounded from the television and grabbed both men's attention. They both shut the hell up as a middle-aged white man spoke into a microphone and reported live from a crime scene.

"This just in! We're outside the Ritz Hotel in Dallas where we've received word that a gunman has apparently opened fire at an election-watch party for wealthy oil giant Viceroy Dominion. As you know, Mr. Dominion survived a catastrophic oil rig explosion less than a year ago, and tonight we have a report of shots being fired inside the suite where his campaign staff was gathered to await the election results. We're waiting for confirmation, but early reports indicate that it was Mr. Dominion himself who suffered the gunshot wound. Details regarding the suspect are sketchy, but it's been confirmed that Mr. Dominion has been shot at least once and is being rushed to St. Joseph's Medical Center. We will keep you updated as more details on this shocking act of violence come in."

"What the fuck?!?" Ruddman bitched. "Damn, fool! So you already went by the Ritz Hotel, huh?" he said in disbelief. "Look what the fuck you did over there!"

Zeke bucked. "Fuck you mean, look what I did? I didn't do *shit!*" he waved the gun toward the television screen, "Yo, that wasn't me, muthafucka," he barked, looking shook as hell as his gun hand trembled. "I ain't even been nowhere near that hotel! I swear to God it wasn't me!"

"You're going to jail, little nigga," Ruddman stated authoritatively. "You just shot up a fucking political event, you idiot! I know your daddy was dumb as hell, but please tell me you're not that fucking stupid!"

"Fuck you!" Zeke raged. "And don't you talk no shit about my fuckin' father!"

"Dumb nigga!" Ruddman ignored him and spit with his lips turned down in disgust. "Your daddy was stupid as hell and so are you. And that's why you shouldn't be walking around pointing no loaded guns at nobody!"

In a flash the older man lunged boldly and grabbed at the barrel of the gun as he tried to overpower the thug.

"Back the fuck up, muthafucka!" Zeke hollered, jerking the barrel away as he gun-checked him. "What? You tryna set me up or something, you grimy bitch? You tryna frame me? Yeah, nigga! I think you tryna set me—"

Ruddman lunged again and a wrestling match ensued. The old lion fought for his life and tried his damnedest to overpower the youngster, but his stamina was low and he was no match for the hard muscles and wiry frame that the hungry young cub was packing.

"Yo, get the fuck back!" Zeke yelled as he struggled to tear away from Ruddman's grasp. He hauled off and smacked the shit outta the wheezing billionaire with his free hand. "Raise up 'fore I split your skull, you fat-headed bitch!"

Ruddman was trying his best to hold on to Zeke's gun hand but he was quickly running out of steam. He made one more bold and courageous lunge for the gat, and as Zeke tried to pull away, the resulting pop and bright spark of heat that shot from the tip of the pistol shocked the shit out of both of them.

"Aggh!" Ruddman screeched as the impact swung him halfway around and propelled him down to the ground. He looked up with his face twisted in a mask of rage and disbelief. "I'll be damned! You shot me, you little thug muthafucka, you! You shot me!"

"Goddamn!" Zeke spit as realization came down hard on him. "Look what the fuck you made me do! Stupid ass! The fuck was you doing grabbing at my piece like that?"

Ruddman was bleeding and he couldn't answer. Matter of fact, it was all he could do not to piss in his silk drawers as he clutched his shoulder and moaned in pain and tried to skooch his fat frame across the floor. He couldn't believe the little bastard had fucked around and shot him and had him stretched out in a pool of sticky blood.

"This is your fault! You did this to ya damn self!" Zeke barked as he raised his knee and slammed his heel deep into Rodney's wounded shoulder, eliciting a painful shriek. "Shut the fuck up!" he snapped as he bent over and dug in Rodney's pockets and stole his cell phone and ten crisp knots out of his wallet. "Who the fuck told your stupid ass to go for my shit anyway, huh? I should shoot ya fat ass again just for being so damn stupid!"

With a cold sneer on his lips Zeke lowered the tip of his pistol and aimed it directly at Ruddman's jiggling belly. The helpless oil baron saw his whole life flash before his eyes as he cringed and clutched his navel to ward off the next round.

"No! Stop it, Zeke. That's enough, son. Don't do anything stupid. You're right. It was my fault and you didn't mean to shoot me, but don't make it any worse. Just call me an ambulance and get me to the hospital right now and I can make this whole thing go away for you."

Zeke smirked and scoffed. "Nigga, please! You think I'm stupid? It was an accident, but I know you ain't about to tell the cops that shit! The minute I call you an ambulance you gonna spill ya grimy guts to the po-po, you bitch-ass nigga! You can tell 'em any goddamn thing you want but you gotta tell 'em from the grave 'cause I ain't going to jail!"

"N-n-nobody has to go to jail!" Ruddman pleaded as a stream of warm blood seeped from his wound and pooled under his body. "I already said this whole thing was all my fault! I swear to God I'll tell the cops exactly that. Just relax and put the gun down, son!"

"Fuck you," Zeke muttered as he headed toward the door about to get ghost. "See you in hell, muthafucka!"

"Wait! You're just gonna leave me here to bleed to death? At least give me back my phone or call me an ambulance before you go!"

Zeke smirked again. "Fuck you, Ruddman. You tried to beat me, muthafucka, and—"

Knock-knock-knock!

The rapping on the front door killed his gangsta talk and sent panic flooding into young Zeke's eyes.

"Mr. Ruddman?" a female voice called out loudly. "It's Priscilla, Mr. Ruddman. Everyone is waiting for you downstairs. Can I come in? Is everything okay in there?"

Ruddman opened his mouth to snitch like a muthafucka and that's when Zeke broke for the door. Flipping the lock, he snatched that baby open and barreled past one of Ruddman's gray-haired secretaries, damn near knocking her down as he hauled ass down the hall toward the stairwell exit.

Grabbing onto the doorframe to steady herself, the elderly secretary stepped inside the suite, stared down at the bloody heap on the floor, then opened her mouth as wide as she could and screamed.

"Oh my God! Oh my God!" she clutched her conservative pearls and screeched so loud Ruddman wanted to cover his ears. "Mr. Ruddman, you're bleeding! Dear Lord, you're bleeding! Mr. Ruddman, please speak to me! Are you okay?"

"Do it look like I'm okay, goddammit?" he snapped. "I got shot, goddamn! Shot! So stop all that hollering and call me an ambulance! That damned fool just shot me! He *shot* me! He fuckin' *shot* me!"

CHAPTER 9

"She shot me, I'm telling you!" he hollered. "That bitch fuckin' *shot* me!"

Members of the nursing staff were huddled around Viceroy's hospital bed in the treatment room, and every head swung toward Selah as Viceroy opened his eyes wide and screamed at the top of his lungs. He had regained consciousness as they were transferring him off the stretcher, and after taking just one look at Selah his violent reaction had everybody shook as hell.

"My wife *shot* me!" he screamed again. He glared at Selah like she was a serial killer and then jabbed his finger dead at her and hollered, "Help! Help! Get this bitch away from me! Get her crazy ass the fuck up outta here!"

"V-V-Viceroy?" Selah muttered as the look of pain and grief on her face was slowly replaced by shock and disbelief. She looked around, puzzled as fuck, peering first over her left shoulder, and then over her right. "Who shot you, dear? What are you talking about?"

"You! *You* did it! You know what the hell I'm talking about! You came up behind me and shot me, goddammit!"

Selah was completely floored.

"*Viceroy!* Don't be silly! You're mistaken, dear! Delirious! You know I would never do anything to hurt you!"

"I don't know *shit!* You killed old Wally Su's ass, now didn't you?"

Selah's eyes widened in alarm. "*Viceroy!*"

Ignoring the pleading look of panic spreading across his wife's face, Viceroy clutched at his bloody shoulder and slumped over in the bed. "Please," he gasped and moaned as the nurses huddled around him and shot Selah hostile looks of disapproval. "Get this bitch away from me!" and then he slumped over and fainted once again.

The younger of the two nurses approached Selah in the treatment room. "Ma'am," she said sternly as she gripped Selah's wrist, "I'm sorry but you're upsetting the patient and you're going to have to leave the room."

"Like hell I am!" Selah balked indignantly. "My husband has been wounded and I'm not leaving his side. You've got a whole lot of damn nerve trying to put me out! The Dominion family donates hundreds of thousands of dollars to this hospital every year, and I want a doctor in here and I want him *now!*"

Selah glared at the nurse with Brooklyn heat in her eyes as she snatched away from her grasp. "And take your goddamn hands off me! My husband is obviously in shock and talking crazy from pain, but I'm not going anywhere!"

"Then I'm afraid we'll have to call security," the nurse said firmly just as a doctor was entering the room.

"Call 'em!" Selah blasted on her. "Call 'em, goddammit!"

"Ladies, ladies, is all of this necessary?" the young doctor asked, looking flustered and confused by the terse exchange.

"I think so," the nurse replied curtly, "because according to our patient, Mr. Dominion, it was his wife here who shot him."

The doctor stared at Selah with a look of horror in his eyes and then looked over his shoulder and screamed, "Security!"

★   ★   ★

GiGi and Barron were feeling good and flying high. They had just left the party at Tess's mansion and Barron was faded as fuck.

They stopped at a local burger joint to grub on some fast food so Barron could soak up some of the alcohol and weed that was in his system and GiGi held him under his arm as they walked inside the well-lit joint.

"You want a burger?" she asked, digging inside her purse for some cash as they approached the counter.

Barron nodded and belched loudly into his palm. "Yeah. Gimme two of them shits. With cheese. And some fries too."

As Barron grubbed on the greasy food GiGi sat across from him watching him like a hawk. This sucker had no idea what she had planned for his ass, and the sooner she got him out of the state of Texas, the better.

Fifteen minutes later Barron had dogged his face out and drained a large Pepsi, and he was ready to go.

"Yo, lemme get the car keys," he said, holding out his hand as they pushed through the restaurant doors.

"Are you sure don't you want me to drive, babe?" GiGi asked in a concerned tone. He gave her a look and she handed over the keys and held onto his arm again as they headed back to the car. "Seriously, though, you smoked up a lotta shit, B. If you're still feeling woozy I can push the whip again. It's really not a problem."

"Nah, baby. I think I'm good now," Barron said as he led her over to the passenger side door and held it open. "I ate my buzz off so I'm straight. I'll get us out of here. Which way do you want me to go?"

That was the kind of talk GiGi liked to hear. Because un-beknownst to Barron she hadn't dragged him to Tess's party just to watch him smile, shimmy, and shake his dick all over the dance floor. No, those shiny bundles of heroin she had copped were about to be put to good use. The plan was to mainline Barron's veins full of horse and use the quality dope to keep him docile and compliant so he didn't get out of line. Barron was her ticket into the millionaire's club, and GiGi wasn't taking any chances with her cash cow. She would shoot his dumb ass up with the good stuff in a heartbeat, knowing she could count on the deadly effects of the drug to keep him in check and even dependent on her, if need be.

Barron climbed behind the wheel of his whip as GiGi slid into the passenger seat and started fixing her hair in the mirror. She re-applied her lipstick and eyeliner and made sure every speck of her makeup looked flawless. Barron side-eyed her and smiled at her vanity. Coming from a high-profile family he understood the need to look on point at all times. He'd seen his mother spend countless hours in front of a mirror, refusing to leave until perfection was achieved.

Thoughts of Selah hit him in the gut. Barron couldn't help feeling fucked up about the way he had walked out on his family without even saying good-bye. He didn't wanna sky up outta Texas on bad terms or nothing, but he knew in his heart that he was making the right the decision. Besides, his father was back on his feet and running shit now, and if push came to shove Viceroy and Suge would make sure the family was okay.

"Okay, I'm ready," GiGi grinned and snapped the overhead mirror closed. "Head north toward the Oklahoma state line, baby," she directed him. "I need to swing by one more friend's house for a quick minute and say good-bye, and after that it's going to be all about you and me and we'll be on our way."

Barron swallowed hard, then nodded like he was down with it. Yeah, shit was about to get real. The thought of leaving his family and everything he had worked so hard for was rough, but like any good gambler he was tossing his dice and putting his money on his woman. He had been with his share of beautiful chicks over the years, but none of them came close to matching up with the drive, intellect, and sex appeal that seemed to surge through GiGi Molinex. Fuck the rest, this bae right here embodied the perfect balance that he had been searching for. She brought out something in him that sparked his drive and elevated him to his maximum potential, and that type of feeling was something that not even the Dominion billions could buy.

Barron kicked back in the driver's seat of the whip, low-riding like a muthafucka. His black Oakley shades accentuated his swagger, and with most of the drugs now leaving his system he was soaring on a natural high.

"A'ight, now. From here on out it's you and me against the world, baby," he said, patting GiGi on her shapely thigh.

"You got that right," GiGi agreed as she turned the radio up then leaned over and kissed his clean-shaven cheek. "It's time to see what this big old world has in store for us. And I promise. As long as we stay together there's not a damn thing that can hold us back."

Barron beamed. "You can say that shit ag—"

"This just in!" The radio announcer blared as the regular programming was interrupted.

"Breaking News from Dallas! Violence has erupted at an election-watch party at the—"

In a flash GiGi spun the radio dial, changing the station. "Let's play a game, baby," she leaned over and ran the tip of her pink tongue over his earlobe. "Let's see who can talk the dirtiest until we hit the highway, okay?"

"Wait, hold up," Barron said, pulling away as he tuned the dial back to the news.

". . . surrounding the wealthy and influential oil baron. According to reports, shots have been fired and Mr.—"

GiGi spun the dial to the left again and country music blared from the speakers.

"Yo, hold up baby! What the fuck did they just say?" Barron barked as he spun that sucker back to the news station and turned up the volume.

"Who the fuck got shot?" he screeched in disbelief as he

pulled over to the curb and hit the brakes. "Are these jawns talking about *my father?*"

"Of course not," GiGi said waving her hand in dismissal. "Calm down, Barron. I didn't hear anybody say your father's name. I'm sure he's just fine, baby."

"Nah, hell no," Barron said as he fumbled with the dial and tried to find another news station. "They didn't have to say his name. He's a Texas oilman and he's at an election-watch party in Dallas! That says enough for me right there!"

"Baby, *please,*" GiGi insisted. "It's just a bunch of bullshit. You know how these radio personalities are always trying to stir up controversy just to help their ratings go through the roof. This is *our* time. It's time for you and me"

"Uh-uh." Barron shook his head. "Something ain't right," he insisted, still fucking with the radio. "Nobody plays stupid games like that just for ratings."

GiGi sucked her teeth then reached out and tapped the dial, turning the radio completely off.

"Just drive, would you, Barron? I'm sure you're getting yourself all worked up for nothing. If there's a problem back at home it's their problem, not ours. *Drive,* Barron. Your father has plenty of people on his payroll who can take care of him. It's time for you to look out for yourself."

Barron side-eyed her like she had little shit balls falling out of her mouth.

"Are you fuckin' serious?" He made a disrespectful sound in the back of his throat then put the whip in gear and pulled off. "I'ma *drive* alright," he muttered as he floored the gas and surged toward a traffic light up ahead. At the last minute he cut a hard left and made a U-turn, nosing his ride toward the southbound entrance of the highway. "I'm driving my ass right the fuck back home."

Something dangerous flashed in GiGi's eyes and suddenly

everything about her changed. "Turn this shit back around, goddammit!"

Barron didn't even look at her.

"Nah, fuck that shit, baby," he said as he merged onto the on-ramp and headed for home. "I know your family is whack and don't give a fuck about each other, but that's not how me and my peeps roll. My father might be a muthafucka sometimes, but no matter what kind of beef or disagreements we may have, I'm still his son. His *firstborn* son. I'm going back."

"Oh no the fuck you're not," GiGi said quietly, and that's when Barron got the iron pressed to his dome.

"Turn this goddamn car back around," she spit quietly. "I want you to get off at the next exit and then head back north, just like I told you to before."

Barron peered at his sweet lil white honey from the corner of his eye and got the shit shocked outta him by what he saw shining from her eyes. Rage. Pure-dee fuckin' rage. It was the same kind of rage he'd seen on her face that night in Denny's when she pressed a steak knife to that racist hillbilly's throat.

"Yo," Barron drawled in a low tone, shivering from the temperature radiating off both GiGi and the cold slice of metal. "What the *fuck* are you doing, baby? What the hell is going on?"

"What the hell does it look like?" she sneered at his punk-ass with her lips turned down. "We had an agreement and we're going north! North, goddammit. *North!* You got that shit? North!"

Oh, I got that shit alright, Barron thought as he side-eyed the psycho bitch sitting next to him holding a .38 pressed to his skull. He fuckin' got it for sure. He pursed his lips, mad as fuck at himself. If there was one thing he could do it was pick a goddamn nut. First Carla, then Pilar, and now this head case right here. Fuck was wrong with him? How the fuck did he keep getting caught up in these crazy-ass trick bags?

Barron pulled off at the next exit and tried one last time. "GiGi. Bae. C'mon now, sugar. Are you really pressing a tool on me, sweetheart? I mean, damn. I give you my heart and tell you I'm down to hand you the whole fuckin' world on a silver platter and all you can think to do is jack me for my ride?" He chuckled. "You can have it, baby. Better yet, I'll buy you one that's even better."

"Just shut the fuck up and drive, Barron," GiGi said coldly, dropping all pretenses as he whipped the car around and headed north on the highway. The icicles in her voice told him she wasn't fuckin' playing, and suddenly Barron understood his situation the same way he understood what it meant for his last name to be Dominion.

"You and your entire ridiculously idiotic family can kiss my ass," GiGi snapped, fed up with the all the acting. "Bunch of crazy assholes with tricked-out ghetto names! Mink the half-naked mole-rat, *great* Dane the pussy-hound-dog, Peaches the pretty punk, and that reality show junkie *Easter* Bunni! You'd just better keep your damn foot jammed on that pedal and the steering wheel aimed straight, Barron the ball-less *bitch,* or I will blow your fucking brains out and make this car your goddamn coffin on wheels, my nigga! Now, drive, moth-erfucker. *Drive!*"

CHAPTER 10

A shooting at one of the most prestigious hotels in all of Dallas didn't go down on a regular basis, and one of the richest oil billionaires in the country damn sure didn't take a hot one in the back every day.

But that's exactly what had happened at the Ritz hotel, and if it wasn't such a scene of mad chaos, and if security had been on their game, then maybe somebody would have seen the slender young woman dressed in a maid's uniform who hauled ass out of the hotel right along with all the other frightened maids and servers and hostesses the moment the bullets started flying.

And if somebody had noticed her, then maybe they would have seen her rushing down the back stairs with a large scarf obscuring her beautiful face as she hit the lobby and blended in with the frenzied crowd of guests and rushed with them toward the parking structure as sirens from the police and approaching ambulance rang faintly in the distance. And had they really, really paid close attention they would have seen her jump behind the wheel of a small black car and zip toward the exit before the other guests had even put their whips in gear good.

And if somebody had taken a stroll past the spot way in the back corner where she'd parked, then they would have seen her phony maid outfit abandoned on the ground as she drove up out of there stripped down to a sleek, fashionable catsuit with a shiny silver gun stuck down in her designer boot.

Barron was sweating crazy bullets in the driver's seat of his Maserati. He couldn't fuckin' believe this shit was actually going down. One minute him and his girl were riding off into the sunset, and the next thing he knew she was pressing a loaded gat to his temple. He was an emotional fucking wreck as he weaved in and out of traffic trying not to crash his shit up and kill the both of them. Try as he might, he couldn't keep a clear train of thought and he figured maybe he should just pull over on the side of the road and plead with GiGi and try to talk her down, but the look in her eyes told the whole story.

There would be no talking her down. He knew from dealing with Pilar that an emotional woman was a dangerous creature. Especially when she was checking you with the business end of a gun. Nah, he didn't want to test his limits with GiGi. The bitch was unstable and unpredictable, and Barron decided to just go along with the program for a minute and do everything she told him to do. He knew he needed to play it smart and bide his time until he could figure out a plan that wouldn't end with him getting his forehead split and falling victim to a crime of greed and passion.

GiGi had flipped the script on him so suddenly that he couldn't get his bearings straight, but he knew he had to try something.

"Yo, where are we going, GiGi?" Barron asked as he played stupid and tried to dial down the tension in the small car. After driving for an hour they had stopped for gas at a lonely service station in a tiny town, and relief had flooded through Barron when he saw a sister sitting at the cash register behind the counter.

GiGi had pocketed the car keys and walked toward the back of the store to get a bottle of water. She was keeping a real close eye on him and had her hand in her purse gripping her heat, but Barron had managed to side-eye the sister at the register and spit frantically to her outta the corner of his mouth.

"Take this number! 972-555-1212! Call my mama!"

"What?" she had turned up her lip and snapped at him. She gave him the evil eye. "You got some nerve rolling up in here with some white chick and tryna holla at me! What? You tryna give me your number so you can get you some black coochie or something? You want me to be your *side-piece?*"

"No, goddammit!" Barron had whined in a whisper as GiGi walked back up the aisle. "I want you to call my mama!"

With GiGi's gun pointed at his spine, Barron had gotten back in the driver's seat feeling more desperate than ever before.

"So what's up now? Can't we forget everything that's happened and just go back to our original plan of getting out of here and building a beautiful life together?"

"Nope. All the plans have changed now, Barron," GiGi said coldly as she kept the gun pointed dead at him. "You should have just done exactly what I told you to do and it wouldn't have had to go down like this."

"Come on, girl," Barron pleaded. "This is me and you. Why don't we stop all this bullshit, GiGi," Barron said as his fear started turning into anger. "I mean, how the fuck am I all of a sudden the bad guy here? You pull a gun on me like some kinda psycho hood chick and threaten to blow my dome off because I wanna be there for my family? What the fuck is up with that? Where's all that sweetness and compassion you used to throw down on me? Where did my gentle baby girl go? I'm sorry, but I just know you ain't serious about all this shit."

"Oh, I'm dead-ass serious, Barron," GiGi said through clenched teeth. She slid on a pair of expensive designer eyeglasses that he had bought her and then started texting on her phone with one hand while holding the gun aimed and steady in the other.

She sent the text and then leaned back in her seat. "You can forget all that bullshit sweet talk, Barron. I've been running ten steps ahead of you this whole damn race, baby. Kill that wishful thinking too, because you're not going to catch me sleeping. I really suggest you think hard before you do anything stupid. If you want to keep your head on your shoulders then keep your silly mouth closed and this car in motion. You dig?"

Barron had no choice but to suck it up and go along with her program, and not much later she directed him to get off the highway and pull into a small plaza of stores that were all closed down for the night.

GiGi forced him to drive around to the back and park way up in a grove of trees, then she demanded that he leave the keys in the car and exit the vehicle. She got out first, then pressed the gun deep into the small of Barron's back and made him walk slowly toward a door that looked as if it was already half open.

It was semi-dark inside and as soon as Barron stepped through the threshold a large figure rose from the shadows and punched him in his stomach so hard he farted in his drawers and doubled over in pain. Barron opened his mouth to holler and a bag was thrown over his head. Then something hard and hot struck him in the back of the neck, sending blinding white light flooding through his brain, and without another thought he faded slowly into the dark arms of unconsciousness.

When Barron came to he was sprawled out across a mattress, ass-naked and dizzy. His arms and legs were strapped down and anchored to the bed. He was disoriented from the blow to his neck, but he could see well enough to make out several half-naked women clad in black leather clothing walking in and out of the room. None of them paid him the slightest attention and Barron's eyeballs were throbbing so damn hard he couldn't even cry out for help. A few moments later GiGi entered the room with a white dude who looked like he was some type of 'roided-up white boy bodybuilder. Judging by the baton that dude was clenching in his hand Barron had a strong feeling that this was the muthafucka who had knocked his ass out.

"So, how was your little nap, Barron?" GiGi wore a shitty smirk on her pretty face as she sat down on the bed next to him. "I kept coming in to check on you and guess what? Your dick was hard the whole time you were sleeping. Were you dreaming about me?"

"Fuck you," Barron managed to mumble as anger surged through his veins. "Where the fuck am I, and what the hell is going on?"

"I got in contact with a friend a mine and he told me to bring you here," GiGi said while still maintaining her grin. "The sign on the outside says it's a massage parlor, but as you're about to find out, it's much, much more than that, baby. See, this is where they film all their undercover dominatrix movies. They make them look so real you'd swear people were really getting tortured. But for some reason there's always a shortage of volunteers who are willing to go on camera, and we thought the son of a billionaire would be a perfect cast member. Would you like to get your ass spanked, Barron?"

Before Barron could object, the burley tanned dude walked over and yanked his forehead head back, then shoved a grimy gag halfway down his throat. Barron bucked and grunted, trying his damnedest to break free from his restraints, but he was stuck like chuck and had absolutely no wins. GiGi clipped him under the chin then laughed and got up from the bed.

"Relax, baby. You will be just *fiiiiine,*" she harmonized. "The lovely girls with the leather whips will take good care of you. Consider this your first major film role and if you perform real good for the cameras I'll make sure your name gets in the credits."

A moment later about six women with whips and chains came marching into the room. They all had spiked dogged collars around their necks and crazy black and white makeup on their faces that made them look like vampires. They giggled and cracked their whips in the air as Barron glared at them wide-eyed and horrified. *What the fuck!* he shrieked in his mind. He was helpless like a muthafucka! He couldn't believe GiGi had hemmed him up like this and he couldn't even bear to imagine what these freaky-looking bitches were about to do to him!

CHAPTER 11

Gutta and Shy had twisted Pilar's little ass up like a pretzel and stuffed her in the trunk of the whip. She had fought like a hoodrat, and Gutta and Shy were both cursing and sweating as they damn near cracked her neckbone tryna cram her down in there good.

They had driven for almost thirty minutes, and now, hiding out in a cheap motel way back off the main road, Gutta ripped the duct tape off Pilar's mouth with enough force to tear the skin from her face and bring tears to her eyes as she shrieked in pain and gasped in terror.

"Gutta! Please stop this madness!" Pilar screamed and sobbed. "Why are you doing this shit to me? I thought me and you was cool! Where the hell am I? You already got the pussy so I know you didn't bring me here to try to rape me!"

"Bitch shut the fuck up," Gutta snarled. "This is way bigger than your little prissy ass. Don't nobody want none of your lil stank trim. We came for the money, yo. What the fuck, you thought I was really feeling you or something?"

Pilar eyes were swollen from crying and her entire body was trembling. She knew what kind of game this was. She got it now, and it hurt to know that this fine mothafucka that she had started catching feelings for had only been using her for a ransom. Yeah, she'd bumped her head on his balls and he had caught her completely off guard, but as she replayed the way they'd met in her mind and remembered how hard he had been clocking her, she could see how the set-up had been sweet from the gate.

"You dirty bastard! I can't believe I actually trusted your ass!"

"See, this is the problem with you rich bitches," Gutta said as he fronted her off and locked the top latch on the motel room door. They had carried her inside a dirty and dingy one-bedroom in a seedy part of town where the clerk didn't ask any questions and the people in neighboring rooms minded their own damn business. "Rich bitches like you walk around with y'all heads all stuck up in the clouds in your own little world, and you think the fucking planet revolves around your pedicures and your hair-weave appointments. Consider this your introduction to the real world, silly ass."

Gutta ignored Pilar's bullshit sniffling as he glanced at Shy, who was cursing at the television as he sat watching the Houston Rockets beat up on the New York Knicks. Gutta shook his head. His boy had the attention span of a ten-year-old and his lack of focus was starting to piss Gutta off.

"Man what is you doing?" Gutta barked. "Fuck that NBA shit, nigga! We 'bout to get down on the most important piece of bizz in our whole fuckin' lives, yo!" Gutta hurled the remote control at the television so hard the back piece flew off and the batteries landed on the floor next to Shy's feet. "Keep your head in this game, muthafucka!"

Shy grinned as he leaned back in the chair and sparked up a fat one. "Nigga you just mad cause you owe me a hundred dollars," he said as he exhaled a cloud of some good Texas smoke and clowned. "I told you your bum-ass Knicks wasn't gonna hold it down."

Gutta was uptight, but he still couldn't help but snicker at his lil homey. Shy was good people. Every time Gutta got too serious or aggressive he would say or do something silly as fuck to lighten the mood. Gutta knew Shy was his man, fitty grand, and he never let him down. Even though he acted like a fucking clown he knew he could trust Shy with his life.

"Yeah, whatever, nigga," Gutta spit as he pulled out a fat knot of money and tossed Shy a crispy hundred-dollar bill. "Here's ya dough, now turn that shit off and get ya shit together. I gotta go make a run real fast so make sure this bitch don't move, ya heard? I don't care if she gotta piss, shit, or vomit you better be in the bathroom watching her."

The New York crooks gave each other daps and Gutta threw his hoodie on and left the room to handle his handle. Shy flipped the latch over on the door and went back to watching the game.

On the other side of the room, Pilar's thoughts were speeding like a pro racer at the Indy 500.

How the fuck am I going to get out of here? Why did my stupid ass fall for this son of bitch? They want a goddamn ransom? Who the hell do they think has the money to be paying for some ransom? Shit, my daddy's wallet is about to jump up out of his pocket and run the hell away! What are these ghetto bastards gonna do when they find out that my side of the goddamn family is dead fucking broke?

Pilar thought about the way Gutta had manhandled her and smacked her all upside the head when he was dragging her out of the car. It was obvious that he was a bitch-beater, and something told her there was a whole lot more smacks where those had come from. That nigga had let it be known that he had no sympathy for her, that she was just a means of getting his hands on some loot in his eyes, and that made him extremely dangerous.

I gotta find a way to get the hell out of here, Pilar thought desperately as she eyed her captor as he watched the basketball game. *Shy might not be the sharpest knife in the drawer, but right now he's my only hope.*

She swallowed hard, then made her pitch.

"Hey, Shy," she purred in a sweet lil voice. "Can I holler at you for a quick minute?"

"Bitch, please," he said without even looking at her. "Don't even come at me with the sweet talk, baby. It ain't gonna work."

"Wait, just hear me out, dude," Pilar pleaded as she tried to pull her emotions together. "Seriously, I'm not trying to play you or anything, I just wanna get out of here. If this is all about getting next to some money then I can definitely get you paid. Just please get me out of here."

Shy turned away from the blowout game and looked Pilar up and down curiously.

"A'ight, I'm listening," he said as he snatched up a bag of chips from the nightstand and smacked on a few. That good weed had his mouth dry as hell and he was dying for some brew. "Tell me what you got in mind."

"Well, how much cash do you need?" Pilar asked. "All you gotta do is get me outta here and I can get you a lump sum. I won't say a word so you don't even have to worry about splitting anything with Gutta. For real. I don't know you or nothing about you, man. You can get paid right quick and just disappear. This shit doesn't have to escalate any further than this. You already know my whole family is connected and powerful. You better believe they're gonna come looking for me, and once the feds get involved there's no way in hell y'all are gonna get away."

Shy looked like he was deep in thought as he mulled over Pilar's desperate words.

"A'ight, say I go along with you. What guarantee do I have that I can make a clean getaway without getting busted by the feds?" Shy asked in a sneaky tone. "I mean, how the hell do I know you ain't gonna gimme the money then turn around and call the man so he can take a bite outta my ass?" He shook his head vigorously. "Nah, baby. I don't trust you like that and you don't trust me neither. Seriously, why the fuck would I get down with you instead of sticking with my manz and the plan he laid out? What's the benefit in that?"

Pilar couldn't help but feel optimistic as she thought at least a little leeway had been made.

"Shy, please. I swear to God you can trust me," she pleaded. "Why would I wanna get you in trouble? You haven't harmed me or anything. In fact, you seem like the type of brother who looks out for sisters. I just wanna get back to my family, that's all! I'll tell the cops that I never even saw your face or anything. Hell, I'll tell them that Gutta snatched me up all by himself. Let me help you get out of this, Shy boo. You look like a reasonable guy, and like I said, you don't need Gutta in order to get the bread. Just let me go right now and I swear to God I'll get you that money and make sure you get outta Texas safe and sound."

Shy got up from his chair and walked over to Pilar with a look of sympathy spreading all over his face. Pilar gazed up at him with her big beautiful eyes, silently pleading with him. Hope surged inside her when Shy reached down and pushed a few strands of hair away from her sweaty face and gently wiped the tears from her cheeks.

"A'ight, Ma," Shy relented. "I'ma get you the fuck up outta here," he said as he began to untie her hands and her feet. "Gutta is a beast and he'll kill us both, so hurry the hell up. I'm telling you, if you fuck around and try to play me I'ma bury yo ass."

"I promise you I'm not playing," Pilar muttered with stark relief. Shy pulled her to her feet and she pushed past him and ran straight for the door where she unlatched the lock and frantically swung the door open and said over her shoulder, "I got you. I meant every word I said."

She turned around to jet out the door and damn near jumped outta her soul when she ran smack into Gutta's king-sized ass leaning against the wall with his arms crossed and an evil grin on his handsome face.

A roar of laughter exploded behind her. That clown-ass Shy was back there cracking the fuck up. Rolling on the damn floor laughing.

Pilar's heart fell down to her feet. These slick New York bastards had played her. Straight-up punked her! The truth was shining bright as fuck from their eyes. She was trapped in the middle of their little get-loot game, and she wasn't going nowhere.

CHAPTER 12

Texas wasn't nowhere near as gully as Harlem, but a kick-door robbery by a crew of stick-up kids was some real funky shit no matter where the hell it went down!

"The security guard said somebody tried to pull a lick on our mansion! I can't believe somebody rolled up on us tryna get sweet!" I gushed, sitting beside Suge as he drove. "Viceroy ain't crazy enough to be keeping no major ends in the crib like that, is he?"

"Just keep calling him!" Suge barked as we hauled ass toward the Dominion Mansion breaking top highway speeds. We had practically torn his damn door off the hinges trying to get outta his crib, and right now I was sitting beside him holding on for my life as he pushed his monster truck down the highway speeding like we had just robbed a bank.

"Alright, already! Damn, I'm calling!"

I had been clutching Suge's phone and pressing the redial button over and over as we tried to get in touch with Viceroy and let him know that somebody had been caught casing the crib, but his phone just kept ringing and ringing until it rolled over to voice mail. "His phone is on, but he's not answering."

"What about Selah?"

This fool was trucking damn near a hunnerd miles an hour and I squeezed my ass cheeks together as I grabbed the overhead strap and held on for dear life.

"I already called her a bunch of times and her phone is ringing off the hook too. Barron's still not picking up either, and Fallon and Jock are outta town."

"Bunni? Can you call her?"

I frowned and hunched my shoulders. "I left my phone in the back of the limo and I don't know her number off the top of my head like that. The whole freakin' family is off the damn grid."

Suge made a sound in his throat like this shit was fucked up big-time.

"That's because everybody's at the goddamn election party. Which is where the fuck I was supposed to be."

I cut my eyes at him. Nigga please! He wasn't whining about no election party when he was ten inches deep in my shit drilling for oil!

I was just about to hit redial and try Daddy Viceroy's phone again when Suge's phone lit up and rang in my hand.

I clicked a button. "Hello?"

It was Mama Selah.

"Suge!" she screamed so loud she damn near busted my eardrum. "Viceroy's been shot!"

"What in the hell?" I screeched back, "Viceroy's been *shot?*"

Suge snatched the phone outta my hand and hollered, "The fuck you mean Viceroy's been *shot?*"

His face went harder than a boulder as he listened to her talk for a quick second. And then suddenly he dropped the phone, jerked the wheel hard to the left, and made the fastest fuckin' U-turn that I had ever seen in my life.

"*Dammnnn!*" My ass slid across the seat and I slammed against the door as his gigantic tires squealed and the monster truck tilted over on two wheels. Suge threw his arm out to brace me and we tore a thick strip of grass up outta the median and burnt rubber up in that bitch! Seconds later Suge nosed the monster truck to the right and bogarted his way into a lane of fast-moving traffic heading in the opposite direction.

"Oh shit! Who da fuck popped Daddy Viceroy?" I hollered as I struggled to catch my balance and sit up straight. "Is he okay? Where the hell are we going now?"

"To the hospital," he muttered, standing up on the pedal and mashing the gas. "To the muthafuckin' hospital."

CHAPTER 13

"Are you having fun yet, my young stallion?" A king-sized blond woman with two milk jugs for titties purred in Barron's ear. "Are you ready for the next round of fun?"

Barron was bound to the mattress and half-conscious as his brain sizzled and blood trickled from his nose. The dominatrix devils that GiGi had let loose on his ass were really doing him dirty. They had cracked him with long skin-slashing whips and whacked the hell out of him with thick wooden paddles. A particularly cruel bitch with spiked green hair and pus-filled pimples between her titties had scorched the tips of Barron's toes with a cigarette lighter.

He had fought against his wrist and ankle restraints like a muthafucka but they had his ass good. The green-haired freak had sat on his face and damn near smothered him as she rode him until she climaxed, while the other one squeezed his limp dick and jacked it so hard that she damn near cut off his circulation.

"Please, lady, please!" Barron had begged her in a hoarse whisper. "I can't take no more. I can't take no fucking more."

"You big bucks are so strong, am I hurting you, baby?" The

woman said as she traced her finger along Barron's biceps then jammed her fingers deep into his armpit and pinched the shit out of him. "I just love it when you're soft and submissive. It makes me feel so powerful."

Barron yelped. He was in pain but he was disgusted as fuck too because the taste of her rancid pussy on his tongue was more painful than the wounds and bruises on his body. The ladies were taking a brief break from abusing him when a huge Samoan dude with man titties and a beer gut walked into the room rattling a chain in his fists.

"Play time is over for now, ladies," he said in a deep voice. "We don't want to wear our guest out too much. Now get out. I'll let you know when you can come back and pick up where you left off."

The women got up slowly and sauntered out of the room smiling and delighted with themselves. The big dude was getting ready to leave too until Barron called him back.

"Hey, wait up, man!" Barron pleaded in a trembling voice. "Lemme holler at you for a minute, my dude!"

The Samoan halted at the exit and turned back around to hear Barron out.

"What the fuck you want from me, man? And make it quick," dude said with much attitude. "I don't get my rocks off on grown men crying so don't start bitching and begging for mercy 'cause you won't find any here."

"Okay, just hear me out, bro," Barron said as he spit a glob of blood out of his mouth. "Please! Let's you and me make a deal. I promise you, it'll be a sweet one."

"How fuckin' sweet?"

"Sweeter than a muthafucka! Yo, I know a nigga like you like money and I got plenty of it. Whatever that bitch GiGi is paying you I can double it! All I need you to do is let me use the phone right quick so I can call my mother. Let me tell her where I'm at and how to get some money to me so I can tear you off real nice."

"What, I'm supposed to just trust you? I let you use the phone and you call the fuckin' cops, right?" dude said, his voice thick with sarcasm. "You could be trying to play me out and get me locked the fuck up for kidnapping. You must think I'm a fucking rookie in this game, huh?"

"Naw man, listen, I got a plan," Barron said wiggling his fingers. These bastards had his wrists tied so tight that his hands were starting to go numb. "On the key ring to my car I have a locker key. The locker contains fifty thousand dollars I keep for an emergency. I will give you the location to it. All you have to do is let me use the phone and let me call my people to get me out of here. Just take the key, go get the money, and disappear. No harm no foul. I don't know you or your name. The locker is in a place that has no cameras. Get the cash and be gone on your way."

The Samoan thought about the deal for a minute and Barron could see the wheels were turning in his head.

"How do I know you ain't on some bullshit?" he asked suspiciously. "How do you know I'm not getting paid more than fifty thousand?"

"I'm in no fucking position to lie to you, man," Barron growled. "I'm laying here talking to you ass-naked tied down to a goddamn bed. Look at this dump! Your ass would be lucky if they was paying you five g's a month. I'd say fifty thousand under the covers just to let me make a phone call is damn sure worth the risk."

"Yeah, alright. You got me. You must be one of those super smart muthafuckas, huh? Y'all rich kids always keep a stash hidden away somewhere." The Samoan grilled Barron with a smirk and then shook his head. "Well you can't be that smart if you got caught up fucking with one of these crazy bitches. Give me ten minutes and I'll get you your phone call, and then you're gonna give me the address and number to that locker. If you try to fuck me over I promise you the next time you see my handsome mug again it'll be the last thing you ever see."

★ ★ ★

Rodney Ruddman was being rushed to the hospital, bitching and cursing all the way. Bleeding profusely, he winced in pain as they loaded him into the back of the ambulance and set off with their sirens blaring.

"Which goddamn hospital are you taking me to?" he demanded.

"St. Joseph's," the female paramedic answered. "We're taking you to St. Joseph's."

"That goddamn punk muthafucka!" Ruddman muttered under his breath as he trembled with rage. He looked up at the paramedics and barked, "Did that bastard think he was gonna take me out? I'm Rodney muthafuckin' Ruddman! Do these fools know who they're fucking with?"

"Please be still, Mr. Ruddman," the skinny female said firmly. "Your pressure is unstable and I need you to calm down, sir. You've lost a significant amount of blood and we need to make sure you don't go into shock and pass out on us."

Ruddman rose up on his elbows and tried to sit up straight. He was swimming in cream and he wasn't used to taking orders from servants. "Don't tell me to calm down! Your ass is on the city payroll and that means you work for me!" he spat. "Baby I got the best goddamn health insurance in the whole damn state of Texas! They call it *cash,* sweetie. Cold green cash! So don't you talk to me like I'm some kinda indigent bum you just picked up off the streets! Treat me with some fucking respect if you wanna keep this two-dollar job, do you hear me?"

"I-I-I didn't mean to imply anything. I certainly wasn't trying to be disrespectful or to imply that you aren't a man of means, Mr. Rodney—I mean Mr. Ruddman."

"Good," he said, wincing as he settled back down. "Now do what you have to do to make sure I don't lay here and bleed to death before I get to the hospital. And I don't really care what you call me. Just as long as you don't call me broke."

Growing weak, Ruddman forced himself to calm down as

the paramedics quietly inserted an IV into his arm and started him on an oxygen treatment. They applied pressure to his shoulder wound to stem the bleeding, and kept his vital signs stabilized until they arrived at St. Joseph's Medical Center.

A large contingent of media personnel were ready and waiting when they pulled up, and Ruddman was rushed from the ambulance and wheeled into the emergency room on a stretcher as cameras flashed and swarms of reporters peppered him with questions about the shooting. The paramedics rushed him through the rowdy mob as they screamed and yelled at him to provide some details and give them the scoop, but Ruddman knew better than to make a statement.

He was whisked into the emergency room and taken to a treatment area where doctors gave him a mild sedative, then examined him, x-rayed him, and cleaned out his wound. They informed him that the bullet had passed straight through him and his injury was non–life threatening, a mere flesh wound. They were just about to take Ruddman to the operating room to have it stitched up properly when a triage nurse ran in and said that five more gunshot victims had just been brought in by ambulance and at least three had critical, life-threatening wounds.

"Well, that bumps you right on down the list," a young doctor told Ruddman as he slapped a bandage over his wound and taped it in place. "We'll get you upstairs as soon as an operating room becomes available and stitch you back together as good as new. Don't worry. You're one of the lucky ones tonight."

"How the hell do you figure I'm lucky?" Ruddman whined as two nurses raised the rails on his bed and prepared to wheel him into the hall. "Some idiot shot me! That little bastard tried to kill me!"

"But he didn't," the doctor said over his shoulder as he hurried from the room. "You'll survive."

CHAPTER 14

Selah had never been so embarrassed in her whole goddamn life. Here she was rolling around on the filthy-ass floor of a crowded emergency room with a cop and two security guards trying to manhandle her and slap the silver bracelets on her.

In his pain-hazed condition Viceroy had these fools thinking she was the one who had shot him, and instead of hearing her out and allowing her to explain, the swishy-ass ER doctor had screamed for security and promptly dropped a dime on her.

"It wasn't me!" Selah screamed as she jetted down the hall in her Fendi dress and designer heels as they chased her past mad patients who were lined up on stretchers and watching all the fun go down. "I didn't fucking shoot him! It wasn't me!"

What the hell? she thought as she dodged an elderly man leaning on a cane and an overweight mother carrying a screaming baby. *I didn't shoot anybody! I can't believe this shit!*

The command hub area of the emergency room was comprised of a square of desks, monitors, and nursing stations, and Selah twisted her ankle and ran up outta one shoe as she circled the perimeter of the room, trucking booty as fast as she could. The two toy cops were hot on her ass, and she felt like she was somehow spiraling through a bad dream as she ran laps around the room.

This can't actually be happening to me! Not to me!

But it was. The elegant Selah Ducane Dominion was hiking up her designer dress and running from the po-po like a common fuckin' criminal!

"Leave me alone!" Selah cried out as doors opened and curtains got pulled back and all kinds of nosy folks started poking their heads out of the treatment rooms to see what the hell was going down. With the security guards breathing down her neck, the real cop doubled back and came at her from the opposite direction, and before she could put her feet in gear Selah almost ran smack-dab into his big red-headed ass. She had whirled around and headed for the ambulance exit when suddenly the door to a treatment room swung open and two nurses exited the room pushing a sheet-covered patient on a stretcher.

"I didn't do it!" Selah shrieked hysterically, running directly into their path.

"Stop right there!" the toy cop barked as the security guards lunged for Selah's ankles and tried to pull her out of the way of the approaching stretcher. The real cop jumped in and tried to get him some too.

"Get your fucking hands off of me!" Selah kicked her feet and wilded out like a child of Brooklyn as she twisted and turned and fought and scrapped with the cop all over the floor. She had never been in handcuffs in her life and she wasn't trying to be in none today.

They tumbled around on the floor together and he wrestled her like an alligator as he flipped her face down, squeezed her hips between his knees, jerked her wrists behind her back, and fought to click the cuffs down on her.

"Stop resisting or I'll pepper-spray you!" the snarling cop threatened. "I'll spray you right in the eyes!"

"Oh yeah?" Selah screamed over her shoulder as she arched

her back and kicked her feet toward her ass just like a baby. "You spray me with that shit and I'll have your fucking job, asshole! I know the chief of police! I know the mayor and the governor too! I'll have you arrested and thrown underneath the damn jail! Do you know who I am? Do you know who the fuck *I am?*"

Suddenly the sheet slid back on the stretcher and Selah's rage and humiliation multiplied like a mothafucka as her arch-enemy Rodney Ruddman opened his mouth and cackled with glee, "Yes, yes! I know exactly who you are! You're that trifling Mrs. Viceroy Dominion, that's who the hell you are!"

We pulled up to the door at St. Joseph's emergency room and Suge hopped outta the monster whip before the wheels could even stop turning. Mad police officers and news reporters were crawling everywhere like roaches, but Suge didn't give a fuck as he grabbed my hand and pushed through the crowd like a giant Godzilla.

Right away some white detective ran up on us and started trying to tamp shit down. I knew he was a DT because I was the type of thief who could spot one a mile away.

"Mr. Dominion, please come this way. Your brother is being prepped for surgery and several of your family members are waiting for you in the lounge."

He led us through some doors and down a long hall, and then opened a door to a big lounge with bright lights. Mama Selah was sitting in a leather chair surrounded by Bunni and Peaches. To my surprise she looked rough as fuck, hair all wild, and makeup smeared, and her banging little Fendi dress had smudges and dirt streaks on it out the ass. She looked up and saw me and Suge coming in and she broke free of Peaches and Bunni and rushed over to us.

"They shot him! Those bastards shot him, Suge!"

I took a quick step backward. Mami looked fugged. Her face

was red and flushed with heat, and rivers of mascara dripped down her cheeks like ugly black tears.

"Who?" Suge barked, gripping her shoulders as the DT opened his mouth and tried to put his two cents in. "Who fuckin' shot him?"

"Sir, we have investigators on the ground trying to answer that question right now. Mrs. Dominion is no longer being detained, but if we could get the both of you to come down to the station and make a written statement we would appreci—"

"Detained?" Suge looked at Selah and then turned his cold eyes on the cop. "Fuck you mean, *detained?*"

Selah's face crumpled and she broke all the way down. "They put me in handcuffs, Suge!" she cried. "Those bastards threw me on the ground and arrested me!"

Suge was so goddamn mad it looked like his head started getting swole.

"*Who* the fuck put you in handcuffs?"

"That fool told everybody it was *me!*" Selah squealed. "He said I was the one who shot him! He actually accused *me!*"

"*Who* the fuck accused you?" Suge growled, turning on the tiny detective like he was about to bite a hunk outta his ass.

"*Viceroy!*" Selah sobbed. "I don't know how he could even think such a thing, but for some insane reason your brother told the cops that it was *me* who shot him!"

CHAPTER 15

Big Suge refused to allow the detective to take Selah down to the station for questioning, so they called in a supervisor and had him take us into a private room and get a statement from her right there.

"Why should I have to give a statement about anything at all?" Selah sniffed with her nose all up in the air. "I'm a tax-paying citizen and I have rights, you know. I didn't do anything wrong."

"Ma'am, we're questioning everyone who was either in the election suite at the time of the shooting, or who may have had access to the suite. We have to take as many statements as we can if we're going to find out who shot your husband."

"Well, *I* certainly didn't shoot him," Selah sniffed daintily again. "I was nowhere near him when he was shot. Everyone in the room can vouch for that."

Just give the damn statement and be done with it! I wanted to holla at her ass. Shit, she was already getting the rich bitch preferential treatment package! The po-po's and DTs were kissing her boojie ass from one check to the other one. If she had'a been suspected of shooting her boo in the hood the po-

po woulda dragged her ass down to the station by the back of her neck and then beat the damn answers outta her.

Me and Suge sat with her while she answered the questions and then signed her statement, and then we met up with Peaches and Bunni back in the waiting room so we could check on Daddy Viceroy and see how he was doing.

"He's being prepped for surgery right now," a giant-sized doctor came out and told us, "and he'll likely remain in the recovery room for most of the night. I have to tell you, though, once we move him to a permanent room he'll probably have a no-visitors order until the police can determine he's safe. Just so you know."

"N-no visitors?" Selah stammered. "B-b-but he's my husband! When can I see him?"

The doctor shrugged. "Probably not until the police clear you, or until he's ready to see you."

"That's bullshit!" Selah jumped up and hollered. "You guys are treating me like I'm some sort of criminal! I have a right to see him! He's my husband! My goddamned *husband!*"

This was turning out to be one crazy-ass night. My heart hadn't pumped this much Kool-Aid since the day Gutta kidnapped me outside the funeral parlor after my fake-mama's funeral, and just like ere'body else I needed me a lil dranky drank to calm my freaking nerves.

Surgery had been performed on Daddy Viceroy's shoulder. The bullet had entered his back and tore some shit up on its way out of his upper chest, and the doctors said he was lucky it wasn't an inch or two lower and to the right. They had posted a security guard outside the recovery room, and once we were sure he was safe and sleeping, we rode back to the mansion for the night.

Suge had gone off to be briefed by the security staff about the attempted robbery that had gone down earlier at the crib, and me, Peaches, and Bunni were in the parlor lounging around on the butter-soft furniture and tossing top-shelf hard liquor down our throats as Mama Selah brought us up to speed on what kinda drama had gone down during the election-watch party.

"I just can't explain it . . ." Mama Selah looked weak and faded as she slurped down her liquor and told her tale. "I mean, it was such an exciting day, and everything happened so damned fast. At first we were all just sitting around together sipping champagne and watching the election coverage, you know, laughing and joking about how Ruddman and all the big-wigs in Austin were gonna shit on themselves when Viceroy won, and basically just having a great time. Then it started getting late and the precincts starting tallying the votes and putting out their predictions. One minute me and Viceroy were enjoying ourselves and kinda flirting with each other a little bit, and the next minute he excused himself and went out into the foyer area to take a phone call. A few seconds later I heard a loud pop, and that's when it got real crazy. One of the waitresses started screaming and everybody started running in all directions. By the time I made my way to him Viceroy was knocked out cold and bleeding all over the place. We called the ambulance right away, and with all the press converging down-stairs waiting for the election to be called they had a field day when they heard about the shooting and saw him being wheeled out on a stretcher."

Peaches pursed his lips, then got up and went to sit next to Mama Selah. He crossed his legs daintily at the knee and started gently massaging her shoulders with his big manly hands. "I'm so sorry this is happening to your family, Mama Selah. Mizz Mink used to get her ass kicked by drug dealers and be up in the hospital all the damn time, so we can relate because y'all are going through the exact type of shit we used to go through in the hood. Are you gonna call Fallon and Jock and let them know they daddy got popped?"

"No," Mama Selah shook her head. "It's too late to call

them right now. Besides, I don't want to alarm them. There's nothing they can do tonight anyway except worry."

"Yo, where the hell is Bump?" Suge stormed back in the room and barked.

My head swung and my eyes bucked at that question and so did everybody else's.

"Oh, shit!" Bunni said jumping up from the couch. She dug down in her bra and pulled out her cell phone and checked it. "I been trying to call him for the longest but he still ain't called me back."

"I ain't heard from him neither," I said, twisting my lips. Shame on that boojie nigga! With Papa Doo knocked on his ass Mr. Barron was noplace to be found.

Mama Selah looked even more worried as she shook her head and frowned. "I don't know where Barron is, Suge, but I'm getting very worried. He never showed up for the election-watch party, although his father and I were both expecting him. Things were so hectic after Viceroy got shot that I forgot about him for a moment, but I tried to call him right after I called you and my call went straight to his voice mail."

"See now, that's a damn shame," Bunni shook her head and twisted her lips right along with me. "Mr. Precious Barron ain't got a drop of shame! I can understand him dissing me and Mink the way he do, but I can't believe he got his head so far up that white chick's ass that he ain't got time for his own momma and daddy."

"Errrm, herrrrm," Peaches agreed, pursing his lips and shaking his head. "Don't make no kinda sense. No kinda sense at all!"

CHAPTER 16

"Get yo silly ass back in that room, bitch," Gutta snarled as he pushed Pilar back inside the hotel room and slammed the door shut behind them. "What? You thought you could just shake ya ass and spit some fly yak and Shy was gonna shit on his manz to save yo dumb ass?"

Pilar's heart had dropped into her ass when she saw Gutta standing right outside the door. She had done her damnedest to sweet-talk Shy into letting her go, just to find out that the two of them were playing head games with her the whole time. She could have kicked herself up the ass for offering that fool everything but her pussy just to find out it was all just a fucking set-up.

"We ain't come out here for that small-time bread," Shy said as he pulled a bag of weed from his pocket and began breaking up the buds. "Besides, couldn't no chick get me to turn on my nigga. You rich bitches are way too gullible. Get used to it, baby. Yo ass ain't going nowhere till we get that big bank."

"Listen to me, goddammit!" Pilar snapped as she felt a fire starting to rise inside of her. "I don't know what the fuck y'all think is going on, but y'all picked the wrong bitch to kidnap. I really don't have all this fucking money that y'all think I do! My side of the family is fucked up right now. We're barely scraping by our goddamn selves, and if something good doesn't happen for us soon our shack is gonna be on the auctioning block and our asses are going to be out on the fucking streets!"

"You *stay* lying," Gutta said as he pulled out his gun and pressed the tip to Pilar's forehead. The mood changed drastically in the room as Gutta amped up the temperature with his aggression. "Don't insult my intelligence bitch 'cause I will put a bullet in that pretty little head of yours. We just left that castle you call a shack. You mean to tell me cheesy niggas like y'all are falling on hard times? Bitch I sure can't tell! I know ya pops got a mean stash hidden somewhere so don't front on me cause I ain't to be fucked with."

"Fuck you, nigga," Pilar said with no hesitation with the gun still pointed at her head. "Matter fact, mothafuck you!"

She sat there smirking as Gutta and Shy exchanged a look of confusion. That scared and vulnerable rich-bitch shit was out the window. There was no way in hell these two idiots were going to kill her. Not if they wanted to get paid.

Pilar stood up and igged the shit out of Gutta as she sashayed over to Shy. She snatched the blunt out of his mouth and took a few long pulls, steaming up the tip. She looked back over her shoulder at Gutta and bucked her eyes.

"What you waiting on, nigga? If you gonna pull the trigger then go ahead and do it! My life ain't worth shit anyway. Like I said, our cash flow is nonexistent, so if you're expecting my pops to pay you a ransom then I'm a dead bitch anyway, and that's real."

Shy jumped to his feet. "Hold the fuck up! How the fuck are y'all broke?" He snatched his blunt back from Pilar and glared at her with the crazy eye. "You related to the fucking Dominions, ain't you? Them fools got enough bread to keep forty-nine generations worth of family happy, healthy, and wealthy. It ain't no way in hell y'all fuckers doing as bad as you saying!"

"Man, fuck them Dominions," Pilar shot back angrily. "My father is Selah Dominion's brother. She's my aunt, but that's as far as it goes. Don't none of them give a damn about me. There's a whole lot of skeletons busting out of closets in that house. They might be rich, but shit ain't as sweet as it looks. So don't think they're going to pay up on my behalf because I'd rather starve before I beg them for a dime. Me and my father are both fucked in the game right now," she said, smoothing her hair. "I just make being fucked look good, that's all."

Gutta was a thorough nigga. He had survived in the game far longer than his competitors because he had sharp instincts and he could read people like a book. As much as he wanted to dangle Pilar's ass out the window like a carrot in front of a horse, his gut told him that she was telling him the truth. And it was that gut feeling that had him about to panic like a muthafucka. Because that gut feeling meant his get-money plan was about to unravel and go up in smoke right in front of his eyes.

He struggled to keep his cool as the truth hung over his head. Pilar was broke as shit, and he wasn't gonna get so much as a crust of bread from her sorry-ass daddy. The thought fucked him all the way up because his pockets were light and the money he had come down to Texas with was starting to get real thin.

"Shit!" he cursed and kicked over a chair. He knew he shoulda stuck to the original plan! All he had to do was snatch Mink's ass up and hit her stash, then head back to New York and spend that shit! Gutta's nostrils flared like a racehorse as he tried to come up with something quick to keep himself from flipping out and doing something that could fuck up everything.

"Yo, I didn't come all the way down here to the boonies to break out empty-handed," he bitched as he placed his gun on the small table next to him and sat down. He put his hands up to his face like he just couldn't believe how bad his luck had been. "Fuck that sucka shit. I want my money and the only way I'ma get it is if I can get next to Mink's yellow ass. And guess what? We gon' get up on that slimy bitch and, Pilar, you gonna help us fucking do it!"

"Help you get next to Mink?" she rolled her eyes. "You didn't have to kidnap me and threaten to murder me for that!" she said. "Doing Mink dirty is a mission I'm definitely down for. I hate the way she just crawled her crab-ass into the family and jumped all in the bank accounts. I'm a blood relative and I've been in the picture my whole life and none of them have so much as offered me a dime. Hell yeah, I'll help you snatch Mink and I can guarantee you my aunt Selah will pay some nice green lettuce to get her back. Hell, a little bit of ransom money won't even make a dent in their pockets. Yep, I'm down, but I'm telling you right now, I want me a nice big cut of the pot or I swear to God I'll lie my ass off and make sure both of y'all get locked up for kidnapping me!"

"Don't get ahead of yourself, lil mama," Gutta said, putting on the brakes. Pilar wasn't running shit up in there and he wasn't the type to submit to no bitch's demands. He dug the fuck outta the way she was talking though, and even through his pride he realized that Pilar could be a powerful asset. "This shit ain't gonna be easy. Mink stays surrounded, and we already tried to bum-rush the mansion. They got that shit on lock."

"Y'all tried to rob my uncle's mansion?" Pilar's eyes bucked as she held out her hand and gestured impatiently for Shy to pass the weed. "You're lucky y'all fools didn't get shot trying to get up in there because Uncle Viceroy ain't the one. Nah," she said, toking hard on the piff and closing one eye against the smoke, "if you want to get next to the Dominion dollars then you have to approach this situation with some smarts and finesse. And that's why you need a diva like me on your team. If

I can lure Mink's ass away from the mansion and get her out in the open, then all y'all need to do is make the phone call, demand the money, and take care of the rest."

Shy's eyes had dollar signs in them as he grinned and nodded his head vigorously.

"But," Pilar cautioned, "this shit has to be done smooth and clean. I'm definitely down to get some money, but I'm absolutely not willing to go to jail for it. So let's discuss our plans and do this thing the right way—fucking Mink up and getting some moolah out of it in the process. That's like smashing two cockroaches with one house shoe."

Shy and Gutta side-eyed each other and shared their silent approval. This was it. This was the angle they needed. There was a reason they had run into Pilar's shiesty ass on their first day in Dallas. All of this shit was already pre-ordained. It was meant to be. Pilar was the conniving little key that was going to turn the golden lock so they could get their pockets right and get at that bitch Mink at the same damn time.

CHAPTER 17

Everything was all messed up with the family and I had to beg Suge to come back to my suite and get some rest. He was real quiet and I could see his brain working and tell he was stressed, but I knew what he needed right then was not to run back out in the streets tryna find no Barron or tryna figure out who had shot Daddy Viceroy. Nah, the only thing Suge Dominion needed right then was the good stuff I was packin' and I was the only chick that could give it to him the right way.

We walked Selah to the master suite so she could go to bed, then we went to my room and took a shower together. Suge lit some candles and rubbed lotion all over my body, and then we laid back on my big old bed and tried to relax as we listened to some soft jazz playing over the speakers. After a few minutes Suge moved down to the end of the bed and began massaging my tired feet real gently. Rubbing them and sliding his fingers in and out between my toes.

I laid there on my back sighing and moaning. It felt so good being touched by my strong, sexy man. Suge's hands were firm but relaxing as he worked the tension out of my feet and left them feeling light and tingly. I moaned out loud as his fingers crept up my bare calves, sliding over my soft skin and cupping my muscles with tenderness. He took care of my ankles, my shins, and even my knees, and by the time he wrapped his pretty lips around my big toe every inch of my body was fire-hot.

I closed my eyes as I enjoyed that moist heat on my big toe as he sucked it between his lips and licked it softly.

I began to moan as his tongue flickered and darted between each of my toes, sending tiny chills up to my naked crotch. Suge sucked and licked the entire sole of my foot, then kissed it like it had a cherry on top before setting it down and touching me on my thigh. I sat up on the bed with my big old titties sitting out in front of me as I stared at his long black dick. My man could go, go, go. We couldn't take our eyes off each other. His eyes were all over my perfect 38 double-Ds with the up-turned nipples, and I stared at his thick, chiseled physique with the hard muscles everywhere.

My eyes dropped down to his manhood again and I had to reach out and grab his arm to steady myself. I had never seen a more beautiful dick in my life and I wanted that shit again and again. I bent over and licked it. It jerked like it was plugged into a socket and had sparks of electricity running from its swollen crown down to his heavy balls.

"Damn, baby," I moaned sexily. It had been less than twenty-four hours since he had dug me out, and here he was stiff and ready again. I took that hunk of meat in my hand and gripped it tight. It was warm and heavy. Like something that had been packed with hot steel. "What you planning on doing with this?"

"Whatever you want me to," Suge said quietly. He reached out and cupped my naked breasts and I gasped out loud and bit down on my lip as he rubbed all over my twins. My nipples were as stiff as darts as he pinched them gently, massaging them with his expert fingers.

I was shivering with pleasure as Suge urged me to turn over, and as I laid there on my stomach he took his time admiring my curved ass in silence.

"Damn, Mink," he whispered under his breath. His hard

dick was pressed against the back of my thigh as he lowered his head and licked up and down my back. "You're fine as hell, girl. From head to toe."

He licked the rim of my ear and sucked the back of my neck as the candles made orange shapes on the walls, and I moaned into my pillow and pressed my hand to my slit. Juice leaked from my honey bun right away and when I reached back and offered Suge my fingers, he licked them one by one.

I turned all the way around and kissed him and he slid two fingers deeply inside me as he sucked gently on my tongue. Then he left my lips and bent his head slightly. He began licking my breasts like they were twin strawberry lollipops and I grabbed his dick and started stroking him, faster and faster. He took it as long as he could, then he moved my hands and cupped my tight ass, guiding the head of his wood to my tunnel and going up in me deep as hell with one long stroke.

He pushed that rock-hard meat up in me as deep as it could go, like he was trying to make the head of it bust right outta my throat. I reached down between our bodies and grabbed the base of his dick, and as deep as he was in my guts, there was still about an inch or two of him left outside my body, and I clenched my pussy muscles tightly and attempted to suck that last bit in too.

Suge stroked me down so good I was damn near in tears. My pussy was overflowing and filled to the brim, and I wanted it to stay that way forever. I vibrated and humped my ass all over him, pumping my hips back and forth and creating delicious sensations in my hot tunnel. Suge drove deeper inside me and I contracted my pussy muscles and squeezed his thickness between my walls.

He reached out and flicked my left nipple and I moaned loudly. That bad boy was swollen and reaching out for him, and he dipped his head, he took it between his lips and bit down gently.

Pure electricity shot through my body and I threw my

head back and humped and grinded. The more Suge stroked and raked his teeth across my nipple, the hotter and slipperier my pussy got.

"Don't stop," I panted like a freak. His tongue lapped and circled my nipples and had my whole body trembling. "Oh shit," I whimpered, grabbing onto his muscle-bound shoulders. Tears ran outta my eyes he was fucking me so good. "Oh goddamn . . ." I threw my head back and moaned. And then my whole body fell loose. Every muscle in my body spasmed as I screamed and nutted like a mothafucka, bouncing up and down on Suge like he was a goddamn pogo stick.

And my man was cumming too. He grunted and jerked his dick outta me real quick, then he spun me around and bent my ass over at the waist. Slapping my ass-cheek he jacked his dick twice in his fist and shot his load in thick hot spurts that landed on my back.

With my body still tingling, we stretched out on the bed on top of the covers, and Suge pulled me into his arms as I dozed off into a happy, satisfied sleep.

It had been a horribly stressful night, but Selah felt damn good to be back in her own bed once again. Even if the other side was empty and Viceroy was laid up in the hospital talking crazy as hell. She had expected her mind to race with chaotic thoughts, or her closed eyes to see that awful image of her husband lying on the floor with a bullet wound in his back, or for her heart to be filled with the intense embarrassment of being tackled to the ground and put in handcuffs like a common hoodrat, but instead she had fallen into a deep sleep the moment her body slid across the fine silk sheets and her weary head touched the goose-down pillow.

The combination of exhaustion and the hard liquor she had guzzled had put her in a semi-comatose state, and when the phone blared from her nightstand Selah was in the very depths of a drunk-sleep as she lunged for it.

"H-h-hello?" Her mouth was dry and her voice was deep as shit. Way down there in truck-driver mode. She struggled to sit up as a strange male voice spoke into her ear.

"Y-y-yes," she said hoarsely, turning her head and using her hunched shoulder to wipe a trail of slobber off her chin. "This is she. Who is this?"

Selah listened for a second and then gazed out the window. It was near dawn and the morning sky was just beginning to lighten up. Clutching the telephone, Selah shook her head vigorously to clear her mental fog because she had to be dreaming. She just had to be. Because there was no way in hell she was hearing what she thought she was hearing.

"What?" she said loudly. "I beg your goddamn pardon, can you say that shit again? My son has been w-w-what? I'm sorry but could you say that one more time for me please?"

Listening intently and tightly gripping the phone, Selah opened her mouth wider than an ocean, and when it registered in her soul that she had heard exactly what the hell she thought she had heard, she let out a scream that was so loud and piercing that it damn near brought the whole house tumbling down.

Me and Suge were fucked out and snoring hard when an earsplitting scream drug me up outta my dream. I had been dancing with Idris Elba in a hotel, but it wasn't really Idris, it was this fine-ass male model who was even taller and sexier than Idris. He had come up behind me at a dinner function and run his hand up the back of my leg. He grabbed my hand to take me to his suite, and I had grinned at all the hater bitches sitting at the table because I was the one who was about to walk off with the prize. But then suddenly it wasn't a hotel no more, it was a jail. And the fine dude who wasn't Idris wasn't taking me to his room, he was trying to drag me into a dark cell and I was kicking and screaming and—

Aiiiighhhh!!!!!

Me and Suge fought the covers off as we jumped outta my

big old bed butt-ass naked and pulled on our soft designer bathrobes. We busted outta the door and hauled ass downstairs to the master suite and rushed inside to find Selah sitting up in bed looking like somebody had slammed her goddamn finger in a truck door.

"They've got Barron!" she shrieked as she clutched her pillow and slung snot all over the place. "Oh my fuckin' God, they've got my son! My son! My mothafucking *son!*"

"*Who's* got Barron?" Suge demanded, scratching his head as we stood around the bed looking half-sleep and crazy and trying to make some sense outta the shit she was talking.

"The man! He said they've got Barron locked up in chains in some sort of smutty sex den, and he can't get out!"

A sex den was all my stripper-ass heard, but Suge heard all the rest.

"Bump is chained up and can't get out of *where?*"

"I don't *knowwww!*" Selah wailed slinging snot everywhere. All that screaming had scared the shit outta everybody and brought Peaches and Bunni running too, and now Selah was babbling some bullshit about Barron getting his freak on with whips and chains with her eyes looking wild and crazy.

"It's a flim-flam," Bunni said, waving her hand as she yawned with her mouth wide open. "Me and Mink used to pull ganks like that all the time."

"No!" Selah's eyes bucked even bigger. "The caller sounded like he was telling the truth! He said Barron gave him my number and begged him to call me! He said Barron promised that I'd give him a reward and he told me to deliver fifty-thousand dollars to a locker at a YMCA! Oh, my *Goddddd* . . . Help me, Lord! I just can't take anymore! Some crazy pervert is holding my baby hostage and they're going to do something crucial unless we get him out of there!"

"Y'all better call the po-po!" Peaches hollered.

"*Nooo!*" Selah wailed again. "He said if I called the police they were gonna *kill* him!"

"Kill him?" Bunni blurted out. She looked at me and I looked at Peaches. This sounded like some real back home in-da-gutter Harlem-shit to me.

"Yo, dial that number back," Suge barked, holding out his hand for the phone. "Dial it back right fuckin' now!"

"I already tried," Selah panted. "I dialed it over and over. Nobody answers. It just rings and rings and rings. They're gonna kill him, Suge! They're gonna kill my *baybeee!*"

"Calm down, Selah," Suge told her gently. "Bump is gonna be okay. Ain't nobody gonna kill him. I can promise you that."

"But where the hell is he? Somebody is holding him against his will! How do you know they're not going to kill him?"

"Because," Suge said, scrolling through the caller ID on Selah's phone. "Because I'm gonna find him."

"How?" All four of us spit at the same time as he snatched his phone off his waist-clip and punched in a number.

"Don't worry about how. I got the muthafucka's number, and that means I got his muthafuckin' *number.*"

"Damn uncle-boo!" Bunni said sounding all impressed. "You nice with the cyber-shit like that?"

"You damn right," Suge said as he tossed Selah's phone down on the bed and turned around to leave. But before he could take two steps Peaches flung himself at Suge's feet and grabbed hold of his ankles.

"Take me with you!" Peaches begged, staring up at Suge in his pink half-slip with a bright yellow silk scarf tied around his weave. The spaghetti strap on his teddy slid off his muscular choco- late shoulder as he clicked his hot-pink press-on nails together and pleaded, "Take me with you, Mister Secret Agent Man!"

Suge snorted. "Nigga you must be cr—"

"Take him, Suge!" I blurted out, remembering how Peaches had saved my ass from Punchie Collins and Gutta and a slew of other niggas I had schemed on and fucked over back in the day. "For real, let P go with you, boo! I know you ain't feeling all the frilly skirts and stuff, but Peaches is from Harlem and he can fight! He ain't no bottom bitch *all* the damn time!"

Selah put her two cents in it too. "Yes, please, Suge. Please let Peaches go with you. I'd feel so much better if you two went together."

Suge looked at ere'last one of us like we were outta our monkey-ass minds.

"All of y'all must be smoking something. Ain't no way in hell I'ma take no goddamn—"

"Peaches can come in handy," Bunni pointed out loudly. "My bruvva is *versatile,*" she said proudly. "He can dip and dive, baby! He can slide all up in the ladies bathroom and a bunch of other places that a hunk of a dude like you could never get inside."

It took a whole lotta begging and pleading, but we finally got Suge to agree.

"Thank you, thank you!" Peaches squealed. "I been bored as fuck sitting up in this dead-behind joint! Everybody else gets to do exciting shit. I'm ready to have me a little adventure too!"

"I tell you what," Suge growled, looking mad as fuck. "You roll with me and you better do exactly what I tell you to do and when I tell you to do it, got it?"

Peaches snapped to attention like a soldier. "Got it, boss!"

"A'ight," Suge said as he turned to walk out the room with a cold look in his eye. "Be out front in fifteen minutes," he barked. "And put on some muthafuckin' pants!"

Peaches was happy as hell that Big Suge had agreed to let him ride shotgun on such an important mission, but then again he had graduated from the school of hard knocks and been the brains behind some of the slickest swindles and schemes in all of New York City. With his eye for opportunity, nose for ganks, and umpteen years of cut-throat experience in the con game, there was no better man for the job.

And he did mean *man!*

"My goodness!" Peaches squeaked in frustration as he stood in front of the mirror and slid his long muscular legs into a pair of tailored men's slacks. Gone were the flared skirts, the slinky tops, the booty-choker shorts, and the colorful wigs. It was time to man-up and put on his big-boy drawers, and he had raided Dane's closet to find some manly gear that he could style.

Humming the tune to "Secret Agent Man," Peaches yanked at the waistband of his trousers until his balls got split east and west by the high seam in the crotch. He had never worn a pair of skinny jeans in his whole damn life, and reaching down into his purple silk panties he gathered his nuts and shifted them babies all the way to the left side, then he changed his mind and rearranged them on the right. Buttoning and zipping his pants, he wiggled his ass around and then jumped up and down a couple of times until his package settled into a nice, comfortable spot.

He felt strange as fuck as he stood posing in the mirror checking out the tall, handsome hunk named Paul. Designer jeans, starched black shirt, paisley tie, silver cufflinks and Italian leather shoes—even as a dude he looked gooder than a mutha-fucka. His muscles bulged underneath his clothes and male or female you could tell he was the athletic type. He was already missing his Remy wig, but his freshly cut hair was lined up to perfection. He peered at his face even closer. His lips felt crusty without his berry-tinted mocha gloss, but he'd ditched the makeup and for the first time in years he was sporting the faint hint of a moustache and the outline of a goatee.

"Baines," he squeaked at the mirror in a British spy accent, and then he checked himself right quick.

"Baines," he growled pushing some bass into his voice as he got ready to play the hell outta his role. "Paul, Baines."

Ready for the world, Paul Baines stepped out of his suite and strode confidently down the stairs to join Uncle Suge and become the man of the hour.

CHAPTER 18

D$_\text{y-Nasty}$ was in a real funky mood as she wandered into the day room at the jailhouse to watch a little television. Earlier in the day the slick Philly grifter had said her final good-byes to that dumb bitch Stanka, who had gotten bailed out and hit the bricks just that morning.

"Bye, hater!" Dy-Nasty had barked as Stanka sashayed past her cell carrying all her jailhouse gear in a dingy-ass pillow-case. "You better be glad I didn't get a chance to put my foot up your ass 'cause your crooked nose would still be dripping shit!"

"Bye, Mink, you low-rated yellow skunk!" Stanka hollered back. "Don't worry 'bout my nose, boo. I'ma still be able to smell your scripper ass all the way from the crib!"

Dy-Nasty walked into the day room with her lips twisted. The first row of seats were the best in the house, but as usual they were all taken. The seats were made of torn brown pleather with the stuffing coming out, and a crew of chicks who ran to-gether like hungry dogs were sprawled out with their legs everywhere, taking up two and three seats at a time.

Dy-Nasty started to walk up on those bitches and start

some shit. She could see herself kicking their feet outta the chairs and making one or two of them raise up and bark, but it was getting late and the fight that was sure to pop off would probably land her in lockup for days.

Taking her funky attitude with her toward the back of the room, Dy-Nasty sat down and tried to get comfortable on one of the hard metal chairs as some local news about a fire in an abandoned warehouse blared from the television screen.

"And now, in other news from around the area, two very strange and very violent incidents are being reported from the DFW Metroplex tonight. Oil billionaires Viceroy Dominion and Rodney Ruddman were both shot by an assailant during their respective election-watch parties tonight. Both men are contenders for the office of chairman of the Texas Railroad Commission, and although they were stationed with their staffers in separate hotels, an unknown gunman or gunmen managed to shoot them both. Each man sustained non–life-threatening wounds and both are being treated at St. Joseph's Medical Center in Dallas . . ."

"Daddy Viceroy got *shot?*" Dy-Nasty leaped to her feet and shrieked. "Get the *fuck* outta here!"

"Shut the fuck up!" One of the troll-bitches on the front row hollered, but Dy-Nasty didn't even pay that heffah no mind. Suddenly all that ass-dragging she'd been doing was done and over with. She was energized and ready to get shit sparking. Something big was going on and she wanted to be in on it. Viceroy and Ruddman *both* taking a hot one? Now how in the *fuck* did that happen?

Without a word Dy-Nasty switched her booty the fuck up outta the day room. There was mad pep in her step and sass in her ass as she rolled her hips down the hall toward the bank of pay phones.

Use everything to your advantage, her dear mother Pat had told her. *No matter what kinda curve balls life throws at you, swing your bat, baby! Aim for the fences and make that shit work for you!*

Ya goddamn right she would!

Dy-Nasty didn't know exactly what the fuck had gone down in those hotel rooms during that election watch, but whatever it was she wanted a cut of the action. The allotted time for making phone calls had passed hours earlier, but Dy-Nasty didn't give a fuck. Them stupid-ass COs could write her up from here to next damn week if they wanted to because she was getting on the phone. Shit, this could be the chance of her miserable little life! Her play daddy had taken him a heat round, and she had to figure out how to make that shit work for her!

Peaches hadn't made it halfway down the stairs when his balls started aching and his dogs started barking. He looked down at the shiny black leather brogans he had taken out of Dane's closet and frowned. It had been so damn long since he'd worn anything except hoe-hopper heels and fuck-me pumps that his feet didn't know how to act in flat shoes.

He paused and wiggled his hips. His nuts didn't know how to act in men's pants neither.

"Oh hell naw," he muttered looking down at himself with a frown. He didn't give a damn what Suge said, his gear was wrong as hell. Uh-uh. Uh-*uh!* These goddamn clown clothes couldn't do a damn thing for him and they just wasn't gonna cut it. They wasn't gonna cut it at all!

Every one of Selah's hopes and prayers were resting on the shoulders of her brother-in-law Suge. The sun was barely up good as she sat alone guzzling gin in the back of her limo while her driver raced her to the hospital so she could tell Viceroy the terrible news about Barron's kidnapping. After Suge and Peaches left to go find Barron, Mink had taken a shower in her bathroom then crawled in the bed with her and the two of them had lain there worrying like crazy and waiting for the sun to come up. Mink had eventually dozed off and started snoring lightly from parted lips, but sleep wouldn't even think about coming to Selah as she lay there crying her eyes out, cursing fate for allowing her life to spiral so far out of control.

It seemed like an eternity ago that she had slapped Wally Su to death and discovered the legal documents that would save her family's fortune were hidden under his mattress. Selah had been feeling mighty fine and proud of herself after that feat. The tide had finally turned in her favor and she'd been certain that Viceroy was going to be crazy pleased and proud of her too.

She'd prayed that Viceroy would let go of all that old anger and suspicion and let bygones be bygones and forget all about her and Rodney Ruddman. She had been dying to get back in her house and back in her marriage bed, and for a minute it looked like that's exactly where her and Viceroy were about to be heading, but then bam! Out of nowhere somebody shoots Viceroy in his goddamn back and he ends up blaming her! And if that wasn't enough to fuck her world up, she gets the phone call that every mother dreads telling her that somebody has decided to kidnap her Lil Bump!

Huddled in the backseat of her limo, Selah reached into her purse and found a lace handkerchief and wiped her face with the edge, trembling as she remembered the intensity in Barron's scream, and the fear and desperation that had been in his voice when he called out loudly for her, his mama.

They were torturing him! Selah thought, shuddering as she bit back her cries. Torturing her Lil Bump! What in the world had she done to deserve this type of misery? What spirit of evil was responsible for the wrath that was raining down full force on her family? Was all this some sort of karmic payback for her many sins?

Selah squeezed her eyes closed and clutched at her stomach. She hated to think it, hated to admit it, but after all the lies she'd told and the dirty shit she had done in her life this had to be either God or the universe reaching out to pimp-smack her with a backhand slap to punish her ass. Because as much as she had been blessed with, all the riches and the finery, she had still been a floozy. A dick-sucking adulteress. A hot-in-the-ass ghetto freak who had chased the enemy's dick right into the pits of hell!

Yes! Tell the truth and shame the goddamn devil!

This plague of bad luck was all *her* fault. She had brought it all on herself, and now her Barron, her oldest and most loyal child, was paying the cost for it.

Dear God, Selah silently begged as the luxury limo ran over a large pothole on the race toward the hospital, *God please forgive me.* Yeah, she was one of those hypocrites who only thought to call on God when she needed him, but she didn't care what anybody called her because right now she really needed Him! *God, please watch over my son and give me another chance. Give me one more chance to atone for my sins and do things the right way. I swear I'm worthy of your grace!*

The hospital was right up ahead and Selah was weeping another wave of bitter tears when her cell phone rang from deep down inside of her purse.

"Hello!" she dug down past her wallet and makeup and balled-up bits of tissue and snatched it out and clicked it, practically screaming into the receiver. "Hello!" she repeated, praying like hell that it was Suge or Peaches or somebody calling her with some good news about Barron. "Hello, goddammit!" she shrieked. "This is Selah Dominion! You called my number now say something, goddammit! Who is this? Who the hell is this?"

"I-I-It's," came a soft, stammering voice from the bitter depths of her past. "It's your sister."

The last time Selah had said more than two words to her baby sister she had been calling her a string of hoe-bitches that was long enough to wrap around the Brooklyn Bridge and stretch all the way back to Texas. Twice.

In some ways it seemed like just yesterday that Selah had walked into Viceroy's New York City office and caught him with his pants down around his ankles and his dick jammed halfway down her baby sister's throat. She had been shocked out of her mind because it had been months since Viceroy had been able to get enough of an erection to have sex with her, but here he was standing in the middle of his office with his joint wet and slippery and looking like it was jam-packed with tiny rocks as baby sis slobbed all over his knob.

Selah had been so traumatized and distraught that she had gone on a drinking binge that had ended up costing her more than she had ever imagined and caused her young daughter to get snatched and abducted right out of her stroller in broad daylight. Little did she know, but it would be twenty years before she laid eyes on her child again, and by that time all the bitterness, guilt, rage, and hopelessness in the world had taken its toll on her and her entire family.

During those long, trying years Safa had attempted to reach out to her, offering apologies on top of apologies for her behavior and her betrayal, but Selah had met each attempt at reconciliation with stone cold contempt. She was through with that bitch. Utterly and totally through. Not only had she felt used and abused as the older sister who had helped raise, nurture, and protect Safa after their mother died, but she had never, *ever,* been able to get that picture of Viceroy's long black dick, rock hard and glistening with saliva as he slammed it to the root into her sister's mouth, out of her mind.

"Yeah, suck it baby, suck it!" her husband had moaned as he stood in his office and pumped his naked hips and clenched and flexed his booty cheeks while baby sister deep-throated him from her knees. "Suck the skin off this dick, baby!"

Uh-uh. Safa could go straight to hell because those words still echoed in Selah's ears like she'd just heard them yesterday.

As her limo driver approached the hospital Selah tossed back her fourth miniature bottle of vodka and shuddered at the memory that had hurt her so bad. Viceroy's soft dick had had her thinking something was wrong with *her*. She'd thought she had lost her sexy and didn't turn her man on anymore. And what else was she supposed to think? Viceroy couldn't stroke up any wood for her, but his shit had been ten inches of brick for her sister as Selah and her small children watched from the doorway.

"Why are you calling me?" she spoke quickly into the phone, all the ugly feelings of betrayal and disgust rising up in the back of her throat. The last time Safa had called she had begged for half of their mother's cremated ashes and Selah had told her what deepest, darkest part of her ass she could kiss. "Why in the hell are you calling my phone?"

"I-I-I just . . . I just saw the news. I heard about V-V-Viceroy. That he's been shot. I'm sorry, Selah. I just called to let you know that I'm thinking about you and the kids, and that I'm here if you ever need me."

"Need you?" Selah turned her lip down in disgust and blasted on her. "You've got a lot of damn nerve calling me with some fake concern about my husband! When I *needed* you, your snake-ass gave me a whole lot more than I bargained for, don't you think? No, boo-boo. We don't need *shit* from you! I think you've given this family more than enough headaches and heartaches, thank you very much!"

"Selah," her sister said quietly. "Wait. Please listen. I know I hurt you twenty years ago, and I've never stopped apologizing or feeling horribly about it. I was sorry then, and I'm still sorry now. But *please*. We're sisters. How much time has to pass before you can find it in your heart to forgive me? Mama's dead and Daddy's gone too. It's just us and Digger left, Selah. And I miss my big sister. I really, *really* miss you."

"*Miss* me?" Selah blurted. She was at the very end of her emotional rope and tears ran down her cheeks as her verbal lashing came straight out of Brooklyn before she could get a grip and slow her roll. "You can *miss* me with that *bullshit*, okay? You wasn't missing my ass back in the day when you were on your knees busy sucking my husband's dick!"

"Selah," Safa said quietly, ignoring her sister's tirade. "This is it. I'm done. I can't do this with you anymore. I think you get some sort of sick satisfaction out of refusing to forgive me, and that's your prerogative. But I'm done. I will never again call you and I will never speak to you again. Never. From this point forward you no longer exist to me. And even if you and Viceroy and the children never see fit to forgive me, God already has. Good-bye, Selah. Good-bye."

CHAPTER 19

I was a nervous fucking wreck knowing that Suge was out there somewhere doing all kinds of dangerous shit to try and find Barron before he got slumped, but Bunni was steady in my ear trying to convince me that there was more to this little story than what Mama Selah was spitting outta the side of her mouth.

"I'm telling you, Mink," Bunni was crunching on some pork skins and smacking all in my face as she spoke, "that grimy bitch GiGi got something to do with this! Trust me. My titty is itching like a mothafucka and you know my girls don't be acting up just for no reason."

I sighed and rolled my eyes at her for the millioneth time. "Bunni, please. I know I'm a suspicious heffah, but you just paranoid for no damn reason at all! Just because GiGi pulled a fast one on us and ran game like a pro, it don't mean she's got ill intentions toward Barron! She seems like the type of white chick who likes to bite on dark meat and chew that shit down to the bone, so why would she set him up for some crazy shit?"

"Because!" Bunni blurted, looking at me like I was stupid

for real. "The bitch is a grifter, Mink! Just like you and me! She tryna get paid, girl. Just watch. I betchu when all this shit is said and done we gonna find out that she was behind the whole damn thing. I seen it in her straight from the gate. You seen how she tried to front me off and play me to the left!"

"But she *did* play you, Bunni! She had you thinking you was gonna get some damn reality show from a station that didn't even exist!"

"Right!" Bunni shrieked, pointing her finger all in my face. "Now if a country bitch like that can grease a gutter pro like me and have me sucking up her fumes and believing all her lies, imagine what she could do to a square like Barron? She got him, Mink! That bitch got his ass by the little tiny hairs on his weak-ass nuts! And I tell you what. Suge better watch his back around that scripper too because I seen the way she was scoping on him. If she can trip Barron up and snag him in a trick bag, she can go for your man Suge too!"

I thought about that shit for a long minute and what ran through my mind was nothing nice. "Nah, Bunni," I shook my head and poked out my lip. I knew Big Suge could handle his like a champ, but I also knew what kinda power was vested in a conniving chick's pussy. "That shiesty heffah better not go at my man's throat because if she do I'ma find that red hot liar and put my foot all up in her ass!"

Viceroy had spent a long, pain-filled night in the recovery room, and when he awoke the next morning he was wheeled into a semi-private room where a pretty chocolate-skinned nurse was waiting for him with a big bright smile. She had pulled a curtain divider across the room to give him some privacy, and then she set about talking in a sweet singsong voice and taking his vital signs while making him comfortable.

"The detectives should be coming to talk to you soon, but until they get here how about a nice cool sip of water, sir?" the slender gem with a million braids said in a lilting West Indian accent. She grasped him expertly under his good shoulder so he could raise his head to drink.

"Shit!" Viceroy complained, wincing as a bolt of pain shot through his injured shoulder. "Hold up, goddammit! That muthafuckin' shit hurts!"

"Just take a deep breath," she instructed calmly. "And have a sip of water."

"Uh-uh!" Viceroy shook his head stubbornly. "I don't wanna take no deep damn breath and I don't wanna drink no goddamn water neither! Unless you gonna throw a double shot of gin in that damn cup!"

Just then the curtain beside the bed fluttered and a gravelly voice drifted across the partition and invaded Viceroy's space.

"Dominion? Is that you, mothafucka?"

Forgetting all about his shoulder, Viceroy frowned and tried to sit all the way up but got slammed back to the bed by another bolt of pain.

"Who's that over there?" he shrieked, motioning for the nurse to pull back the curtain. "Who in the hell is that?"

Suddenly the curtain was yanked all the way back from the other side, and to Viceroy's surprise it was none other than his arch nemesis, Rodney Ruddman, laying in the next bed and staring at him with his ashy frog face and bugged out eyes.

"The *fuck* are you doing in my room, sucka?" Ruddman slurred, morphine-drunk but still mad enough to talk cash shit. "Get the hell out."

Viceroy was pissed. "Fuck you nigga, I was here first!" he roared. "Nurse!" he motioned toward the West Indian cutie. "Get this trickster out of my room before I snatch him out that bed and kick his fat ass up and down the hall! Get him the fuck outta here!"

The nurse shook her head. "I'm sorry, gentleman, it was an extremely busy night and we're packed to capacity today. There was a large gang fight and several bad accidents, and we have more patients than we can handle right now," she explained.

"We're doing our best to free up some single suites to accommodate you, but we're short-staffed and we have a lot of critical-care patients to deal with at this time."

"I don't give a damn about your other patients, lady," Ruddman spit. "This mothafucka right here is probably the one who set me up to get shot! Get his ass away from me! Where's my assistant? I want a security guard! Hell, no. One of us gots to go and it won't be me."

"Nigga are you drunk?" Viceroy shot back with a look of bewilderment on his face. "*You* probably set *me* up to get shot, you fucking coward! Lord knows you don't have the balls to run up on me yourself! Yeah, you knew I was about to beat the hell outta you in that election race so you sent one of your flunkies to snuff me out, didn't you?"

"You wasn't about to beat shit but your *dick,* nigga!" Ruddman fired back gutter-style. "You were about to *lose* that race, my friend, and once I took over the commission I would've sanctioned your company so hard you would have had no choice but to bow down and kiss my ass! I don't need to get a flunkie to take you down, Viceroy. I can get out of this bed and fuck you up all by myself!"

As the insults continued to fly back and forth between the two injured billionaires the nurse darted from the room to go get some help. And a moment after she left Selah Dominion walked into the room and stopped dead in her tracks, confused like hell at the sight of the two men who had caused so much turmoil in her life sharing the same space.

Ruddman spotted her first and he was all over that shit.

"Hey, sexy! Come on in! Look, Viceroy, I bet you can't guess which one of us this whore is here to see! Me or you?"

Ruddmn gazed evilly at Selah and chuckled. "Mrs. Dominion. Come on over here and give Papa a kiss. May I ask where your ring is, darling?"

Viceroy yanked his IV straight out of his arm and swung his shaky legs over the side of the bed. "Muthafucka," he screeched,

balling up his fists, "I will knock the black off your ass!" Forgetting all about his shoulder, he slid his naked tail off the bed
and limped toward Ruddman in a murderous rage. "You lucky
you caught it in the chest and not in the head because you're a
dead man, you crispy fat fucker! A dead man!"

"Viceroy, *no!*" Selah grabbed her husband's arm. "Baby,
please! You're too weak to walk, honey. Come on. Let me help
you get back in bed."

But it was too late for all that rational talk. Viceroy stumbled toward Ruddman with his hospital gown flapping in the
back and his naked ass exposed as he rushed at the man who
he knew for a fact had fucked his wife! He loomed over Rodney and they both got to swinging their good arms and ex-
changing weak, one-handed blows.

"You fucked my *wife*, you slimy bastard!" Viceroy muttered
as he fought to stay on his feet and tag Ruddman with his left
fist at the same time. "You took what was mine, you crispy
frog-faced muthafucka, you!"

"That I did," Ruddman agreed as he dodged and tried his
best to swing back with one fist. "That I did!"

Selah tried to get between them but Ruddman caught her
with a right hook and Viceroy tagged her with two clobbering
blows too. She fell against the wall stunned, and she was mad
grateful as two hospital security guards rushed into the room
and pulled the old men apart. The security guards lifted
Viceroy back into his bed, then began wheeling him out of the
room as he flailed his arms and legs and called Ruddman a
string of ugly muthafuckas.

"Yeah, yeah, yeah! Talk all that shit but get the fuck out!"
Ruddman screamed back from his bed. "Go, asshole, go! And
ain't nobody gonna miss you neither! That's why your wife
had to come crawling to me to get the good wood, sucka!"

Ruddman's words stabbed Viceroy in the heart like pointy
steak knives, and like a good soldier he twisted them shits
deeply into his enemy's wounds. "Your package must be short

as shit, nigga! Short, short, *short*! Your wife is on fire and your hose ain't long enough to put it out! You should have seen how fast that bitch came running to me! Crawling and *begging*! How do you think I got a'hold of her cheap little ring?"

In one furious stride Selah was at Ruddman's bedside swinging blows. "Shut the fuck up!" she punched him dead in the lip, busting that shit like a grape as she tried her best to knock the truth out of his critter-looking mouth.

Ruddman's eyes bulged as he yelped and recoiled in pain, and Selah whirled around and caught up with her husband as they wheeled him toward the door. She grabbed his good hand and searched his eyes with desperation in her heart.

"Viceroy, look at me!" she pleaded as she ran around and stood in front of his stretcher. "Please, *look at me*! Don't listen to him! That fool is lying! He's just trying to hurt you. There's nothing going on between us and he doesn't have my ring! He's *never* had it! He's *lying* to you, baby! Lying!"

"Liar!" Viceroy roared, glaring at Selah like he could barely stand the sight of her. The heat in his eyes was enough to scorch the breath out of her throat, and she was relieved when he turned away from her and screamed over his shoulder, "Eat a dick, you fat bastard!" he barked at Ruddman as they wheeled him out the door. "You grimy, toad-hopping bitch! Forget dining on worms, muthafucka, go eat your own dick!"

"Oh, I would," Ruddman said, licking blood off his busted lip as he snickered and said something so foul and nasty it ensured him the last and grimiest laugh of them all. "I'd eat my own dick, but your pretty little wife already slurped it up and swallowed it whole."

CHAPTER 20

Things went from bad to worse for Selah after the verbal ass-kicking Ruddman put down on Viceroy, and when he was wheeled into a private suite on a higher floor, the first thing Viceroy did was arrange for a private security firm to post someone outside of his door twenty-four/seven, and the next thing he did was demand a telephone so he could call his lawyer.

"I want a divorce, goddammit," he barked into his attorney's ear with authority and finality. "I want Selah out of my house and out of my life, so draw up the documents and serve that bitch with papers and serve her NOW!"

Cooper Costner Esquire, Attorney at Law, was a shark-ass lawyer who worked for one of the state's most powerful families, and whatever his boss wanted he made it his business to deliver. Usually.

"You're going to want to think about that," he warned in a neutral voice. "We're talking multiple liquid assets well into the billions, here. Land, stock, bonds, and oil royalties. Selah's going to want half of everything you know, and if she gets the right judge she just may get it too."

Viceroy bitched. "So what the hell am I paying you the big

bucks for then goddammit? Who the fuck cares if she gets the right judge? I have the right lawyer, don't I?"

"You certainly do, Mr. Dominion," Cooper said smartly. "You certainly do."

The phone call from Cooper Costner had caught Selah totally by surprise.

"Look, I shouldn't be talking to you but we've been friends for nearly thirty years and I just thought you should have some time to prepare yourself."

"Prepare myself for what?" Selah stammered. She had huddled in the backseat of the limo and cried all the way back to the mansion, and as soon as she hit the door she'd dragged herself up the stairs and crawled back into her bed. She'd started not to answer the phone when it rang, but when she glanced at the caller ID and saw who it was she'd picked it up right away.

Costner was primarily Viceroy's business attorney, but he had handled a few personal matters for Selah as well over the years, and in addition to his brilliant mind Selah trusted him as a confidante and a friend.

"Viceroy's filing for divorce," he said point-blank, hitting her with a gut shot straight, no chaser. "He's claiming it on the grounds of infidelity, fraud, theft, and everything else he can think of. He's prepared for this whole thing to be public and he's prepared for it to be messy. But most of all, he's prepared for a fight and he's actually looking forward to you giving him one."

Selah could only sit there like a deaf-mute as she stared up at the ceiling like the roof had just crashed in all around her. As bad as things had been between her and Viceroy she couldn't believe what the hell she was hearing. She just couldn't believe it!

"Th-Th-There must be some mistake," she finally stammered softly. "My husband is not feeling well. He was shot, you know! It's the medication. It has him talking all kinds of craziness out of his head, but he doesn't mean it. He doesn't mean any of it."

"Oh, he means it," Costner assured her in a deadpan voice. "He told me he wants you out of his life and he wants to shove his foot up your ass on your way out the door, and he means every word of it."

Selah swallowed hard as agony and embarrassment pulsed in her blood. After all these years divorce had never even entered her mind, especially not when Rodney Ruddman had pressured her to do it, and to hear about it like this, from someone else instead of from her husband was devastating. Viceroy *had* to be tripping. No matter what they were going through he had to know it was only temporary. They were committed to each other. They were in it for the long haul, to the very end. Sure, their marriage was complicated and had its share of problems just like most marriages did, but they had moved up to the big time together and neither one of them had ever thought about hustling backward and leaving any of it behind!

"My assistants are putting together some preliminary paperwork to send you as we speak, but I can assure you that Viceroy is willing to be very generous. I can't give you any specifics, but I can say he'd be willing to consider beginning negotiations at about ten percent of his net income, excluding certain assets of course. Now, as your friend, what I recommend you do, Selah, is hire yourself a very fine lawyer. Of course no matter who you find he or she won't be nearly as skilled or as shrewd as I am, but you at least want someone who can put up a decent fight. Since I'm representing Viceroy this will have to be our final conversation, but I want to tell you what a pleasure it's been serving you over the years and I wish you good luck."

Selah could barely breathe as Costner disconnected the call and the phone went dead in her hand. What in the hell was Viceroy thinking? A divorce? Could this be real? Could it be that her husband didn't love her anymore and he wanted a goddamned divorce?

No, Lord, *no,* Selah screamed in her mind as she threw the

phone to the floor and bolted straight out of the bed. Clutching her quaking stomach, she rushed into the bathroom and coughed and heaved until she ejected the traces of hard liquor that were left from her guzzling spree in the back of the limo, cringing at the taste of bitterness and defeat that filled her mouth and coated her tongue.

When she was finally done retching she leaned over the sink and rinsed her mouth vigorously and splashed cold water all over face, and when she finally raised her head and looked into the mirror it wasn't her own hazel eyes that she saw staring back at her. No, they were the eyes of her sister. Her only sister. Her *baby* sister.

Safa.

"Oh God!" Selah cried out as the weight of the last twenty years came crashing down on her. She had been done so dirty. She had been done so damned *wrong*! But for the first time ever she was acknowledging to herself at least, how dirty and wrong she had been too! Her life was a hot-ass mess! Every damn thing that could possibly go wrong was going that way. Maybe God was trying to tell her something. Maybe He was punishing Viceroy and her poor darling Barron because of *her* sins!

It was hard to think it, and even harder to own up to it, but alone with only her own fears and her demons to blame, Selah had no choice. Yeah, her sister had fucked up, but she had fucked up too. Damn right, Viceroy had hurt her and cheated on her, but she had done the same damn thing to him. Hell, it was only right that God was punishing her. Teaching her a lesson! She had been so damn desperate for Viceroy's forgiveness and grace, but she hadn't been willing to extend her own to anybody else!

The truth be told, in her heart of hearts Selah had forgiven her sister long ago. As a woman she had always known that Viceroy was her man, not Safa's. With her eyes full of dollar signs, she had been dying to marry his black ass, and standing before God they had made certain vows and commitments that they'd both promised to honor.

But it was *Viceroy,* not her damned sister, who had lost his head and violated the sanctity of their marriage. It was *him* who had laid his mack game down and convinced a naïve young girl to come across town to his office and suck his dick down to the meat bone!

Yet, Selah had stayed with him. She had cut her sister off, and stayed married to her unfaithful-ass man. She had slept with him, supported him, loved him, and even sucked that same old cheating dick of his too! So, if she had found the room in her heart to forgive her lying husband, why hadn't she been able to do the same for her sister?

Fucking hypocrite!

That's what she was, and that's why she was being tested! Because she was a hypocrite! A liar and a sinner. She was all those grimy low-down bitches she had accused her sister of being, and more!

But now she finally had some clarity and she knew exactly what she needed to do. Selah had to forgive Safa. She had to forgive her baby sister. As hurt as she had been, and as mad as she still wanted to be, she had to let that shit go. She could and she *would!* And, Selah prayed, once she opened up her heart and offered forgiveness to her sister, then maybe God and Viceroy would both forgive *her.*

Hell yeah. Selah knew exactly what she had to do. Like she had told Safa, words were empty. They didn't mean a goddamn thing. It took action and deeds to show a true change of heart, and she knew exactly how to prove to her sister that her heart had been changed.

These were the thoughts on Selah's mind as she stumbled out of her bathroom and headed back to her rumpled bed. On the way past the fireplace a glint from a glistening crushed-glass purple urn caught her eye. She froze in her tracks as she stared up at it.

The exquisite glass urn had been sitting on her mantel for many years, untouched. It contained her mother's cremated ashes, and Selah couldn't count the times that her sister had begged her to divide them up in thirds and send a portion to her. Selah had refused that simple request over and over again. Her anger wouldn't allow her to send Safa shit. Not only wasn't she going to desecrate her mother's remains by splitting them up, she wasn't about to share them with her sleazy low-down sister neither.

But now, Selah walked over to the urn and ran her finger over the yellow butterflies on the rough, etched surface. The glass was made from the prettiest combination of lavender and deep purple that she had ever seen.

The time had come. She would do more than divide her mother's ashes in thirds. She would send the entire urn to her sister as a peace offering, and then go to church and pray at the altar for forgiveness.

Selah dressed quickly in some casual clothing and called downstairs and ordered a servant to bring up some packing materials and a sturdy box. And for the next thirty minutes she secured the urn and snuggled it tightly in foam packaging and addressed it to her sister.

It was really a damn shame that after all these years her sister was still living in their old apartment on Broadway right under the El, while Selah lived a life of luxury and magnificence that could put royalty to shame. On impulse, Selah reopened the box, then went to her nightstand and retrieved her checkbook. She scribbled out a check for a hundred thousand dollars made payable to her sister, then stuck it inside the box and resealed the whole thing back up again.

There, Selah thought as she rang for her personal assistant and instructed him to have a courier service pick up the box for overnight delivery. Hopefully Safa would accept their mother's ashes and her sister's apologies too, and in time maybe she would come to forgive her big sister for being so damned unforgiving.

CHAPTER 21

"A'ight, so what's the plan for putting the clamps down on this trick?" Gutta asked Pilar with a grimy glint in his eye. The tables had turned and Pilar was now on Gutta's winning team. At least for now anyway. "You wanna keep my foot outta ya ass then you better be cookin' up a mean cuisine for Ms. LaRue."

"Chill the fuck out and let me think," Pilar responded with her attitude on high as Shy sat in the corner and laughed his ass off. Pilar didn't trust these low-life mothafuckas for a second, but she was determined to get the last laugh. First things first though. "I already told you, I got this. I just need a minute to think about all the possibilities."

Pilar knew what had to happen. She was going to have to devise a scheme that would draw Mink out in the open and lure her into a trap. But knowing that shiesty Harlem hustler, tripping her up was gonna prove to be easier said than done. It wasn't like Pilar could just hit her on the cellie and say, "Hey girl, it's me, let's go out and have a spa day" or some shit like that. Pilar couldn't stand Mink's high-yellow ass, and Mink damn sure wasn't feeling her either. Hell, nah. That wasn't gonna happen.

For a brief moment Pilar considered reeling Mink in with

some fake get-money plot, but how could that shit work? Now that Mink was officially a Dominion she was rolling in cream and already had everything she could ask for under the sun.

The only thing left for Pilar to do was to switch up her strategy. As far as she could tell, the only thing besides money that Mink gave a damn about and could be used against her as a weakness was the family. Even as conniving as Pilar was, she wasn't trying to involve her aunt Selah in no low-down schemes, and she wasn't about to get in no tussle with that hoodrat Bunni neither. That gutter chick carried razor blades in her mouth and there were no wins in that, only a sliced up face. Jock and Fallon were out of town, and Dane stayed too high to give a fuck about anything, and she seriously doubted if Mink would go out of her way for Barron or that ugly bitch Dy-Nasty either.

Nope, none of them would do at all, and the only other person Pilar could think of that was consistently up Mink's ass and in her corner was Uncle Suge. Yeah, Suge. That fine-ass buffalo-built nigga was like a hound dog, always tracking something down. If she could find a way to get at him and catch him sleeping and fuck him up, then maybe Mink might jump in all amped and hyped to help get his dick out of a sling.

The more Pilar racked her brain and thought it through, the more Uncle Suge was looking like the best angle she could twist to come up with some leverage against Mink. Yeah, Pilar admitted with a frown, Suge was her uncle too, and he had loved her and looked out for her and her father big-time over the years, but somebody had to pay a fucking price to get next to Mink, and crossing Uncle Suge up and putting him in a trick bag was a price she was willing to pay.

Ignoring the two New York gangstas who were staring down her grill like a murder scheme was about to jump off her tongue, Pilar picked up her purse and pulled out her cell.

"Yo! What the hell is you doing, girl?" Gutta barked as he rose up off the bed and stepped up on her looking like the chocolate Hulk. "Fuck you think this is? You better run ya lil plan by me before you start making decisions and putting in calls!"

Pilar smirked calmly and placed a finger over her mouth, motioning for him to be quiet as the phone rang in her ear. She wasn't pressed by all that growling and snapping this nigga was doing no way. She was a master at manipulation and she didn't have time to explain every little detail to these lame New Yawk mothafuckas!

"Hello?" Mink said as she answered on the other line.

"Hey, Mink, how's it going? This is Pilar."

"Yeah, and?"

"Well, I don't mean to bother you," Pilar said trying to keep her tone light and even. "But I was wondering if you had a minute because I need to talk to you about something that's kinda important to both of us."

Mink and Pilar didn't have a damn thing in common, and back at the mansion Mink palmed her cell phone and stared down at that shit, wondering what in the fuck this thirsty bitch wanted to speak to her about. Her and Pilar didn't run in the same circles, they didn't get down on the same streets, and they damn sure didn't smoke blunts and chat. So what in the world could be that important to both of them?

"Something like what?" she finally snapped.

"Oh, so, you *do* have a minute for me then?" Pilar said patiently, like she wanted to clarify that she had Mink's full attention before she gave up any info.

Mink smirked. "A'ight, you want one of my minutes? Cool. But I only got one for you so you better make it snappy. What you want?"

"Well *I* don't want anything because this is really not about me at all," Pilar said sweetly as she dropped her tone. "It's about Uncle Suge."

Silence. Pure-dee silence.

Boom! Pilar pumped her clenched fist in the air. That blank silence on the other end told her every damn thing she needed to know! Yeah, she had struck a real big nerve up in that camp for sure because the cat finally had Mink's slick-ass New York City tongue and the yak-mouthed bitch was all out of words!

On the other end of the line, Mink sat straight up in her bed and kicked the silk covers off her body. Just the sound of Suge's name had her shook as hell, and Pilar immediately had her attention.

"What's going on with Suge?" Mink said, trying to front like she wasn't nervous. "He ain't here right now because him and Peaches went to look for Barron. Are you trying to say something is wrong with him?"

Pilar was amped like a mother! Her hunch had paid off and this lil troll was about to get played big-time. Fuck all that fronting. Pilar knew what it was like to love a nigga's last week's dirty drawers, and she could hear every ounce of that worry and concern that Mink was fighting so hard to keep out of her voice. This is exactly what Pilar had been hoping for and counting on, and it was going to help her get Mink's ass right where she wanted her. Caught in a trap.

"Well, see, I was kicking it last night with this old head politician who's been sniffing around my ass and dying to get at me for the longest time," Pilar said as she started painting a picture using colorful lies.

"I mean, I should have known better than to go anywhere with his old ass from the gate, but he just kept begging me. Anyway, the night started out really sweet at first. He told me he brokered a lot of deals and rubbed elbows with a lot of rich people so I ain't gonna lie, I was on his heels. He took me to this icy restaurant and we were guzzling champagne and having a real good time, but then the more he drank the looser his old dentures got, and finally he started talking some crazy shit about Uncle Viceroy and basically hating on our whole entire family."

"So?" Mink said impatiently. "Viceroy got a lotta haters out there. You know his mouth is always wide open and he likes to talk big smack. Papa Doo is a certified gangsta, but not ere'body is gonna think he's the coolest G in town. But why is you telling me all your bizz for anyway, and how is Uncle Suge wrapped up in all of this?"

Pilar almost chuckled out loud. She had this ghetto bitch and she had her real good. "Well, the guy just kept going on about how Uncle Viceroy was gonna go down in flames at the end of this election," Pilar said, getting into character as the lies rolled off her tongue.

"Then out of nowhere he slipped up and said that he had a tape that was gonna take the whole damn family down."

"What kind of tape?"

"He said it was a tape of Uncle Suge. Murdering someone and stuffing them in the trunk of a car. The old dude claims he's gonna send it to all the cable outlets and get Uncle Suge locked up and thrown underneath the jail."

Mink's heart was jumping around in her chest and she started feeling weak. "That don't even make no sense, Pilar," she said, trying not to freak out and lose her fucking head. "Who was filming and got it on tape? Why ain't nobody else heard this story? Besides, who in the world was Suge supposed to have killed?"

"Listen, Mink," Pilar said before she could start asking more questions. "I know me and you aren't on the best of terms, but Uncle Suge is cool as hell so you gotta know we both wanna look out for him! I mean, that old bastard politician told me if I didn't act right he would call 9-1-1 right then and there and then leak the tape to the press too! I'm telling you he was about to straight up take Dominion Oil to the mat. Send the whole damn company to the shit house! So I played it real cool and finished the date, because I didn't want that fool to freak out and do nothing stupid that could get our favorite uncle locked up. I mean, that shit was real hard on me because I had to tongue kiss that wrinkled-up white fool and give him a hand-job too!"

Mink felt her breath catching in her throat. She wasn't tryna let Pilar know she was catching vapors over no nigga, but any damn thing that affected Big Suge damn sure affected her too.

"Okay, I'ma need you to run that whole story by me again, okay? Start over and talk real slow this time so I can make sure you saying what I think you really saying."

Pilar sucked her teeth. "Oh, so you think I'm lying or something? See, I knew I shoulda just called the cops and left your scary ass out of it! Ain't nobody got time to be repeating shit they done already said once. If I had known you was a hider instead of a rider I wouldn't have wasted all this time with you. I'm about to hang up and call the police and let them handle this whole shitty thing."

Mink's shook ass started back-pedaling like a mutha. "W-w-wait, Pilar! Hold the phone, dammit! Don't hang up, cousin. I heard what you said, I'm just tryna let it all sink in. I know me and you ain't the best of friends, but we are family, so let's put our petty bullshit to the side for now, okay? This here thing is way bigger than the both of us. I'm not trying to win no points, I just wanna know how in the hell we can help get Uncle Suge out of this situation?"

"We have to get that *tape*," Pilar said flatly. "I didn't call Barron and tell him nothing because his weak ass might raise an alarm. And I didn't want to get Aunt Selah involved either because she's already going through a lot. You're the only person I could think of to call without fucking it all up. That old politician is crooked as hell, but he has a thing for pretty young black chicks and with your help I think we can get the tape and set this son of a bitch up to get taken down too. Me and you working together might be able to help Suge get outta this mess, but we have to do our work under the table and keep it on the low."

There was a cold silence on the phone line and Pilar knew Mink was weighing her options. *I'll wait bitch*, she thought, grinning inside. If Pilar was right about how hard Mink was clocking for Suge, then this was an offer that she could never refuse.

"Alright, I'm down," Mink practically whispered. "So what's the plan? How are we gonna roll up and gank this old cracker and when are we gonna do it?"

"How about we meet up tomorrow and talk about it in person?" Pilar asked quickly. "I don't trust these phones because you never know who's listening. We just need to get together in the same room and come up with something and we have to do it fast. I shouldn't have to tell you to keep all this under your hat, though. This has to stay just between us, so don't go blabbing your mouth to anybody else, you hear me? Uncle Suge's life could be on the line, and if anybody finds out what's going on he could end up in the bing on a murder charge."

"Who you think you talking to?" Mink snapped, back to her old gutter self. "You don't have to tell me how to keep my mouth closed, boo-boo. I ain't the country bitch from the 'burbs, baby. You are. Don't tell me what the hell to do. Just tell me where you wanna meet."

"Let's hook up and put our heads together tomorrow at the Starbucks in the plaza downtown," Pilar said firmly. "I'll be busy most of the day so let's get together around nine p.m."

"Okay, I'll be there," Mink agreed.

"Fine. I'll see you then."

Pilar hung up the phone and looked up at Gutta and Shy and smiled real big.

"Damn Mink must really be about that nigga," Shy said with an uncontrollable grin. "She fell for that shit like somebody punched her in the back of the head!"

"I told y'all I could get that bitch," Pilar said smugly. "Now let's see how y'all get on *your* fucking grind. I set the trap and that dummy is gonna stick her big-ass head in it. Now it's up to you two fools to make sure it snaps closed and breaks her neck. Tomorrow night is when it all goes down."

CHAPTER 22

Selah couldn't believe this shit. Viceroy had pulled a slick move on her and called in an armed security team. They had posted up outside his hospital room and threatened to flatten her to the ground if she so much as inched her toe across the threshold to his room.

"But Viceroy!" Selah had wailed from the doorway, horrified out of her mind. So much shit had gone down that she was whipped to the bone and her poor lil heart just couldn't take no more. "I'm your *wife*!" she shrieked from the hallway as she peered at him with hurting eyes. We're a family, baby! I just want to talk to you. I stood by you through thick and thin, and after everything we've been through how could you do me like this?"

"You's a stone cold *liar*, Selah!" Viceroy bitched loudly from his hospital bed. The security guards' eyes were shifting left to right, from Selah to Viceroy, like they were watching a ping-pong match. "And that's why I'm putting some papers on your ass! I want you out of my house, and I want you to stay your lying ass right out there in the hall!"

"But *I'm* not the liar!" Selah cried out. "I'm your wife and

you should know me better than that! *Ruddman* is the liar. He's
all in your head! *He's* the one who's trying to mess you up
with all this bullshit!"

Viceroy cut his eyes at her and smirked. "All right, then.
You say that muthafucka's lying?"

Selah nodded, wide-eyed.

"Then I say prove it!"

She threw her hands in the air. "How? How am I supposed
to prove something like that? You're willing to take your worst
enemy's word over mine, so what kind of proof would even
satisfy you at this point?"

"Your *ring*, Selah," Viceroy said coldly. "If that bastard is
lying, then cough up your muthafuckin' *ring*, goddammit! And
if you can't do that, then you need to have your trifling ass and
everything you own out of my house by the time they let me
out of this damn hospital bed, because unless you come up
with your ring I'm filing for divorce!"

Selah had broken up out of the hospital in a panic. Being
tossed out back to the pool house was one damn thing, but
getting evicted out of her home completely was something
else!

She rode in the back of the limo in silence, biting down
hard on her lip as she pondered and schemed on a way out of
this mess. Fucking Rodney Ruddman had put her in a trick
bag that it was going to take a miracle to get out of, but she
just had to find a way. The first thing she needed to do was get
her goddamn ring back. Viceroy had made that shit real clear.
Unless she could produce the ring that Ruddman claimed he'd
taken off her finger twenty years ago, she had no alibi, no de-
fense, and not a damn thing to lean on. If she didn't get that
ring back she would be heading straight to divorce court!

Selah closed her eyes and willed herself to consider all her
resources. There was one avenue that kept pushing its way to
the forefront of her mind, and even though the mere thought
of asking that trifling young bitch for help made her shudder

and twist her lips in disgust, it was looking like she was going to have to bite the bullet and scrape her manicured fingernails down inside the bottom of the grimy basket.

In a twist of shitty fate, Dy-Nasty Jenkins, Mink's twin and the greediest bitch on the lighted side of the planet, had picked Ruddman up as a trick one night. The two of them had spent the night fucking and as a parting treat Ruddman had blessed the girl with a small gift: Selah's engagement ring.

Just the thought of how low she'd felt that night was enough to make Selah's blood boil in her veins. Dy-Nasty had come home fucked out and funky as all get out, hyped and excited to show Selah and Mink the beautiful gift that she had just received.

It had been a long time since Selah had seen the precious engagement ring that she'd left in a hotel bathroom more than twenty years ago, but she recognized it right away. Viceroy had bought it for her when he made his first real hunk of cash, and the sentimental value it had held for both of them came from the heart and was off the chain.

But somehow, during one of her hot nights with Ruddman, Selah had taken the ring off and forgotten to put it back on. That fat, froggish bastard had found it and kept it under his saggy nuts for twenty damn years before handing it off to that trifling hooker Dy-Nasty Jenkins, who promptly turned around and tried to blackmail Selah with it.

Selah had been trapped between a rock and a hard spot. Dy-Nasty had put the screws to her for two million big ones, and if it hadn't been for the family cleaner-upper Suge and his brilliant mind, the nasty little Philly 'rilla would have gotten away clean.

But even with the two million dollars in her bank account, the natural born liar Dy-Nasty Jenkins was still a criminal-minded crook all down in her bones. Instead of playing nice and sticking to their agreement, Dy-Nasty had tried to double-cross Selah by leaving a slummy piece of toe-ring on her pillow instead of the

million-dollar jewel she had agreed to return, and Selah had
hit the roof.

Dressed in war clothes and with Vaseline caked up on her
face, Selah had run up on that dirty rotten liar and caught her
at the airport and put a Brooklyn-style ass-whipping down on
her that was one for the record books! She had gone to town
wailing on Dy-Nasty's ratchet ass, and she'd enjoyed pounding
her with every single lick. And when the cops came and the
stupid little con artist was arrested and tossed way back far underneath the jail, Selah had figured that was the end of that.

Except now it wasn't.

"I might just have to bail that young bitch out," Selah muttered furiously under her breath, "but I swear to God if she tries
to cross me again I'll beat her shady ass down to the gristle!"

Dy-Nasty's trifling tail was still parked in the county jail,
and she had been writing Selah half-illiterate letters begging
like crazy to be bailed out. The letters were so damn ridiculously ghetto that Selah had laughed as she read each one and
then crumpled it up and tossed it in a trash bag and stuffed it
in the back of her closet, but now it was looking like she was
going to have to help Dy-Nasty get that thing she wanted
more than anything else right now: her freedom.

Selah hated to do it. Just the thought of it irked her all
down in her bones. Because the truth was, Dy-Nasty was sitting right where she deserved to be sitting. She had tried to
shit on Selah and gank the Dominion family out of two million dollars, and for that she should have been locked up someplace cold and dark for a real long time.

But now that Ruddman had brought all this drama back
into her life Selah was in a serious bind. If she had any chance
of convincing Viceroy that she'd been faithful to him and had
never strayed with his number-one arch-enemy, then she
needed her ring back and she needed it back right goddamn
now, and unfortunately Dy-Nasty Jenkins was the only person
who knew exactly where it was.

That gutter bitch, Selah thought bitterly as the limo pulled up in front of the mansion and the driver got out to open her door. She strode upstairs to her freshly cleaned suite of rooms with a single-minded purpose, and once she was safely behind closed doors she dug Dy-Nasty's letters out of the bag in her closet and reread every single one.

Hell yeah, Selah finally conceded, lowering her eyes in defeat. She was going to have to do the last damned thing she wanted to do. She was going to have to go against her inner voice, her intuition, and her baser nature. She was going to have to dig deep into her pocketbook and bail Dy-Nasty's black ass out of jail.

CHAPTER 23

Selah was way too embarrassed to ask her regular driver to take her, so she hopped in her whip and drove herself down to the county jail. Thanks to Barron's old lawyer friends Dy-Nasty's bail had been set at five hundred grand and that meant it was going to take a ten percent cash bond to get the treacherous little hoodrat sprung.

Parking her midnight-black Mercedes outside of a bail bondsman's office right down the street from the jail, Selah slipped on her designer shades and walked quickly across the sidewalk as she ducked her head down low and jetted inside.

She stuck her hand inside her pocket and felt the pages of one of the countless half-illiterate letters that Dy-Nasty had written her from the county jail, begging Selah to bail her out. Half the letters were so jacked up with spelling errors and shit that they were practically unreadable, and in most of the others the ghetto troll had used a combination of numbers, letters, and pictures to get her point across. The letter Selah pulled out contained a picture of a big-headed stick figure crying an ocean of tears and saying, *Ma-Ma Selah. I rilly hope you donut h8t me.*

Selah shook her head in disgust as she walked down the hall and into the crowded office. The joint was jam-packed full of people who had come ready to put their homes and their last dimes on the line just to get their loved ones out of lock-up, and after visiting with Dy-Nasty a few days earlier Selah couldn't blame them. The girl had looked torn down and defeated, and after crying her eyes out and telling Selah how she'd been getting jumped on by other inmates and beaten up while the guards turned their heads and pretended not to notice, Selah had decided Dy-Nasty's dumb ass was getting exactly what she had coming to her, and that there was no way in hell she was gonna go in her pocket and plunk down her cash to help the grimy chick get out.

But that was before Viceroy had gotten shot, and it was damn sure before Ruddman had shown his natural black ass up in that hospital and started spitting all their sexual secrets out of his disgusting mouth! It was hard for Selah to even believe that she'd ever been sprung on his ugly ass, foot-long dick or not. And now that he had Viceroy all riled up about that damned engagement ring again, Selah had no choice but to make some moves. Her hand was being forced and she needed to get her goddamn ring back!

Hot rage directed toward Dy-Nasty flooded through her heart and beads of sweat popped up on her nose. All of this could have been avoided if the little ghetto troll from Philly had just upheld her word and given Selah her damned engagement ring back like she promised. That little stunt she pulled had backfired on both of them, but now that Viceroy was ready to walk out on her after all these years the stakes were even higher and Selah was beyond desperate.

The look of pain and betrayal that had flooded Viceroy's eyes as Ruddman rubbed his dick problem all in his face had been enough to stop her heart in the middle of a beat. No matter how pissed off she had been at her man, no matter what he had done all those years ago to hurt her, none of it mattered anymore, and giving Ruddman all that revenge pussy had been a big waste of her time.

Which was why she now had to help Dy-Nasty get out of jail. Selah knew if she had any chance of saving her marriage she had to produce that goddamn ring, and unfortunately she had to go through Dy-Nasty Jenkins in order to get it.

At first Selah had considered calling the district attorney's office to ask if she could just drop the criminal charges that were pending against Dy-Nasty and forget all about her crime, but then she thought better of it. The young schemer had already double-crossed her once and Selah didn't put it past her to try that shit again. But this time, if Dy-Nasty made any slick moves Selah had an ace in the hole. She had her bail deposit, which she could always revoke and have a warrant put out on Dy-Nasty's tail and have her sent back to county to await trial at anytime.

After placing the fifty-thousand-dollar bond that would secure Dy-Nasty's release, Selah stuffed her receipt in her pocket and jetted back outside to her ride. The bondsman had informed her that the payment would be posted to Dy-Nasty's account in a matter of hours, and that more than likely she could be picked up from the jail later that afternoon.

With a couple of hours to kill, Selah drove down the streets of Dallas with a heavy heart. This thing between her and Viceroy had gotten way out of hand and she didn't know how in the world she was going to fix it. Underneath his designer suits and expensive cologne, she knew her man was as hood as could be, but never had Viceroy acted so downright gutter toward her. Pushing her away was one thing, but low-rating her and calling her a murderer in public was something she'd never thought he had it in him to do. Let alone ask for a divorce!

To tell the truth, Selah wanted her man back more than she ever had before. Hearing that gunshot and seeing him stretched out on the floor with blood all over him had made her realize that dick problems or not, she loved the shit out of Viceroy Dominion. All those lonely nights sleeping out in the pool house by herself had shown her how badly she really wanted to be back tight with her husband again. Plus, seeing him laid up in a hospital bed again had also done something to her sense of stability. It had lowered her defenses and made her weak. If Viceroy hadn't gotten so fucked up in that oil rig explosion there never would have been room in Selah's life for her to go rushing back into Ruddman's bed like a sex-starved freak in the first place. If her big dog hadn't been away, her hot little cat would never have come out to play, and Selah felt horrible behind the damage that she'd done to her marriage in her mad pursuit of a rock-hard dick.

And to tell the truth, although she had held her head high and put on a brave front for her children, she had cried every night when she laid down in that lumpy-ass bed out there in that pool house, but she refused to come back into the main house to sleep until her husband came out there and gave her a personal invitation. Barron, bless his heart, had ordered her a brand-new bed and he'd called in a design team to redecorate the area and make it as comfortable for her as money could arrange, but still. The fact that she was sleeping out in the backyard while the rest of the family slept in the mansion was a low blow to Selah's heart and to her ego too. She went to bed every night begging God to change Viceroy's heart, and she woke up with a headache and a heartache every morning when her prayers remained unanswered.

Selah hadn't felt this bad since that horrible day that she lost Sable, and back then drowning her troubles in a bottle of vodka had become her way of blocking out the pain. But these days she wanted more out of life and she refused to live out of the bottle again, and that's why she knew it was time to do something drastic. There was no way for her and Viceroy to fix their broken wagon on their own, and he wan't about to see a counselor no matter how much she begged. Selah wasn't one for putting her business out in the street, but desperate times called for desperate measures, which is why when she found herself pulling up in the parking lot outside the pastor's entrance of the Church of the Blessed Redeemer and climbing out of her car to go inside, she didn't stop to think and she didn't turn back. No, she had a few hours to kill and she was ready to lay this burden down on a pair of shoulders that were far broader than hers. She was ready to confess to her sins and seek help from a healer. She was ready to tell the truth and shame the damned devil.

Standing at the entrance Selah smoothed her hair back and looked up at the plaque that was nailed over the door. Her lips moved as she read the inscription and she knew without a doubt that she was in the right place.

Come unto me all who are weary heavy-laden and I shall give you rest.

Yes, *rest,* she thought as she found her hand twisting the doorknob and her feet carrying her inside. That's exactly what she needed more than anything else right now.

Rest.

"Pat!" Dy-Nasty was filled with excitement when her mother answered the phone. "You so freakin' smart, Mama!" she gushed. "All them stupid letters you made me write really-really worked! You was dead on it about Selah and all the rest of them rich mothafuckas!"

"Is that right, baby?" Pat said with a chuckle, sounding real proud of herself. "See, I told you them high-siddity bitches like for you to beg them for every damn thing! They wanna see you on your knees like a servant and make the whole damned world be about them, them, *them!* So, when is she getting you out?"

Dy-Nasty twisted her lips. "She *claimed* she was coming up here this morning but her ass ain't got here yet. But she's coming, though. I know she is."

"How you know for sure, baby?"

"Because," Dy-Nasty said slyly, "I got something Miss Prissy-ass wants!"

"And what's that?" Pat snickered.

"Her ring, remember? I got her million-dollar engagement ring! I hid that shit right up under her stupid-ass nose, and now she's feening for it just like a crackhead! Since she's posting my bail do you think I should just go ahead and give it to her?"

Pat snorted. "Chile, do a pimp break hisself in church?"

"Huh? What you saying, Mama? You know them holy bitches be wanting to fight me every time I go to church!"

Pat snorted again. "Dy-Nasty Ann Jenkins, I swear sometimes I wonder is you really minez or not! You act like you was raised out in a barn with a bunch of dumb dairy cows sometimes! How many times I gotta tell you what to do with a pair of sweaty nuts when you juggling them in your hands?"

"But Mama that ring is *hot*! I ain't gonna be able to sell it to no—"

"Fool! Who said anything about selling it? What I'm tryna tell you is, when you got a pair of hairy balls in your hands you don't rub them shits and pat 'em up and fondle them thangs to death now, do you?"

"No, Mama."

"Hell no you don't! When you got a pair of balls in your hands you gotta *twist* them shits, baby girl! You gotta do exactly like I taught you to do! Squeeze 'em, and crush 'em, and rip them shits off at the root!"

Two hours after walking into the Church of the Blessed Redeemer and laying her burdens at the altar, Selah walked back out feeling brand-new. The pastor, Chuckie Sanders, was a middle-aged ex-football player who had turned to preaching the gospel after falling into drugs and poverty when his playing days were over and his money was long gone.

His large congregation consisted of mostly black and Latino inner-city Christians, and many came from backgrounds that were the exact opposite of Selah's pristine boojie life. But as a child of Brooklyn, Selah's roots ran deep in the ghetto and despite the diamonds and pearls she dripped, she knew how to get down with folks from all walks of life.

Especially church folks.

She had given the pastor a fake name and lied big-time about visiting the city to attend a two-day conference and suddenly finding herself in spiritual need. As a result, she had been led up to the altar by the pastor's dumpy, wide-hipped wife, and the church couple spent several hours listening to Selah as she poured out the grimy half-truths of her twisted tale of betrayal and adultery. Selah was in need but she wasn't stupid. Most of what she told them was true, but in order to protect her identity and avoid revealing anything that could be used against her, she made up names and locations and held back certain details to make sure she kept her secrets safe.

"So you killed him?" the pastor's wife cried out when Selah finished telling them the part about questioning the billionaire Wally Su as he lay dying in his hospice bed and her finding some crucial documents from Dominion Oil under his mattress.

"N-n-no," Selah had stammered, "I didn't kill him! I mean, I slapped him around until he kinda passed out, but I didn't kill him!"

"So, you slapped him into a coma and then he died, right?"

Selah hunched her shoulders and nodded. "Yeah, I guess you could sorta say that. It must have been a real short coma because he died right after I hit him, but you get what I mean."

The church's first lady had run her fingers through her old-fashioned press and curl, and then together her and the pastor had held Selah in their arms and prayed mightily over her, passionately begging the Lord to forgive her sins and to cast a healing down on the spirit of her broken marriage.

Selah left up outta there soaking wet from tears and sweat, and feeling like she had been thoroughly baptized in the River

Jordan. Her burden had been lifted and forgiveness had been rained down upon her, and by the time she drove back to the county jail Dy-Nasty's bond had been approved and they were preparing for her release.

She waited another thirty minutes for the girl to process out of the facility, and then suddenly Dy-Nasty was free, standing right there in front her, grinning like crazy and swinging everything she owned in the whole wide world in a ripped jailhouse pillowcase that was so yellowed it looked like somebody had peed all over it.

"Whew! Thank you so much for getting me out, Mama Selah," she said, looking whipped and worn. Her high-priced weave was now natty and hanging by a few threads, and she was wearing the same tiny pink skirt that she'd had on the day Selah had jumped on her at the airport and given her a serious beat down.

"You just don't know how rough it was up in there. I had to fight them studs off 'ere single day! These country bitches down here are skanky as hell and I hope I don't never see none of their ratchet asses no dammit more!"

Selah turned away slightly and nodded as she wrinkled her nose. Dy-Nasty was kinda ripe. Hell, the girl was funky as all get out. She just flat-out stank! The chick smelled like she hadn't showered or splashed a drop of water between her legs or even taken a bird-bath the whole time she'd been on lock.

"Well, I'm sure none of this was a picnic for you, Dy-Nasty," Selah remarked as they walked out of the jail together. "But I need you to remember what kind of criminal behavior led to you being arrested in the first place. And I also need you to remember why I agreed to get you out."

"I got it," Dy-Nasty said as she slid her funky ass across the soft leather seat of the luxury ride. She sighed deeply as she pushed her headrest back and reclined, enjoying the smell of new leather and the sensation of sweet finery.

"You say you've got it," Selah cut her eyes at the girl and

frowned, "but I need to *know* you have it. Look, I want my ring back, Dy-Nasty. And that's word to the mother, as we used to say back in my day. Without that ring our deal is off. Before you can blink twice I'll revoke my bail money and send your black ass straight back to jail, you dig?"

"Dagg, Mama Selah!" the girl rolled her eyes and flopped around in her seat tooting her ass out toward Selah as she faced the window. "I already told you a hunnerd times! I got it!"

Surrounded by a cloud of funk and musk, Selah held her breath and hit a button to roll down all four windows at once. She flipped a switch and turned the air-conditioner on full blast and then pulled off into traffic praying for a strong breeze to come by and blow Dy-Nasty's rotten booty odor the hell away.

Selah drove out of the parking lot and pulled off into traffic, ignoring the girl sitting beside her as she focused her mind on the restoration of her marriage. She felt so much lighter with all her secrets now safely unburdened in the house of the Lord, and all she wanted to do was find out where Dy-Nasty had hidden her goddamn engagement ring. And once she had that precious jewel safely back in her hands she could go up to that hospital and show Viceroy that she wasn't the dick-sucking cheater that Ruddman had made her out to be after all. And after that, once she was properly reunited with her husband and secure in her marriage, then perhaps together they could start working on fulfilling the prophecy of hope that Pastor Sanders had revealed to her.

CHAPTER 24

While Selah was pondering on the prophecy of hope that Pastor Sanders had revealed to her, Zeke Washington was hitting the good pastor with a couple of revelations of this own.

"Y'all know that was Selah Dominion, right?" he asked, standing near the front pew with a look of amazement on his handsome face. "The wife of the richest black man in the whole fuckin' state of Texas?"

The Sanders were his godparents and Zeke had been hiding out in the church basement ever since the night he accidentally shot Rodney Ruddman, shitting bricks and expecting the po-po to come drag him out and slap the cuffs on him at any moment. But after several days with no knocks on the door and no static, and then hearing on the news that Ruddman had denied getting a good look at his assailant, Zeke had relaxed a bit and started making short trips above ground and venturing back into the streets.

"I'm serious," he told Pastor Sanders. "That's her. Viceroy Dominion's wife!"

"Get the hell outta here! She said she was in town on business and told us her name was Deidre Aston."

"Bullshit," Zeke said shaking his head as the pair ran down the entire convo they'd had with the mystery woman. "That's Selah Dominion. I know that bitch's face like the back of my hand."

Pastor Sanders' jaw stiffened. He hadn't always walked around in church robes. There was a time in the not so distant past when he had sported a gun strap and a bandana, and just the sound of Viceroy's name brought back some real old and real bad memories.

"I'll never forget how dirty that bastard fucked over your father," he said bitterly, reaching up to loosen his white preacher's collar from his neck. "Muffucka shoulda got served righteously straight off the bat. With a fuckin' forty-five."

"What the hell was she doing coming up in here?" Zeke wanted to know.

Betty Sanders shrugged. "She showed up outta nowhere talking about she needed some spiritual guidance. Said she was going through a lotta turmoil in her marriage and she needed the Lord's blessings and some guidance to see her through."

"It ain't just her marriage that's fucked up," Zeke said bitterly. "Her husband's company was about to take a hit in the pockets too. Back in the day they paid off some old Asian dude to help forge the papers that cost Daddy his share of the company, but before he could give me the hook-up and slide me the documents, he ended up dead."

"Well I sure didn't know about none of that," the pastor's wife said shaking her head. "Like I said, she told us she needed some spiritual guidance to see her through."

"Yeah, I'ma see her ass through alright," Zeke said, his eyes narrowing as his blood got to boiling all over again. Just because that greedy bastard Wally Su had fucked around and croaked it didn't mean their business was finished. "I'ma damn sure see her through."

With all the recent drama going on in the Dominion family there was no way in hell Selah could allow Dy-Nasty to stay at the mansion. Not only wasn't the girl welcome to show her face within ten miles of the joint, Selah would have been way too embarrassed to be the one to bring her ratchetness back into their midst. So Selah had called in a favor from a friend. They were close enough that she could trust him to keep his mouth closed, but he was distant enough from the family that their little arrangement wouldn't get back to anyone by mistake.

"You do remember Pilar's ex-fiancé Ray, don't you?" Selah asked Dy-Nasty as she drove the luxury car down the highway. "Nice guy. Kinda heavyset, bald head, big smile?"

Dy-Nasty giggled. "Oh *hell* yeah! I remember Ray-Ray." She covered her mouth and snickered slyly. "Hell yeah I remember his ass!"

"Well, with all the conflict and confusion going on at the mansion right now I thought it would be best if we not tell everyone that I'm helping you, okay? I mean, Mink is still pretty pissed off at you and honestly, so is everybody else."

Dy-Nasty yawned and tooted up her lips. "So what?"

"So," Selah said slowly, "we're going to keep our little arrangement under our hats for now. And that means you won't be staying at the mansion. You'll be staying at Ray's condo. He has an extra room and he's agreed to let you crash with him until you decide to go back home to Philadelphia."

There was big-time silence in the car and Selah was ready for the explosion that she just knew was coming. But to her surprise Dy-Nasty thought for a moment and then nodded in agreement.

"Okay, cool. I'll go stay at Ray's crib. I ain't got no problem with that but don't think I give two damns that the whole family ain't speaking to me! I wouldn't wanna stay at the mansion no way and have to look at Mink's ugly-ass face."

Selah kept her eyes on the road and nodded. She wasn't fazed at all by Dy-Nasty's tough talk. If she showed her face on the estate or darkened their doorstep with that stank booty and her raggedy weave there was no telling which one of the Dominions would start swinging on her first.

Selah took a shortcut to Ray's condo and called his cell phone as she pulled up outside. While she was waiting for Ray to come downstairs to get Dy-Nasty, Selah took the opportunity to remind the girl who the hell was really in charge.

She leaned her head out of the window and took a nice deep breath, then turned toward Dy-Nasty and said, "I'm sure you're eager to get yourself situated and settled down and take a nice long bath and brush your teeth, but I need you to keep a few things in the forefront of your mind."

Dy-Nasty shot Selah a strange look from the corner of her eye and muttered, "A few things like what?"

"Like what we agreed to."

"Yeah, and what was that?"

Selah's nostrils flared. "Look, bitch," she said quietly with the wrath of a murderer flashing in her eyes, "don't fuck with me, okay? I want my ring back, and I don't wanna hear any 'what ring' shit out of your nasty mouth either! I want the ring you tried to jerk me out of when you bribed me for two million dollars!"

"Mama Selah!" Dy-Nasty wailed as her jaw dropped down to her chin. "Where you get that mouth on you from? Why you gotta talk to me like that and get so ghetto wit' it? I know what ring you talking about and I'ma tell you where it is, too. You ain't gotta go all hood on me. The ring is right there in your room at the mansion, dang!"

"In my room?" Selah blurted incredulously. "Are you serious?"

Dy-Nasty nodded. "Yeah. I told you I was gonna leave it for you and I did! You the one who tried to stunt and went back on your word! You gave me the two million and then took it right back again when I was the one who stuck to our agreement!"

"I took it back because you left that crusty, moldy-ass green toe ring sitting on my pillow! Damn right I took my money back!"

"But you tried to fight me and you got me locked up for nothing! I put the ring in your room just like I said I would."

Selah sighed sweetly, busting Dy-Nasty's move.

"Oh, I didn't try to fight you, my dear. I *whipped* your mothafucking *ass*! And I'll whip it again too, unless you tell me right here and now where my goddamn ring is."

A funny look came over Dy-Nasty's face and she cocked her ear the way a dog does when he's hearing something important. What Dy-Nasty was hearing was her mother Pat's voice echoing in her ear.

Make it work for you, baby! Aim for the fences and make that shit work for you!

"Yeah okay," she crossed her legs and smirked. "You talking all that mess, but what you gonna do if I don't tell you where I hid the ring?"

Selah shrugged and said quietly, "I guess I'll do whatever I can."

"Like what?"

"Well, like get your bail revoked and have you sent back to jail."

Dy-Nasty's lips went up in a toot as she leaned back in her seat. "I don't care about no damn bail being revoked! You think I'm stupid enough to stay down here in Texas? You revoke my bail and my ass will hop on a bus and be out, baby. *Out.*"

"Well then," Selah said, reaching across to the glove compartment. She clicked it open and extracted a cool slice of dark metal and pointed it at Dy-Nasty's dome.

"Then I guess I'll just have to make sure your ass doesn't leave Texas then. Ever."

Dy-Nasty sat up straight and hit her with the crazy look. "Mama Selah! You pulling a gat on me? I knew it! I *knew* that shit! You DID shoot Daddy Viceroy, didn't you?"

"You goddamn right I shot him!" Selah spit as her lips trembled in rage. "And I shot Ruddman's monkey-ass too! Now if you wanna see what a piece of this hot lead tastes like then just fuck with me, Dy-Nasty! I *want* you to fuck with me!"

"Okay, okay!" Dy-Nasty blurted, eyeing the heat as her hand snaked toward the door handle. "Put that burner down, Mama Selah, before you mess around and hurt somebody! You ain't even holding that thing right!"

"Oh, my grip is good, baby girl. I guarantee you if you jump outta this car and try to run I swear I'll shoot you in the ass first and then blow out the back of your head! Now if you think you can outrun these bullets, jump on out and beat your feet."

For the first time since she'd gotten in the car Dy-Nasty looked unsure of herself. The wheels in her head were turning around and around, and she was trying to figure out if she should save her ass or make another push for the cash. The last thing she wanted to do was to have to call Pat and tell her she gave up the damn ring without getting nothing in return, but if Selah flew her brains outta her head then she wouldn't be calling nobody never again.

Resigned to her fate, she took her hand off the door handle and poked out her lip and muttered, "It's in your pretty ashtray."

"What?"

"You heard me! The stupid ring is in your pretty ashtray, damn!"

Selah looked straight up bewildered.

"*What* pretty ashtray, Dy-Nasty? You know me and Viceroy don't smoke and we don't keep any ashtrays in our room! What in the world are you talking about?"

Dy-Nasty sucked her teeth and bucked her eyes out like Selah was a numbskull.

"That ashtray you keep on the shelf over your fireplace, stupid! The pretty purple one with the yellow butterflies all over it!"

This time it was Selah's jaw that hit her damn chin.

"Are you talking about the urn? The urn with my mother's ashes in it?"

"The *what*?"

"The glazed glass urn! It's lavender and purple with corn-colored butterflies etched into the glass! I had my mother's body cremated after she died and her ashes are stored in there."

"Duh, boo-boo!" Dy-Nasty glared at her and smirked. Clicking the lock, she flung her door open and swung her legs around, then scooted her funky ass to the edge of the pristine luxury leather seats and frowned over her shoulder. "I *said* it was in the purple fuckin' ashtray!"

Selah was cursing up a blue streak as she stormed out of the master suite and headed down the winding stairs. It had seemed like such a simple fix to a gigantic problem, but once again her ass was in a sling and she had to depend on the kindness of others to get it out.

Finding out that Dy-Nasty had been stupid enough to toss a million-dollar ring into an urn full of cremated body parts was mindboggling, but after putting in a call to her sister Safa to ask her to dig her hand down in the urn and see if she found anything, her sister's reaction was even worse.

It was bad enough that she'd had to call Safa three damn times only to have the phone ring until it switched over to voice mail, and after leaving a couple of long, pleading messages where she had begged her husband's dick-sucker to pick up the phone and talk to her, Safa had finally answered her phone.

"Hello Safa? It's Selah—"

Click!

Selah had stared down at the phone in her hand like it had shot electricity into her body. *I know this chick didn't just . . .*

She dialed her sister's number again, and when Safa answered on the second ring Selah's words came tumbling out of her mouth.

"Safa! This is your sister! Selah! Did you just hang up on me?"

Safa's voice was colder than a New York winter. "I told you I would never speak to you again, Selah. I *told* you that."

Selah was both shocked and pissed when the phone clicked in her ear for the second time, and she didn't know whether to call her sister back and curse her out or call the pilot of the Dominion Diva and tell him to get that bitch fired up so she could roll up to Brooklyn and kick that ungrateful chick's ass!

But instead, she had stormed out of her room and was heading downstairs to the bar when she changed her mind and decided to go back upstairs and call her sister one last time.

"What can I do for you, Selah?" Safa answered the phone with ice chips in her voice. "The last time we spoke you let me know exactly what you thought of me. So why are you blowing up my phone?"

"I-I-I," Selah stammered, "I just wanted to know if you received what I sent you in that box. You know, Mama's ashes."

Sweat beaded up on Selah's nose as she listened to the long pause of silence on the other end.

And then finally, "Yes. I received it."

"Whew!" Selah gushed and let her breath out in a long sigh. "I didn't know if it had gotten lost in the mail or if some fiend had stolen it off the front stoop or something!"

"No," Safa said quietly. "I got it."

"Well, that's good to know," Selah said with a short laugh. "Because I need you to send it back to me."

"You need me to do *what?*"

Selah had originally planned to ask Safa to find her ring and send it back to her by express courier, but after the way Safa was fronting her off the last thing she wanted to do was put herself at her sister's mercy. Especially after the way she had treated the girl when Safa was at hers.

"Send the urn back to me. But only for a day or so. I need to do something with it real quick, but after that, I promise you I'll mail it right back to you again and Mama's ashes are yours to keep forever."

"Are you serious?"

"Yes, Safa. I am. Now, you've been wanting Mama's ashes for a very long time and I sent them to you out of the goodness of my heart. It was my way of telling you that I apologize for being so hard-hearted and that I forgive you for everything that happened in the past. All I'm asking you to do is send me the urn back for a day or so, and I swear I'll return it to you. It's been a very long time since we've talked and this could be a start to renewing our relationship. Besides, you owe me."

Selah tried to keep the begging out of her voice, but getting that ring back was her last and best hope of proving her worth to Viceroy, and she wasn't about to blow it.

"Selah, I tried my best to pay you what I owed you a million times over the last twenty years. But like I told you, I'm done now. I've worked my steps and apologized, and whether or not you've forgiven me has always been up to you. I've forgiven myself and I'm healed. I've moved on with my life, Selah, and I hope you find a way to move on with yours too. Good-bye."

"Goddammit, Safa! Don't you hang up the phone on me! Don't you dare hang up on me! I'm your older sister, dammit! I took care of you. I *sacrificed* for you! And you betrayed me! Now you send me Mama's urn back, you hear me? You send me that goddamn urn or I'll come up there and put my foot in your ass like I should have done twenty years ago!"

"Are you done, Selah?"

"What?"

"Are you done?"

"*Bitch*—"

"Good-bye, Selah."

Click!

CHAPTER 25

Suge and Peaches were hot on Barron's tail, sniffing him out like a pair of hungry bloodhounds. After plugging in the address that Selah had gotten from the mysterious caller, they'd hit the highway hauling ass north as fast as Suge's monster truck could take them. Suge was still mad as fuck about Peaches showing up to ride shotgun in a sky-blue skirt and heels, but right now finding Lil Bump was the major thing on his mind.

According to Selah's info Barron was being held in a sex den. His boy at Verizon had narrowed the call area down to a few square feet a couple of hours north of the Texas state line, and Suge had contacted a few of his homies in that area and alerted them to the situation.

"Is that right?" his manz Ugly Ollie had spit when Suge finished laying out all the details. Ugly Ollie was a gangsta nigga who had made a lot of money tricking bitches and pimping hoes all over the Southwest, and when Suge described the red hot liar who had ganked Barron outta his cash and had him chained by his balls, all Ugly Ollie could see was red hair, white pussy, and green dollar signs floating in the air.

"Yeah, come on up, man and let's get ya nephew straight and let me check out that broad. I'll meet you there."

Suge had been pushing his whip for a long minute when the GPS alerted him that he would be arriving at his destination very shortly.

"A'ight," he turned the stereo down and elbowed Peaches. "I'ma tell you how this shit is gonna go down, and you're gonna wanna make sure you follow what I'm saying real close, dig?"

Peaches nodded, his blond wig bobbing as his bangs fell across his forehead and into his wide eyes. "Dig!"

"When we get there I'm gonna park around back and case the joint out. And once I get the layout, I'll go inside and find Bump."

"Ermmm-herrmmm, now please tell me, what am *I* gonna do?" Peaches asked, batting his eyes and humming the tune to "Secret Agent Man."

Suge cut his eyes hard to the right and spit out the corner of his mouth. "You ain't gonna do shit, you hear me? Your ass better not move! You're gonna stay your ass right here in that lil blue-ass skirt and wait for me and Lil Bump to come out!"

Suge Dominion was a gully muthafucka and he was comfortable blasting his way out of a bar fight or running into a burning building and rescuing shit.

Leaving Peaches sitting in the car with strict instructions not to move his powdered black ass an inch, Suge was like a cat burglar as he cased the massage parlor from the outside and scoped out everything he needed to see. After checking his burner, he waited in the shadows of a grove of trees and watched as customers parked their cars discreetly around back and then approached a side door and quietly knocked to gain entrance.

Fifteen minutes later Suge was at the door knocking and looking around sheepishly, just like a guilty-ass trick.

"You hab appointment?" a young Asian woman said as soon as she opened the door.

"Er, no," Suge said quietly. "I'm just passing through and wanted to spend a little money."

"What you looking for?" she demanded.

Suge turned on the charm and grinned down at her. "Just some company. Maybe a nice massage from a pair of small, hot hands."

The lady sniffed the air and peered at him through suspicious eyes.

"No," she said pursing her lips firmly as she attempted to close the door. "No new customers. Sorry. We close for the night."

"Is that right?" Suge growled, his hand snaking out like a whip as he caught her by the throat and barreled her backward, farther into the room. He kicked the door shut behind him as she struggled and fought in his grasp, and he had raised his pistol and was just about to knock the shit outta her with it when a blinding white-hot pain exploded in his back and every muscle in his body contracted into a gigantic knot and froze.

"Looking for me?" a cool female voice sounded in his ear as the stun gun that was pressed against his flesh sent mega volts of electricity coursing through his body. GiGi Molinex squeezed the trigger and hit him up again, and Suge dropped his piece and yelped as his back arched into a C shape and he went down stiffly to his knees.

The next burst of electricity was applied to the back of his neck, and he grimaced as his eyes bulged and drool ran from his mouth. The smell of burning flesh filled the air as Big Suge Dominion keeled over and collapsed on the floor, his body now slack, his consciousness all gone.

Peaches wasn't hardly feeling that wait your ass in the car shit.

Suge hadn't been gone for more than twenty minutes when Peaches opened the door and swung his well-defined legs out the car. Humming his tune, he slid his muscle-bound booty to the edge of the seat and stood up smoothly, adjusting the hem of his sky-blue mini skirt so that it wasn't flapping up on his powerful ass.

He was a vision of manly loveliness in his church hat and halter top as he swayed his hips up to the front door of the joint and tapped on the door. The cover to the peephole slid open, and a few seconds later a tiny Asian chick wearing glittery stretch leggings and a white smock opened the door.

"You late!" she snapped, and yanked him inside.

Peaches fell into the coolness of the foyer as his eyes crawled over the dim room. It was small and smelled like ginger, honey, and dirty feet. The windows were covered by black plastic bags and there was a table against a wall holding a bouquet of fake flowers.

"I ask you for tree o'clock!" she snapped, holding three fingers up to his nose. "Tree!"

"Uh-*unh*! When you ask me that?" Peaches blurted.

"On Craigslist! The ad say for tree and now it past six. You not get paid for late, mister!"

"Mister?" Peaches muttered under his breath as he tossed his weave and smoothed down his skirt. "Who the hell is you calling mister?"

The muscles in his dark legs flexed as he balanced in his heels and followed the lady down a dim, narrow hall. She took him inside a room that looked like a medieval war chest. An assortment of whips and collars and chains and other instruments of sexual sadist and S&M torture hung from hooks on the walls.

"Here," the Asian chick motioned toward the whips. "We have many clients waiting for service now. You choose."

Peaches' eyes lit up as he selected a wire-studded whip, a pair of pliers, a heavy link chain, two locks, a blow-torch, and a small electric drill. He giggled inside as she looked up at him with mad approval.

"Okay," he said pushing past her as he carried his tools of torture from the room. "I'm ready, goddammit! Where my pain sluts at? Who in here needs to get they ass whipped? Raise your hands!"

CHAPTER 26

After trying every trick in the book to convince her husband that she hadn't betrayed him, this is what it had come to. Selah was defeated. She was at the end of her rope and there was only one thing left to do: start climbing up.

She had called Viceroy at the hospital and told him she was ready to tell him some things that might be painful for both of them. The decision to confess had been surprisingly easy to make, and once her mind was made up it felt like an entire universe had been lifted off of her shoulders.

Just tell him the truth, Selah, the simple words had come out of nowhere and echoed through her mind. The truth is the light. Tell it and let the chips fall where they may.

And that's exactly what she was going to do. She was going to go up to that hospital and throw herself on Viceroy's mercy. She was going to give her husband exactly what he had been asking her for all this time. *The truth.* Yes, it was going to hurt like it was known to do, but there was no way around it and it was the last chance she had of saving her marriage.

Her mouth was desert-dry and she was shaking like a leaf when she got off the elevator on the private floor. She approached Viceroy's room with her heart beating like a drum and the sound of her blood rushing through her ears.

"I'd like to have a word with my husband," Selah told the armed security guard in a serene voice. "I'd appreciate it if you'd go inside and ask him if he could spare a few minutes to spend with me."

The security guard did as he was asked, and a few moments later Selah found herself standing in the room and facing her husband, whose eyes were so cold and hard she felt like she was standing in front of a firing squad.

"Viceroy," she took a deep breath and began. "I asked to speak to you because . . . I mean, I came here to tell you that—"

I am no better than you. I'm a liar and a cheater. I fucked your worst goddamn enemy and I loved every stroke of it!

"I, um," Selah stammered, trying her damnest to spit the words out of her mouth. "Well, I just wanted you to know that I . . ." *There was no way in hell. No goddamn way she could utter those words and not expect them to haunt her for the rest of her life!*

Viceroy's voice was icy. "Whatever you came here to say, Selah, make it the truth. I want the *truth!*"

Nigga, you can't handle the truth!

Without another thought, the classy and gracious Selah Dominion took a deep breath, then looked her husband dead in the eye. And lied.

"I've been a good wife, Viceroy. I've been faithful to you and I've stood by your side. I know it might take some time for our marriage to heal itself, but I'm willing to put in the work and I hope you are too."

"Get out, Selah," Viceroy said coldly as he nodded at the security guard and pointed toward the door. "Get the hell out."

Mink had been crawling around down in the dumps ever since Pilar had called her with the news about Suge. As scared as she was for her boo, she just couldn't shake the feeling that something didn't feel right. She didn't know if it was because she didn't like that bitch Pilar or because she was genuinely afraid for Suge, because Mink wasn't stupid and she knew how Suge got down when he was about his bizzness.

He didn't go around talking about the work he did, but Mink could just imagine all the dirt he had cleaned up and helped make disappear for the Dominion family over the years. It made sense that some power-hungry political hater had finally caught the family pit bull slipping and wanted to smash his nuts in a trap. After all these years of being the go-to guy and making everybody else's troubles disappear, Suge was now the one who needed some protecting and Mink wasn't gonna let her man go out like that. She loved her some Suge and she was gonna ride out for him no matter the cost.

She usually told Bunni everything, but this time she didn't feel like hearing none of Bunni's scatter-brained schemes so she had kept her plans under her hat.

"Mink! What you in here doing, girl?" Bunni had busted up in Mink's room like she did every morning. "Time to get yo ass up, Ms. Domino! We gotta go make some moves, baby. I'm tired of you dragging ya damn chin on the floor, Mizz Minaj! Let's go shopping and see don't a couple a pairs of new shoes bring some Harlem fire to this gloomy-ass joint!"

"A'ight, I'm down. Actually, that's a damn good idea," Mink said as she slid out of bed and went inside her bathroom and shut the door. "I'll be dressed in a few and we can head out, a'ight?"

"Nuhh-*uhh,* bitch!" Bunni said with a smirk as she followed right behind Mink and pushed her way into the bathroom with her. "Who you think you agreeing with? The last time you jumped outta bed this damn fast was when Punchie Collins threw that lighter fluid on your ass and tried to strike a match. Why you got that broke scripper look in your eye? What the hell is wrong witchu?"

"Damn, Bunni!" Mink bitched as she sat down on the toilet. "Can I take a goddamn piss in peace? Get the hell out! The bathroom is supposed to be off limits!"

"Girl, stop that old bullshit," Bunni said as she twisted her face up. "I been coming in the bathroom with you since we was thirteen years old. I know how all your farts smell and ere'thang. Hell, I know *you*, Ms. LaRue, so just spill the goddamn beans please and stop stalling."

"I'm trying to spill my urine, Bunni," Mink said, fronting her off as she tried to stay focused. "Now get gone so I can throw on something fly and we can hit the mall, okay?"

"Whatever, heffah," Bunni said whirling around on her heels. "Just be ready to roll in thirty minutes, ya dig? You know a chick like me needs to get her eat on before I walk outta here."

Mink and Bunni did a little shopping at the mall but all Mink could think about was the meeting she was gonna have with Pilar later that night. Bunni practically bought a whole new wardrobe, but all Mink got was a big cheesy-looking TEXAS belt buckle for Suge since he was the only thing she could think about. It was huge and made of pure silver and the letter X was way bigger than all the other letters.

"You getting that ugly thang for Suge?" Bunni asked.

Mink nodded as she paid for it. Yeah, the heavy-ass buckle was ugly and tacky and she had started to put it back, but fuck it. If he loved her he would wear it, and if he didn't . . . then she would know.

Bunni kept trying to pry in her thoughts but Mink stuck to her guns and kept her mouth shut. Suge was in trouble and she didn't need Bunni all in her ear. Mink planned on hearing out Pilar's plan first and if it sounded legit then Mink would let Bunni know what was going down. Mink kept Bunni out shopping and running the streets as long as possible. She encouraged her girl to throw down on hot dogs, fries, candy apples, and two great big cinnamon buns. Bunni chewed all that shit with her mouth wide open, moaning as she got a sugar high that was out of this world. Mink grinned inside. At this rate her girl would be nice and sleepy by the time they got back to the house and she'd be able to make her escape.

They weren't home for more than twenty minutes when Bunni got to yawning. "Girl, I'ma go hang my new shit up," she said as she sat on the couch rubbing her sore feet. "Then I'ma go take me a quick nap. Your aggy ass look like you could use some beauty rest too, Mink. Maybe it'll cure that ugly look you done had on your face all day."

"Yeah, you right," Mink lied. "I'm about to take it down for a little bit my damn self. I'll check for ya when I get up."

Mink's plan was working to perfection. Bunni would be snoring loud as hell in no time, and as soon as she was asleep Mink was gonna be outtie. She hated keeping her girl in the dark but Bunni's mouth was big as hell and Suge's ass was on the line! *Her man facing jail time for murder?* Uh-uh. She had to go at this one alone. She couldn't chance fucking nothing up and she knew she was making the right decision.

Fifteen minutes later Mink had changed her clothes and laid Suge's gift out on the bed for him, and now she was on her way to the Starbucks where her and Pilar had agreed to meet. She had called the chick just as she was leaving the mansion and everything was still a go.

Mink's mind was racing a million miles a minute as she rode in the back of a taxi clutching her cell phone and worrying like crazy. She hopped out of the cab in the shopping plaza, and after handing the driver a fifty-dollar bill, she walked toward the coffee shop looking around to see if she could spot Pilar's ride. Mink was crossing the street to head up Starbucks' walkway when a silver car darted out in front of her and in a flash the backseat occupant jumped out and snatched her by the neck and yanked her in.

"What the fuck?" Mink screamed and bucked as her Harlem instincts kicked in and fear flashed through her. She couldn't believe who the hell she was tussling with but she knew this was gonna be bad. "Nooooo!" she screamed as he got the door shut and leaned on her until she was forced to crumple down to the floor of the car. "Nooooooo!"

They'd snatched her ass up so fast that the few people who were in the parking lot were oblivious to her plight. Just as fast as the little silver car had zipped in, that's how fast it zipped back out too. There were absolutely no traces left of Harlem's Mink LaRue. Other than the scent of her perfume in the air and the cell phone that she'd dropped on the pavement.

A thunderous back-handed smack almost rocked Mink clean out of the chair she was tied to. She opened her swollen eyes but she was surrounded by darkness and all she saw was black stars. She tried to scream but it came out muffled, and she damn near peed on herself when she realized that a plastic bag had been wrapped tightly around her entire head. She was helpless as fuck and she wilded out in a panic as she gasped for air and it became harder and harder to breathe inside the plastic.

And when the powerful smacks finally ceased and the bag was ripped off, Mink found herself bloody and staring into the last face on earth that she had ever wanted to see.

"Fuck is you crying about, lil mama?" Gutta crooned. "Daddy's home and he's got you now!"

"Oh my God!" Mink cried out, her eyes wild, wide, and terrified.

"Naw bitch, it ain't *God,*" Gutta said with a smirk. "It's ya dude *Gutta,* baby!"

"Gutta, *noooo!* You ain't supposed to be here!"

"What? You thought you could run, duck, and hide from a nigga like me forever? Ain't no roach-hole on the face of the earth that's too far for me to hunt your ass down, Mink! I came down here to get what's mine!"

A look of pure defeat fell over Mink's face and she was sweating and breathing so hard her chest burned. Gutta was making true on the deadly promise he had made to her a long time ago. He had told her he would beat the stankin' dog shit outta her if she ever crossed him up or fucked with his loot, and that's exactly what he had done too.

Mink trembled in fear, knowing exactly what time it was. She had just been lined up and snatched off the streets by one of the most deranged niggas she had ever pulled a scheme on, and she knew her days, minutes, and hours were numbered. There was no way in hell this psycho nigga was supposed to find her way down in Texas! Gutta was a scary-ass ghost from her past, but this was supposed to be her *new* life! It seemed like no matter how far she ran or how hard she tried to switch her game up and do shit a different way, she just couldn't escape the ghosts from Harlem.

"How in the hell did you find me?" she bitched. "Nigga, why you gotta keep on showing up in my life?"

"Shut the fuck up, Mink," Gutta growled as he walked over to a table and poured a glass of Remy. He walked back over to her and smacked her upside her head, then leaned in close to her ear like he was about to lick her neck and whispered, "You make it sound like I'm chasing you for summa dat sweet pussy or something. You must don't remember me. You still ain't learned that I'm not one them trick niggas you can curve and run game on like you been doing your whole life, huh? I'm the grimiest nigga you ever gonna meet, Mink. I'm that Gutta slanga from the streets of Harlem, bitch, and you shoulda never crossed a thoroughbred gangsta like me."

"I didn't cross you!"

"Yes you did, you half-slick ghetto bitch! Thought you could shit on my game and fuck over my dough when I got sent upstate, didn't you? Thought I wasn't gonna roll outta the joint and smash your ass! You dipped on my product and spent up all my money, just like a lil fuckin' thot, Mink! You gets no mercy from me, bitch. You gets the death penalty for that type of shit! Yeah! I should murder your grimy ass!" His eyes blasted her as he growled. "Hell yeah! I should plant your dirty ass deep down in them fuckin' bushes out there right fuckin' now!"

Mink trembled as she swallowed a big clot of snotty blood that ran down the back of her throat. Her nose was massively swollen, her left eye was black, and one of her front teeth felt loose. She already knew this mothafucka didn't have no intentions on letting her go. He had warned her a million times not to fuck over his cash, but her greedy trifling ass just had to get her shop on, her drank on, and her swerve on too!

"Okay, I crossed you, but Gutta I swear I ain't like that no more," she shook her throbbing head and pleaded. "I've changed my whole game up since I came down here. I swear to God! I know I was outta pocket to do you like that, and I'm sorry. But if you let me go I can get you your money back. I can get you double what I owe. Triple, goddammit! Just fucking let me go!'

Mink felt the last shred of hope inside her die as that nigga cut his evil eyes at her with his nostrils flaring out like a mad bull. She could feel the hatred he had for her just rolling off his ass, stinking up the whip as it poured off him in his sweat.

"You can get me triple?" he said with a sneer.

"Yeah!" Mink nodded, her head bobbing up and down like a motherfucka. "I can get your ass ten times triple! Twenty times triple! We *rich*, goddammit! My peeps got boo-coo cash coming out the ass! Just let me go, Gutta, and they'll give you any amount of bank you want. Lemme make a quick call to the Dominions and I swear your ass'll be gwapped out and swimming in cream for the rest of your fuckin' life!"

Hope was born again inside Mink as Gutta turned his lips down like he was thinking about that shit, but when he turned to look at her again she knew her ass was grass and all this talking him down shit was a wrap.

Mink trembled and squinted her eyes closed as she braced herself for another brutal smack to the head, but to her surprise it never came. Instead, Gutta unloosened the straps that bound her wrists behind her back and let her arms go free. Mink's eyes fluttered open and she broke out in a cold sweat and terror soaked her scalp as she watched him walk away. She figured he was going for his gat but instead he sat down at a small table.

Gutta igged her ass as he tossed his liquor back and gazed around the room. That little rinky-dink motel where him and Shy had taken Pilar to and held her captive wasn't the move. They'd had to fly up outta there because the joint was too hot and attracted way too much attention due to the low-level local hustlers who pushed their work from the cheap rooms. Getting in Mink's shit the right way was crucial and he had needed a spot that was more secure, so Gutta had gotten in contact with one of his old prison connects who used to get money in Texas. Gutta told him that he needed a tucky spot to conduct some business in and his manz had made a few phone calls and got Gutta a meeting with one of his associates.

Gutta had hit the associate off with a few of his last green-backs and was given the keys to a two-bedroom bungalow way in the back of a gated community. It was just the type of lay-low hut that Gutta needed. The place was barely furnished and had a cold and empty feeling, but it was secluded and it smelled like mad bleach and disinfectant. Gutta had a feeling the joint was so clean because this was where his boyz chopped up bodies and got rid of their criminal evidence. He was willing to put some money on it that if he shined a blue light up in that bitch it would glow like a muthafucka. But that wasn't his concern.

"Alright, Gutta, you got me," Mink surrendered weakly as she shifted her booty and tried to switch positions in her chair. She knew this nigga and she knew it was time to keep it real with him. If she went on a lying spree or tried to bullshit him she could end up in a crime story on the ten o'clock news. "I fucked up and you win, okay? I'm sorry. You know what kinda ratchet chick I am. You know my scheming ass is always caught up in some kind of stupid misadventure. My whole game was fucked up back when we was kickin' it and you got knocked. I mean, I was scratching and scrambling just like everybody else in the hood was. I wasn't trying to disrespect you or play you for no fool, Guta-boo. I promise you I had good intentions to keep your money in the safe for you, but the streets got the best of me and I fucked up. But I'm better than I used to be now. I swear I am."

Gutta threw his head back and laughed his ass off. "Bitch, I know a lie when I hear one," he said as he turned his Remy up and slammed that shit down his throat. He grilled Mink with cold, hooded eyes as he studied her from head to toe and analyzed her body language.

"The crazy thing about it is, you been a fucking liar since the day I met you so the truth actually sounds funny coming outta your mouth. Ere'thang you just said sounded real upfront and righteous, but too bad you said all that shit too late. I gives a fuck if you got down here and found religion or how much your scandalous ass done changed. It's too late for all that shit, Miss Slimy Mink LaRue."

"Look Gutta, I already told you I can get you the money that I owe you," Mink pleaded. We ain't gotta do no whole lot of talking and going down memory lane, just take me to an ATM and let me tear you off a couple of dollars so you can go back to Harlem in style and we can put this whole thing behind us, bet?"

Gutta jumped up outta his chair and crossed the room in two steps. He drew his hammer fist back and punched Mink in the stomach so hard that she vomited instantly. Coughing and gagging, Mink slumped over and fell to the floor with a thud. She lay there and farted real loud and gasped for air like a fish outta water as Gutta put his boot on her head and started applying crazy pressure.

"Bitch you still think you the fucking one running shit, don't you?" he snarled as he crushed her face under his foot and growled down at her. "First you fuck over my dough and lose my shit and have me looking crazy in the streets, then you take my money and dip up outta town and make me chase your ass a thousand miles away. Them rich people ain't shit to you! You's one of them project-ass *LaRues,* just another dirty bitch from around the way, and them damn Dominions don't give two shits about you."

"They do too," Mink croaked, grimacing in pain as that big nigga damn near stood on her head. "They my f-f-family and they care about me!"

"You's a *con artist,*" Gutta barked, coming up off her grill. "Some kinda way you tricked up on a DNA test and ran yourself the gank of a lifetime, but you must forget I know your ass! You ain't shit but a two-bit thief and a stripper, Mink! Them muthafuckas ain't your goddamn family!" he spit in a rage. "You don't even belong down here. I grabbed your ass right from under their noses, and you don't see none of them rich bastards out here looking for you, do you? Your face ain't ringing no bells on CNN, ain't no DTs going door to door showing your picture, and ain't no police helicopters flying in the sky throwing down searchlights neither. You on your *own,*" he taunted her, "and you better believe it. Shit, you been down here sucking up these cow fumes so long that you got your own head all gassed up. But there ain't nothing nice waiting at the end of the road for you, baby, and I can promise you that. I told you what I was gonna do if you fucked with my money, and I meant it. Ain't no happy endings for a grimy bitch like you, Mink. You belong to Harlem, baby. You belong to *me.*"

Mink was laying on the floor feeling like shit when Gutta reached down and snatched her up by the back of her shirt. He slammed her up against the wall then got up in her face and pressed his nose all up on hers.

"You got one thing right, Mink. I'ma get my muthafuckin' money outta that fake-ass family of yours," he spit. "I'ma cash in on your yellow ass for all the shit you put me through and for all the time and dough I wasted coming down here to get your grimy ass back in my grips. And check this shit out, baby girl. Once I get hold of that gwap your ass is coming back home to New York! You try to buck and I promise you I'll run up in that mansion and murk ya whole damn fam in they sleep! I swear to God I'll lay every last one of them Dominion bastards down. And that's my word."

"Fuck you!" Mink screamed at the top of her lungs. She sniffed deeply through her nose and then spit a slimy lugi dead in that nigga's face. "You talking about touching my fam?" she shrieked. "Fuck around and try it! I'll slump your ass, Gutta! I'll fucking murder you!"

Gutta went off. He cocked his fist back and let the hammer fly. He laid an ass-whipping down on Mink that was ten times worse than the one he'd given her after kidnapping her from her mother's funeral and stashing her in a warehouse in New York. He busted her lip and blackened both of her eyes. He pounded noogie knots on her forehead and tried to kick her spine through her chest. He tossed Mink's ass from wall to wall and wiped up the whole fuckin' floor with her. Mink was a bloody swollen mess, and Gutta had just picked her up again so he could slam her head straight through drywall when somebody pounded on the door.

Gutta froze. He was breathing heavy with one hand wrapped around Mink's throat and the other one ready to fire. The banging at the door sounded again and he growled reluctantly as he let Mink's battered body drop to the floor.

Mink moaned and curled up into a fetal position and prayed like hell that somebody had heard her screaming and sent the cops to rescue her. She turned her head toward the door as her heart pounded hard in her chest. Her whole face was dented and both of her eyes were swollen halfway shut, but when Gutta opened the door she managed to peep through her right eye good enough to recognize his boy, Shy.

Mink wanted to cry. She should have known this fool was down here too. His hyena-looking-ass never left Gutta's side, and he was stupid enough to go along with anything Gutta had up his sleeve. But it was the next person to step through the door who made Mink's heart plummet way down into her cervix.

It was Pilar. Dressed to the tee and sporting a real slick grin.

That fucking bitch!

Realization hit Mink like a speeding A train to Harlem. She had been set up lovely. That bitch Pilar was in on the whole thing, and she had lured Mink into her trap like a spider casing a fly.

CHAPTER 27

Staying at Ray's condo had ended up being a boss move for Dy-Nasty. Passing a blunt back and forth, they were laid up naked and tangled in the sheets after an hour-long bout of freaky sex. Dy-Nasty's clit was throbbing like it had a delicious toothache after Ray had whipped it back and forth then fucked the shit out of her with his foot-long tongue.

"So how long are you staying in town?" he asked as he put his arms under his head and stared up at the ceiling in an after-sex bliss.

Dy-Nasty turned over on her side and looked at him. This nigga could fuck like a champ but he was one fuggly-ass mess. There was so much meat on his cheeks, chin, and forehead that Dy-Nasty coulda ate off his face for a whole week. His exposed armpits were overgrown with wiry strands of black hair that were so damn nappy it looked like crabgrass. His long, jiggly man titties had slid halfway off his chest and were hanging under his arms. His stomach was ashy and bloated, and it actually laid on the bed like a chocolate mousse puddle on both sides of his body.

Yuck, Dy-Nasty thought. *Yuck!*

But that ain't what came outta her city-slick mouth.

"Sheeiit, I'm free as a breeze, baby! Gimme a good reason and I'll stay down here witchu as long as you want me to."

Ray reached over and grasped her thick yellow thigh and squeezed it. Her hour-glass figure turned him the fuck on. Her bulging breasts with the pert nipples were the prettiest he had ever seen. "Well, I *have* been pretty lonely," he admitted softly. "I sure could use some fine company like yours."

"Boy you ain't even gotta ask me twice," Dy-Nasty said eagerly as she spread her legs and inched his hand up toward her damp pussy. She could tell by his lil condo setup that Ray was doing okay for himself, but he wasn't rolling in cream the way she wanted to be rolling in it, and that meant she had to find a way to get back at those goddamn Dominions.

"What's your story, Dy-Nasty?" Ray asked as he stroked her kitty and played in her tangled hairs. "I mean, I got the boot from the Dominion family because Pilar got the hots for her own cousin and dropped me like a bad habit, but what did you do to piss that whole bunch off?"

"I didn't do nuffin!" Dy-Nasty spit angrily. She grabbed his wrist and flung his hand outta her hot box and then snapped her banana-colored thighs closed tightly. "All them hater-bitches living large up in that mansion is just *jealous* of me, especially Mink! She got them dumb mofos under her spell like she some kinda royalty but they don't know she's really just a low-budget scripper who used to crotch-polish poles up in New York!"

Ray nodded. "Yeah, it seems like the Dominions have some sort of selective vision. Like they pick and choose what they want to see and believe."

"They so fuckin' stupid!" Dy-Nasty spat. "Ere'last one of 'em! I tell you what, you can best believe that before I leave up outta here I'ma fuck them Dominions up! I'ma get what's coming to me and put my foot up that whole fuckin' family's ass!"

Ray got real quiet for a minute and the air seemed to go

cold in the room. Suddenly Dy-Nasty wanted to kick herself.
She wished she could bite her stupid tongue off and take
her idiotic words back. Pat was always telling her to watch
her mouth and to make sure she didn't go around talking
herself out of a good thing. She knew how tight this nigga was
with the Dominions. He had been around them for a long
time, and because of his thang with Pilar he had stayed packed
up their rich asses like doo-doo tryna win him some brownie
points.

And now he was looking kinda pissed in the face. Like she
had fucked around and said the wrong damn thing.

"Yo, check it out, Ray," Dy-Nasty said, sliding her fingers
under the covers to jerk on his soft, sticky dick. "I'm sorry. I
ain't mean no harm, okay? I mean, I know you down with
them Dominion mothafuckas and you prolly ain't like what I
just said but—"

"Nah," he cut her off quietly. "Actually, I dug what you
said, and I feel where you're coming from. Yeah, I used to be
real close to that family at one time but I was never blind to
them. I've watched them get away with all kinds of under-
handed shit over the years and they never seem to get caught.
And even when they do get caught, they still never seem to get
punished. At least until now."

Dy-Nasty's eyes got wide.

"What you talkin' bout, Ray-Ray?"

Ray pulled the sheet up to his chin and then swallowed
hard and said, "I can't give you any real specifics, but that family has a strong criminal background that could get them in a
world of trouble. My new boss is handling a major court claim
against them that could put them on the front page of the
news and blow their bank accounts wide open."

"What?" Dy-Nasty gasped in glee. "Why?"

Ray shook his head. "I mean, it all seemed so damned in-
credible when I first read the charges, but I was actually dating

Pilar when the crime occurred and the more I thought about it the more I remembered some of the details."

By now Dy-Nasty's mouth was open, her eyes were glinting, and she was salivating like a dog about to fuck up a T-bone steak.

"Details?" she demanded. "What goddamn details?"

Ray pursed his lips and shook his head. "Sorry. I'm a licensed attorney so I can't divulge any privileged information, but I can tell you that this thing is big. Very big."

Dy-Nasty squinched up her face and tee-hee-hee'd like a mothafucka!

"Big? How big? Tell me! How fuckin' big? Big enough to put them boojie-ass bitches on blast?"

Ray nodded. Wide-eyed.

"With my new boss on the case it's big enough to send their boojie black asses to jail!"

CHAPTER 28

Big Suge came awake slowly. His mind was in a fog, and every cell in his body was screaming out in pain. He was buck-naked, and he felt something warm touching his ass. He opened his mouth to protest and realized why his jaw was aching. A rope had been tied across his open mouth, and a thick rag had been stuffed damn near down his throat.

As he regained more of his consciousness, he realized that wasn't his only damn problem. He was trussed up. In a reverse hog-tie. He was bent with his bare chest resting against a wooden barrel. His wrists were secured tightly behind his back, and his knees were bent upward with his feet tied to his hands.

He felt something hot bite his ass again and his roar was muffled by his gag as he arched his back and heaved backward with all his might.

"Quit bucking!" a heavy voice shushed him. "I'm trying to burn these damn ropes off so I can get your ass outta here," Peaches snapped as he ignited the blowtorch and let the heat fly.

"Hold still, Uncle Suge!" Suge recognized his nephew Barron's voice and grunted. Fuck what he had said about that girlie dude. Peaches had come behind him and cleaned shit up. Not only was he right on time to get Suge's ass out of a jam, he had found Bump too. Relieved, Suge braced himself and took the pain as the heat from the blowtorch burned through the thick ropes and blistered little bits of his ass at the same time.

Moments later Suge's feet were freed from his hands and he fell over on his side and gratefully stretched his aching muscles. His arms were still jacked up and tied behind him, and they trembled with relief when Peaches set his upper body loose too.

"We good now," Peaches whispered as him and Barron hauled Suge to his feet. Barron passed his uncle a checkered piece of cloth he'd taken off a small table and Suge pressed it to his crotch and covered up his business as Peaches gripped his arm and helped him hobble toward the exit.

With their eyes peeled for GiGi and the pyscho Asian chick, Peaches and Barron supported Suge's weight as they hit the door and stumbled outside. They were climbing in the whip when Peaches saw what time it was.

"Oh, no. Hold the fuck up," he said. He pointed at the slashed tires and growled, "Ain't this a bitch?"

Suge was exhausted as he stared at the four flats on the whip. The tires were drooping like a muthafucka and there wasn't a drop of air left in them bitches.

"Shit." Peaches sucked his teeth. "Somebody got our asses. We stranded like a muthafucka! What the hell are we gonna do now?"

Barron nodded. "I got this," he said as he led them quickly around toward the other side of the building where GiGi had forced him to park his whip way up in the treeline and leave his keys in the ignition. "My shit is right up here and I got a full tank of gas. I told that big Samoan dude to take my keys, but it's all good because I got an extra one in the ashtray."

★   ★   ★

GiGi Molinex burst through the door just as her human ATM and her ball-swinging hostage were peeling out of the driveway and sending a spray of gravel flying in the air.

"Motherfuckers!" she screeched as she stepped outside and slammed the door so hard the raggedy little building shook. This wasn't how this number was supposed to go down, and rage wasn't the word for what she was feeling as she watched her chance in the big leagues slip right out of her grasp.

"Those black *bastards!*" she fumed as she wracked her brain trying to come up with her next step. "Those rich mother-fucking black bastards!"

She had been ready for that super nigga Suge Dominion when he came knocking at the door, and she'd had three stun guns waiting on his King Kong-sized ass. She'd peeped his game as soon as his car pulled up on the property, and she had watched from the darkness of a second-floor window as he snooped around outside.

The moment he was in the house good she'd had the dominatrix devils sock it to him and light him up with elec-tricity until he passed out at their feet, and then they'd dragged his giant body into one of the dungeon-like rooms and tied his ass up over a barrel like a black cow that was about to be slaugh-tered.

GiGi cursed out loud as she stomped back inside the house and headed for the telephone. Yeah, she'd gotten the drop on Suge, but she had messed around and slept on that goddamn he-she Peaches and he had gotten the drop on her!

Or at least that's what his glamorous ass thought!

GiGi walked over to the front counter and snatched the phone off the hook.

She cupped it in her palm and punched in three num-bers. 9-1-1.

"Hello?" she said breathlessly when the phone was answered on the other end. "Oh my God, I need help," she moaned.

"Please! I was kidnapped and robbed by two big black men! They're drug dealers, and they forced me to get into their car! They threatened to sell me to a white slavery prostitution ring somewhere down in Dallas, and I'd probably be dead right now if I hadn't jumped out while the car was moving! It's a black Maserati with Texas plates. They're traveling with an extremely ugly transvestite prostitute, and they're carrying a shitload of drugs too. Hurry! Please catch them before they kidnap someone else!"

Suge's jaw was set in a hard line and his temper was doing a slow burn. He had stinging blisters on his neck and back from the electric heat of the stun gun, and raw burns on his wrists and ass from the blowtorch that Peaches had used to set him free. The little bit of pain wasn't shit to him. Nah, it was the fact that somebody had caught him sleeping and stripped him outta his drawers that was really eating him up inside.

"How the fuck you let that bitch get you hemmed up?" he demanded of Barron, shaking his head.

Barron could only shrug and sit there looking like a chump in the face. "I don't know, Unc. She fucked me up, man. She fucked me up!"

Of the three men rolling, Peaches was the only one who wasn't fucked up in some kind of way, so he had taken the first shift and started off driving toward Dallas. They'd stopped a few minutes out and pulled over behind a small gas station so Suge could grab some clothes out of Barron's suitcase and cover up his balls, and once he was dressed, Barron stretched out in the backseat and Suge took the wheel in the stylish Maserati, while Peaches sat beside him and once again rode shotgun.

Suge hadn't been pushing the whip for much more than five miles when he heard the wail of a police siren and saw the telltale flashing red lights coming up on him in his rearview mirror.

"Uh-oh," Peaches said, glancing over his shoulder with his dolled-up eyes wide as fuck. Suge checked out the cop car in his rearview mirror and slowed down as he pulled to the right and let his tires hug the edge of the road.

"What them fuckers stopping us for?" Peaches said, sounding like a paranoid New Yorker.

"Don't say shit," Suge warned quietly as he coasted to a stop and kept his hands on the steering wheel.

Barron stirred and sat up in the backseat. "What's going on? What happened? You speeding or something?"

"Naw," Suge said coldly, his hard gaze plastered to the country cop who had exited his squad car was now approaching them from behind. "Don't say shit."

The cop walked up to the window and motioned for Suge to roll it down.

"Good evening, sir. How's everything going for you?"

Suge shrugged and stared straight ahead. "It's going."

Dude shined his flashlight inside and peered at Peaches in the passenger seat.

"Picked up a little company for the night, huh?" He laughed. "I see you got you a big old flashy gal!"

"What the hell is he tryna say?" Peaches muttered, batting his eyes.

"Nice car," the cop turned his focus back to Suge. "Is it yours?"

Suge grunted. "I'm driving it, ain't I?" He glanced in his rearview mirror and saw two more squad cars rolling up with their lights flashing.

"Then can I see your license and registration?"

"What for?"

"Routine stop," the cop claimed, inching one hand toward his holster as he shined his flashlight inside the car. "Lemme see that license and registration now, big fella. And don't you make no sudden moves."

"The registration is in the glove box," Barron said from the backseat. "Give it to him, Uncle Suge."

"I ain't giving him shit," Suge said, scoffing as three more police cruisers pulled up and joined the party. One car stopped behind the three that were already behind them, and two other cruisers pulled in front of Suge, boxing them in.

Suge chuckled. He was Texas born and bred, and he had known what time it was from the moment the first trooper put on his lights.

"Okay, outta the car, motherfucker," the cop said, fed the fuck up as three of his blue brothers ran up to the car holding dope dogs on leashes and joined him. "Get your black ass outta the goddamn car right now!"

"Take me out," Suge dared him. He was pissed like a muthafucka behind getting stunned and burnt and tied up like a hog with his ass in the air. The next muthafucka who put their hands on him was gonna catch a bad one, and he didn't give a fuck who it was.

"You don't want no trouble tonight, boy," the first cop said menacingly. "Now, if I have to come in there and get you I'ma bust ya black fuckin' head wide open for you!"

"Bust minez and yours gonna get busted too," Suge promised with a growl.

But the good-old-boy country cop must not have believed him because he swung his flashlight and smashed the window, then reached through the shattered glass and hit the lock. He flung open the door and reached inside to grab Suge by his thick, muscle-bound arm and pull him out, and that's when the muthafuckin' party got started.

CHAPTER 29

Ugly Ollie had been tenderizing his ass on a bench at the precinct for the longest as he waited for his manz and his fam to get released from police custody. He had posted cash bail for Suge, Barron, and Peaches, and these old country crackers were almost ready to let them go.

After catching several reports of the incident on the news Ugly Ollie had been waiting on Suge's phone call. The male reporter had seemed astounded during his live report over the air, and it had immediately captured Ollie's attention.

"What started out as a routine traffic stop on a long stretch of highway in southern Oklahoma turned out to be some sort of strange ménage à trois between an uncle, his nephew, and a transvestite prostitute . . ."

Suge had been hit with charges of resisting arrest, assaulting a police officer, and soliciting prostitution, and when Ugly Ollie caught a glimpse of their mug shots he damn near hollered. Barron looked scared shitless. Peaches was styling his blond wig and trying to look cute. And Suge's mug was twisted up like, "Really, muthafuckas? Really?"

Don't worry, my nigga, Ugly Ollie thought as he waited.

He knew Suge was good for the bail money so he wasn't worried about that. His main concern was getting the three black men out of that small town as quick as possible, and as soon as they were released that's exactly what he did.

"For real, Mama Selah. I know Mink like the back of my hand. That chick is hooked on her damn cell phone like a fiend on crack," Bunni declared as she plopped down on the chaise lounge beside Selah and poked out her lip. "I'm telling you, for her not to be picking up when I call means something real."

"All it means is that she doesn't want to talk to you," Selah said firmly. "Now go ahead, Bunni. Suge should be arriving home with Barron in just a few minutes and I've got a blinding headache that I'm trying to get rid of. I promise you Mink is fine. Just keep calling until she picks up."

Bunni had been running off with the mouth and bugging her about Mink for a couple of hours now, and Selah honestly didn't know how much more she could take. She was at her wits end and her head was banging like a drum, but she did her best to mask her anxiety with a look of confidence. She sat with her feet up in the large family room with a copy of Okrah's latest magazine spread out on her lap. She'd been thumbing through it and looking at the pictures to calm her anxiety until Bump was safely back at home, but Bunni and her incessant drama about Mink not answering her phone was just adding unnecessary stress to her load.

And if that wasn't enough stress, every so often one of Viceroy's bodyguards walked past on his security check and asked her if she was okay. The Dominion mansion had been on high alert ever since the shooting and attempted break-in, and the chief of security had implemented much stricter security measures. The sight of armed guards in the background roaming the grounds and protecting the property was nothing new, but having them inside the house was beginning to make

Selah feel like a prisoner in her own home. It made her feel eerie and even less safe. And now Mink was suddenly noplace to be found.

"I'm telling you, Mama Selah, my left titty is itching like crazy, and that means something ain't right!" Bunni insisted as she jumped up and started pacing the floor. "I'm getting a signal," she said, scratching at the side of her perfectly rounded left boob. "A signal-sign. That crazy-ass heffah is in trouble. I just know she is."

"Bunni please sit your behind down," Selah said, patting the seat beside her. "There's absolutely nothing to worry about. Maybe Mink's cell phone battery died, or maybe she's taking a call and doesn't want to click over. In any event, let's just thank God that Barron and Suge and Peaches are on their way home. I'm sure Mink is okay, and she'll be calling or texting you in just a few minutes. I mean, everything was just fine when you guys came home from shopping earlier, right?"

Bunni frowned and nodded. "Yeah. Shit was cool, but we was tired so we both went upstairs to take naps. But Mink musta got right back up. The security guard said she was dressed up and talking on the phone when she rushed outta the house and jumped in a cab. She didn't even wake me up or leave me a note or nothing."

"But if she was talking on her phone then that means her phone was working when she left. And she probably didn't wake you up because like you said, she knew you were tired."

"Yeah, yeah, I get all that," Bunni said as she gave Selah a look that said, *what's your fucking point?* "But if she was talking on her phone when she left, then why is that bad boy off *now*?"

"Listen, Bunni," Selah said trying to sound calm. "I know you two are best friends and how do you say it, 'homeys' and all, but it sounds to me like Mink might have needed some alone time. She is a grown woman, you know? As much as we both love her, and as protective as we might want to be over her, she has the right to come and go as she pleases."

Selah smiled gently, hoping Bunni would leave her the hell alone, then continued. "I know Mink had a rough life full of twists and turns, but it's not dangerous here in Dallas the way it is in New York City. At least not for the most part. I'll tell you what. I'll have a little talk with Mink about keeping her phone on at all times so that we can get in contact with her, but I can't allow myself to go off into panic mode with you every time Mink leaves the house to go do something without you." Selah smiled and added sweetly, "My blood pressure just wouldn't be able to take it."

Bunni hit her with the stank look. She could tell that wasn't nothing she said getting through to this chick, but that wasn't gonna slow her down. Bunni was born with a sixth sense and she was rarely wrong about her gut feelings. Her left titty was talking to her. Real loud. That bad boy was itching like hell, but in order to convince a chick like Selah she was gonna need much more than a skin rash. She was gonna need some hardcore *proof*.

"A'ight, Mama Selah, if you say so," Bunni said reluctantly. "Ain't nobody trying to get your blood pressure up. I'm just trying to find out what's going on with my girl. But you right. Mink is grown and she can swing her ass any which way she wants to. My bad for getting you all worked up. I'm carry my ass back to my room now, but if you hear anything from her could you holla real loud and let me know?"

"No problem, sweetheart," Selah said gently. "If I hear a single word, I'll holler at the top of my lungs."

Selah sighed and closed her eyes as Bunni left the room, grateful for the peace and quiet. She had just dozed off and was dreaming about a black cat biting at her ankle when her cell phone rang from the glass coffee table beside her.

She came awake with a start, and snatched it up and stared at the screen. *What the hell?* she thought groggily. *Another unavailable number?*

Selah's stomach sank as she prayed it wasn't someone calling with more bad news about Barron. He should have been
home by now, and her stomach started churning so badly that
Selah had to force herself to answer it before the call rolled
over to voice mail.

"Hello?"

"Is this Ms. Dominion?" a gruff-sounding voice asked
right off the bat.

"Well, y-yes it is," Selah admitted as she sat straight up on
the couch. "Who's speaking and how may I help you?"

"Oh don't be worrying about who I am. Who I am ain't
none of your fuckin' business," the man said in such an evil
hood tone that it made Selah's skin crawl. "You know, bitches
like you should really keep a closer eye on your children. There's
all sorts of crazy shit a kid could get caught up in and force their
parents to have to pay the price for. Do you get what I'm saying, Selah?"

"N-no," she stammered, coming all the way awake now.
"No, I'm sorry but I don't."

"Look, we got your skank-ass daughter, a'ight?" another
voice cut in. "We got Mink's grimy ass and you gonna have to
get up off a million big ones in order for us to cut the bitch
loose!"

"Pardon me?" Selah said loudly, her voice full of indigna-
tion. She reached over and snatched her half-empty glass of
vodka off the coffee table and drained that shit dry.

"What do you mean you've got Mink? You must be kidding me!"

"Bitch, do I sound like I'm fuckin' kidding?"

New York! The first man was back on the line and Selah's
brain exploded at the familiarity of his tone and lingo.

Hell yeah. That accent was straight out of New York.

"Um, I-I'm afraid I don't understand," Selah stammered
and tried to stall as she jumped off the sofa and hurried into

the kitchen to search for a piece of paper to write on. "Why in the world would you want to kidnap my daughter?"

"Why the fuck do anybody kidnap anybody else?" he exploded in her ear. "*Money*, stupid ass! You 'bout to get up off some of them oil vapors, baby! I want a million hot ones for this chickenhead trick. A million hot ones!"

Selah was suddenly as sober as a judge. Déjà vu came raining down on her and she knew exactly what she was up against. Bunni had been right. Mink was in trouble and some fool had snatched her. He had her and now he wanted a ransom. Memories of Mink's kidnapping at the age of three flooded her heart and Selah balled up her fist so hard that the nail on her middle finger snapped off and blood flooded the palm of her hand. She fought back her rage and horror and kept her voice neutral so she wouldn't excite the dirty bastard who had taken her daughter.

"How do I know you haven't already done something to her?" she asked quietly. "Let me speak to Mink," she demanded. "I need to know that my baby is alright."

"A'ight, that's fair enough," the man on the phone snickered. "Just make this shit quick because we got some gwap issues to discuss."

This man was definitely from New York. Either that or north Jersey. Selah was a native New Yorker and she could pick out that urban east coast slang from anywhere. A few moments later she heard a rustling noise and suddenly Mink was on the phone.

"Mama Selah, it's me," Mink panted like she'd been crying for hours. "I'm sorry for getting myself into this shit. I'm so sorry!"

"Mink," Selah said soothingly, relieved that Mink was still alive. "Just relax, baby. Whatever's going on, it's not your fault. Are you alright? Did they hurt you, baby?"

"I-I'm okay," Mink muttered, and Selah could tell she was

trying hard to keep her voice from cracking. "These crazy niggas ain't nothing nice, but I'm okay."

Selah's heart pounded. "Can you tell me where you are?"

"Hell no she can't fuckin' tell you where she at!" the man's
voice boomed in Selah's ear. "Fuck you think this is, Mama? A
goddamned joke? You want me to fuck this bitch up again
right fuckin' now?"

"*No!* Please don't do anything stupid. Don't hurt her!
Whatever you want, just tell me and I'll make sure you get it.
Please. We just got our daughter back and we don't want to
lose her again!"

"You about to lose this bitch alright!"

"*Mama!*" Mink cried out like she was in pain.

"Just stay calm, Mink," Selah begged her, ignoring the man
as she realized she was on a speakerphone. "I love you and I'm
going to get you back safely. Whatever they want I'll give it to
them, okay?"

"Now that's what the fuck I'm talking about, Mama," the
man laughed ruthlessly. "That's more like it! You just make sure
you keep twelve out of this and stay by the fucking phone."

"Mama please just do what they say," Mink added, sounding distraught. "These niggas are crazy, Mama! They've *always*
been crazy! Just please cooperate, okay?"

"I'll cooperate," Selah promised breathlessly. "I swear I will!
I love you, Mink. Your whole family loves you!"

"Y'all rich niggas better love her," the kidnapper said hap-
pily. "Y'all better love her trifling ass to death!"

"I love you too," Mink cried out, and a knot twisted in
Selah's heart. "I love you too, Mama Selah!"

"A'ight, that's enough sweet-talk!" the man snapped. "Your
conniving-ass daughter is safe and sound for now, but I'ma tell
you right now. You better not do nothing stupid like calling
the goddamn po-po. Don't you bring them blue boys into our
lil bizzness 'cause if I feel like you fucking with me, Selah, I *will*
fuck this bitch up. I'll chop her up in pieces and start mailing

all kinds of body parts back to that big pretty mansion of yours. Starting with the cheeks of her phat yellow ass!"

Selah ignored his vulgar insults as she made another mental note on the slight bit of information that Mink had let slip. Selah wasn't sure if Mink meant to say it on purpose, but it was definitely a distinct possibility.

"*They've always been crazy.*" That right there told Selah that Mink not only knew her captors, but she had known them for a long time, and that meant that they were more than likely from Harlem.

"I'll do whatever you say," Selah told them, her voice firm. "You want a million, you've got it. Just tell me how to get my daughter back, and I'll make sure you get your million dollars."

"Tree million," a shrill voice blared from the line. It was the second man who was speaking now, and it sounded like he was clowning.

"Pardon me?"

"We want tree million now," he snickered. "Matter fact, make it tree million, seben hunnerd thousand, fiddy-two dollars and leben cents."

"Three million, seven hundred thousand, fifty-two dollars and eleven cents?" Selah asked incredulously.

"That's right," he said chuckling. "Write that shit down, Mama. We'll call you back and tell you where to drop it off and you better make sure you don't come up a penny short."

CHAPTER 30

Selah was sitting on the sofa with her face buried in her hands when Barron, Suge, and Peaches walked in the door. She raised her head slowly and the intense pain and misery was so evident on her face that they immediately rushed over to her with concern in their eyes.

"Mama what's wrong?" Barron got to her first and he sat down beside her and cradled her slender form in his arms. "I'm home now," he soothed her. "You can stop worrying. Peaches and Suge came and got me and everything is okay."

"No," Selah shook her head slowly. Her voice sounded like it was coming up out of a cold, wet grave. "Everything is not okay. Mink has been kidnapped. Somebody is holding her for ransom."

"Oh, *gawd no!*" Peaches flailed his toned arms dramatically and then clutched his chest and crumpled down to his knees. *"Miiiink!!!"* He rushed over and hugged Selah around her ankles and pressed his face down into her lap. "Somebody got hold of my *Miiiink*!!! I raised her up from a small child! I taught her everything she knows! *Miiiink!*"

"Shut the fuck up!" Suge crossed the room in three strides

and blasted on Peaches, yanking him out of Selah's lap. "Run that by me again, Selah?" he said, cocking his hand behind his ear like he knew for damn sure he hadn't heard what he thought he heard. "What the hell did you just say about Mink?"

"I said," Selah said weakly, swallowing hard against her grief and pain, "She's been kidnapped. Somebody snatched her and they won't let her go. I got a call from a man who says he's holding her hostage. He said he's going to kill her if we don't pay him over three million dollars."

Barron groaned. "What the hell is this? Kidnap a Dominion Week?"

"Oh my gawd!" Peaches shrieked again. Tears ran down his face and his neon-pink bra strap slid off his broad shoulder. "Whoever he is, pay him, Selah! Pay his ass! Pay him any amount of money he wants! Hell, y'all are rich! We gotta do whatever it takes to get Mink back!"

"Did he say anything else?" Suge demanded. "Did he tell you where he was holding her, or where he wanted us to drop off the money?"

"Yeah!" Peaches piped in. "Did he say anything to give you an idea of who he might be?"

Selah's eyes lit up as she nodded her head vigorously.

"He said he was going to call back with more information about where to deliver the money, but I can tell you this: he was from New York!" she said emphatically. "That much I know for sure. That bastard had a New York City accent, and he sounded evil as all hell!"

The mansion was in an uproar.

Peaches had called Bunni downstairs to tell her the bad news, and she came storming from her room mad as fuck at Selah and screaming at the top of her lungs.

"See I told you! I fuckin' *told* you! I knew it! I *knew* some shady shit was up! My left titty wasn't itchin' for nothing, goddammit!"

"I'm sorry!" Selah said tearfully as she grabbed at Bunni's hand. "You were right, Bunni. I should have listened to you. I just couldn't imagine something like this happening twice in a row!"

"Yo, how the fuck did this happen?" Suge demanded of no one in particular. "First Barron, and now Mink! What fuckin' slime holes are these animals crawling out of?"

"I don't know," Selah said, "but I swear this family is cursed! Generationally!"

"Cursed, hell," Peaches said with a smirk. "Somebody got some 'mo' on y'all asses!"

"Hell, naw," Suge shook his head. "The only m-o this here shit is about is m-o-n-e-y goddammit!"

He turned to Bunni. "Yo, Mink is your homegirl. When's the last time you seen her?"

"Right after we came home from shopping," Bunni said. "We both went upstairs to take naps, but when I got up Mink was ghost. I kept tryna call her ass to see where she was, but she never answered. About an hour later my titty started itching like a mug, and that's when I knew something wasn't right. I came down here and tried to tell Selah that something off-brand was going down, but she fronted me off like I was crazy or something."

Suge grilled her. "So what the hell you saying, Bunni?" he barked, clearly agitated like a muthafucka. You tryna tell us that you and Mink are thicker than grits, but she dipped out on you without saying shit? Did y'all have an argument or something? A lil cat fight? Who the hell do you think she went to see?"

"Why you barking on me? What the fuck do I have to hide?" Bunni blurted out. Suge was acting like he was coming for her on some sideways shit! "Yeah, me and Mink is thick, and the only time she ever dips off like that is to go see yo— whoever the hell got her nose open, I guess."

Bunni glared at Suge with the *nigga I wish you would* look

in her eye. She had damn near slipped up just now and blurted some shit out, but she caught herself just in time.

Suge busted the move and backed off a little bit. Now wasn't the time to mess around and let it slip out that him and Mink were mashing it up.

"Barron," Suge turned to his nephew. "Wassup, man? I know you just got outta some real deep shit yourself, but maybe that scheming chick GiGi is behind this thing too. Can you think of anything she might have said or done that could have been directed at Mink? Do you remember anything at all that might help us out? Anything at all?"

Barron had been sitting beside Selah pretty quietly but now the raw pleading in his uncle's voice made him drop his head down into his hands.

"FUCK!" he muttered bitterly. "I can't believe this shit! How fucking stupid could I be?" He knew it. He just fucking knew it! The New York accent, all that shit he talked about Mink . . . it all came flooding back. He had even seen that muthafucka! He had *seen* him!

"Lil Bump," Suge said quietly as he loomed above him. "You know something we don't know? You got something that you wanna tell us, nephew? Mink is in trouble, goddammit. Spit that shit out!"

The room got hot as shit. Peaches, Selah, and Bunni were all staring at Barron intently. Bracing themselves for whatever he had to say.

"I think I know who took her," Barron finally admitted as he looked up into Suge's hardened eyes. "I think it's that slimy son-of-bitch Gutta. From Harlem."

"GUTTA?" Bunni shrieked at the top of her lungs. "Aw, *hell* no! Not Gutta! Not that psychopathic criminal-minded murdering mothafucking *Gutta!*"

"Oh, *gawd!*" Peaches moaned and sank down to his knees again.

A look of pure terror was in Bunni's eyes as she turned to

Selah and gripped her by her shoulders. "How the fuck did he find us? Oh *God*, Mama Selah! We gotta find Mink! We gotta get her away from him because if we don't that cray-cray nigga is gonna *kill* her!"

"Wait a damn minute, hold up," Suge shut Bunni up and turned back to Barron with a wave of fury rolling off him. "Who the hell is Gutta and how do you know him?"

"I met him in New York," Barron admitted and lowered his eyes. He could feel the disappointment coming out of everybody's pores, and he didn't blame them one bit because he was disappointed in himself. "I hired him to do a job for me before I knew that Mink was really my sister. I thought she was trying to con the family out of Sable's fortune. So I gave Gutta some cash to get rid of her. I told him to tie a concrete block around her ankles and throw her in the river."

The air was immediately sucked out of the room.

Suge bucked. "Muthafucka you paid somebody to kill Mink?"

Bunni covered her mouth with both hands and gagged. Peaches rushed over and wrapped his sister in his arms as her body shook with sobs. Selah leaned over closer to Barron and slapped the shit out of him.

"What the fuck is wrong with you?" Selah spit through clenched teeth with fire shooting from her eyes. "What kind of fucking idiot are you? Mink is your *sister*, Barron. She's my daughter and *your* sister!"

"Let me get my ass outta here," Bunni spit, throwing a foul look and some real nasty shade at Barron as she broke free from Peaches and stomped toward the door. "Before I bust a cap in this fool's ass! My girl is out there getting her skull cracked by public psycho number one, and this slimy mothafucka probably helped set it up!"

Selah let loose with the tongue and hit Barron with a barrage of foul language too, going hard in his ass. Suge held up one hand to check her, and when that didn't work he crossed the room to restrain her.

"Calm down, Selah. There'll be time for all that later," he said quietly. "Right now we need less questions and more answers."

Yeah, answers. He would swing his hammer and put the wrath of fury down on his nephew's ass later on, but right now he needed Barron because Mink's life was hanging in the balance.

"Bump," Suge said quietly. "Who the fuck is Gutta and where can I find him?"

Barron shook his head. "I don't know how to reach him, but I did see him recently."

Suge moved in close. "Oh yeah? When and where?"

"It was a couple of weeks ago. I saw him with—he was here at the mansion. At one of our cookouts. He walked up on me with some real crazy attitude and threatened me a little bit. I fronted him off and he . . . he left."

This time it was Selah who had to leave the room.

"I can't even *believe* what the hell I'm hearing!" she muttered under her breath as she grabbed her cell phone and headed from the room, her face a mask of bitterness and disgust.

"Where are you going?" Suge demanded.

"I don't know but I'm getting the hell up out of here before I mess around and have to knock this damn fool over his head with something!"

Suge whirled around to Barron with a blazing fire shooting from his eyes. "What the fuck was that nigga doing in this house?" he barked as he reached down and snatched his nephew up by the collar. He lifted Barron in the air and slammed him up against a wall, pinning him with his grip. "Why the fuck didn't you tell somebody? Why didn't you let somebody know that a nigga you paid to kill Mink was right here in this fucking house?"

"I-I-I," Barron stammered, helpless and about to shit his drawers. He glimpsed Suge's inner beast peeking out and knew this was the last muthafucka on the face of the earth whose bad side he wanted to walk on. But there was no excuse he could think of that would be good enough to satisfy his uncle. Or his mother, or Bunni, or even his father, who was sure to go off as soon as he found out Mink was gone again.

A security guard who was making his rounds poked his head in the living room when he saw Suge raging with Barron still in the air all yoked the fuck up.

"Is everything okay in here, sir?" the guard asked.

"Get the fuck outta here!" Suge blasted on him. "Get gone, muthafucka!"

Without another word the guard walked off. Everybody knew Suge was a deadly muthafucka about his business, and nobody wanted any parts with him. Suge turned his attention back to Barron, who was hung up on the wall looking guilty in the face.

"Yo, let me down, Uncle Suge," Barron gasped. He wasn't begging and he wasn't pleading, but he *was* asking. "C'mon, now. We have to talk about this shit rationally so we can figure out what to do, so c'mon, man. Let me down."

Slowly, Suge released his grip and allowed Barron to slide down the wall until his feet hit the floor. Suge's face was twisted in a mass of murderous rage, and Barron was damn glad they were family because otherwise he wasn't sure he would have survived this shit.

"Who the fuck took Mink and where the fuck can I find him?"

Barron sighed. "I don't know, Unc," he said truthfully. "All I remember is that big nigga Gutta being in my face—talking all types of ill shit and trying to flex on me. He walked up on me outta nowhere and knocked my plate out of my hand and I acted like I didn't know him. I wasn't scared of that nigga, but I knew that I had gotten down with him on the grimy tip in the past, and I didn't wanna cause a scene and risk everybody finding out what I'd done. So I kinda played it off and honestly, I didn't even think about him anymore."

By now Suge damn near had smoke blowing out of his nose. He wanted to straight up rip Barron's face off for being so goddamn stupid!

But he couldn't.

He couldn't afford to. He was the fixer. He was the family problem solver and he had to do whatever the fuck it took to keep the family together and get his Mink back.

"Stay your ass here and take care of your mother," Suge barked as he released his grip on Barron and headed toward the stairs. "Make sure Selah stays by that phone at all times, and if they call back, stall them. Tell Bunni to sit her ass still and keep her mouth closed. And make sure nobody says shit to Viceroy, at least for right now. If anything else pops off call me right away."

"But what about the money that fool is asking for?" Barron asked. "Should I get in touch with our accountants and arrange for some cash to be bagged up and delivered when they call?"

"Hell fuckin' no," Suge said as he stormed upstairs to get his gat so he could jump in his monster truck packin' big heat. "We ain't paying that muthafucka shit. Niggas like him don't deserve no payoff. That bitch-ass muthafucka won't be getting a dime from this family because that nigga ain't gonna live long enough to spend it."

CHAPTER 31

As sore as Barron was from the beating he had taken from those Dominatrix bitches, his physical pain didn't have shit on the mental beating he was putting down on himself. When Suge stormed out of the mansion Barron had dragged himself upstairs to his suite with his tail tucked between his legs like a boot-kicked dog. He had leaned up against his mini bar in exhaustion, and poured himself a double shot of hen-hen. In ten seconds flat he had tossed that shit back and chased it down with a nice hot shot of gin, and now he stood in the shower with his head all fucked up as scalding hot water rained all over him, stinging his battered muscles and his rope-burned skin.

All kinds of crazy thoughts were running around in Barron's head. The hot water was washing away the dirt and grime on his body, but it couldn't touch the guilt and shame he felt in his heart. He had gotten played like a muthafucka. Chumped by yet another white chick. It was just like Bunni had said. He had a weakness for them bitches that he just couldn't shake.

Right about now he wished he could go back to his boring-ass life with Carla. He should have married her ass and called that shit a day. But still, it wouldn't have stopped him from getting dick-strung on GiGi's delicious piece of ass, and it damn sure wouldn't have kept him from going at Mink's throat before he was sure that she was really his sister.

But as much as he had hated Mink, Barron had never imagined the ramifications of the shady actions he'd taken in New York would come back to hurt his family like this. He had exploited his power and used his endless supply of cash to manipulate circumstances and do his share of off-balance shit before—from hitting that Mexican kid with the car and trying to cover it up, to getting arrested and taking a mug shot dressed like a tranny drag queen, to letting his dick lead him into lusting and trusting that red hot liar GiGi Molinex, which is why he was in the shitty situation he was in right now.

Barron had been in tight spots where his nuts were gripped at the root before, but it was the look on his mother's face when he had admitted that he had paid Gutta to get rid of Mink that had damn near broken his spirit today. He hated hurting his mother more than anything else in the world, and just remembering the kind of joy that had filled her heart when she found Mink and realized her daughter was alive, it just tore him up inside.

Of course, at the time Barron had thought he was doing the right thing. With Viceroy in a coma, it was his job to protect the Dominion empire and he had wanted Dy-Nasty and Mink's scheming asses as far away from the family jewels as possible.

So yeah. He had gone to New York City and hired Gutta to do a job that never got done, and now Barron's secret had come back to haunt him and his whole fucking family.

He cut off the water and dried his sore body with a king-sized cotton-ball-soft towel that had been imported from Egypt. His large, lavish suite was a model in luxury and finery, but right now Barron didn't give two shits about all his wealth and extravagances. He had to figure out how to fix what the fuck he had broken, and the only way he was gonna do that was to find

that bitch Pilar and figure out why Gutta had suddenly decided to reappear in their lives.

Barron got his ass in gear and threw on a pair of black
slacks and a collared D'eregino shirt. As always, his clothing
was expensive as shit, but today he made sure his gear was also
loose and comfortable because he had a feeling he was gonna
need some room to move.

He had held back on telling Uncle Suge that Gutta had
used Pilar to get close to the family because he wanted to give
her the benefit of the doubt. But if he found out that her crazy
ass had been scheming with that fool . . .

Barron didn't even wanna think that shit. He knew Pilar
was a thirsty chaser who could be hostile, fiery, and defensive
when she didn't get what she wanted. But could she cross her
own family up like that? Could she get down with a low-
down trench-nigga like Gutta and bring blood down on her
own people?

Barron couldn't be sure about the answer to that question,
but he had already decided that no matter what happened he
wasn't leaving up out of Pilar's crib without getting the answers he needed.

As he was heading downstairs he bumped into Bunni dragging herself up the steps. The vibrant swag that Bunni brought
to the house was totally gone. Her ass looked whipped.

She raised her gaze toward him and immediately twisted
her lips and glared at him like he was a stinking pile of dog
doo-doo.

"Yo, Bunni, I-I-I'm sorry," Barron began.

"You goddamn right you sorry!" she said hotly. "Got my
girl out there in the hands of that jailhouse beast! Asshole! Did
you hear back from Suge yet?"

"N-n-naw," Barron stuttered stupidly. "No, I haven't." He
frowned and clenched his jaw tight. He could barely look Bunni
in her eyes. Although him and Bunni didn't really rock with
each other too tough, Barron knew how close she was to Mink.

"But I'm about to go make a couple of moves myself and see what I can do."

Bunni's whole face started trembling as she looked up at him with big fat tears in her eyes, and then she did something that was so unexpected it fucked Barron's whole head up. Bunni reached out and wrapped her arms around Barron and gave him a great big hug.

"You gotta find her, Barron!" she sobbed. "You gotta bring my mothafuckin' girl back home! Ain't no telling what that bastard Gutta is doing to her right fuckin' now! He's prolly whipping Mink's ass like she picked his goddamn pocket! I mean, yeah okay, in a way she did kinda pick his pocket, but you know what I'm saying! That maniac is prolly kicking Mink's ass up and down the street and straight fucking her dome up!"

Barron stood there as stiff as hell. He didn't know what in the hell to do as Bunni stood in his arms crying with her plump titties pressed all up against his chest, but then slowly he raised his arms and hugged her back.

"Don't cry, Bunni. Just calm down, a'ight?" Barron said patting her back. "I'm going to find out where Mink is. Don't trip. I swear to God I'm gonna find her."

Barron dipped out of the mansion and headed over to his Porsche, and in just a few minutes he was burning rubber down the highway and aiming straight for Pilar's crib. He pressed a button on the console intending to call ahead and make sure she was home, but then he changed his mind and decided against it. Rolling up out of nowhere and catching that slick heffah with her guard down would give him a big advantage. If she knew he was coming she'd have a chance to prepare and get her attitude on so she could come at him from the wild side. But showing up unannounced would kill all that shit and give him a chance to put the pressure on and come at her with mad aggression as well.

Barron shook his head as his foot mashed the gas. Pressure and aggression were the only things a chick like Pilar understood. Well, that and money, of course. But she had been putting some real aggressive pressure down on him hard the whole time they were fucking around. And now it was time for him to turn the tables.

By the time he pulled up into Pilar's driveway Barron was fired up and ready to fight. He put the car in park and didn't even bother to turn it off because what he had come to do wasn't gonna take long. He strode up to the front door and after beating on the wood with some iron-fisted nigga knocks and a couple of jabs on the doorbell, Pilar snatched the door open and looked at him like she was expecting someone else.

"Barron! W-W-What in the world are you doing here?" she stammered, poking her head out the door and sounding like he was the last person in the world who should have been standing at her front door. She turned her lips down nastily and looked him up and down. "What the hell do you want?"

"Pilar," Barron said with fire in his voice as he pushed past her and barged straight into the house. He slammed the door and locked it behind him. "I'm gonna ask you this one time and one time only. Where the fuck is Gutta, and when is the last time you saw him?"

Immediately her attitude turned savage. "Gutta? Do some damn body named Gutta live here? I don't know what the fuck your problem is Barron, but don't come busting up in my crib like the Dominions pay the bills around here! I don't know where the hell that fool Gutta is! If you were so worried about him then you should have asked him for his address that day when he was about to give you a beat down in your own backyard!"

Barron looked away like he was defeated. She'd always had a sharp tongue and she had no problem testing his pride. He wondered what the hell he had ever seen in her. But today it wasn't about him. Today there was nothing Pilar could say to fuck with his manhood, because today it wasn't his pride that was on the line.

It was his sister.

"Yeah, just like I thought," Pilar said smugly. She put her hand on her hip and started walking dead at him, knowing damn well he was going to back down as usual. Pilar was grinning as she eyed Barron like a predator who sensed weakness in her prey. She didn't know it, but this time she was wrong. Dead-ass wrong.

"Get to stepping your ass out of my house, Mister Softie! Trust me, you don't want no parts of Gutta. A nigga like him will chew you up and spit your punk ass out!"

Barron pounced on Pilar like a panther on a fresh kill. In a flash he gripped her by the back of the neck and lifted her straight up off her feet and chucked her into the air. She bounced off her father's leather recliner and then landed ass-first, hard on the floor.

"Bitch! Does it look like I'm fucking playing with you?" Barron roared in her face as he straddled her waist and grabbed a fist full of her hair and swung her around. Pilar was stunned as she spun on her ass like a top.

"That grimy muthafucka took my *sister*! My muthafuckin' *sister*! Do you hear me?"

Pilar was scared as fuck as he manhandled her but she wasn't ready to bow down and kiss his ass just yet.

"Get your hands off me, you crazy fuck!" she screamed. She tried to buck up and swing a couple of punches from the floor but she was too light in the ass to do any damage. "So Mink is your sister now, huh? You weren't feeling all brotherly toward her when you were having wet dreams and shooting off in your drawers over her ass! Fuck that bitch! Even if I knew where Gutta was holding her I wouldn't tell you! Just pay him his three point two million dollars and go on about your business. That ain't but a drop in the bucket baby because the Dominions have plenty of dough to spread around!"

"Pay him how much?" Barron said as he eyed her closely. "How you know Gutta is trying to get some money out of us? Where'd you get the three point two million from, Pilar? How the fuck do you know what Gutta wants?"

"I *don't* know what he wants!" Pilar said hotly, catching herself and trying to clean shit up as she played it off. "I'm just saying when people get kidnapped it's usually for money, duh!"

"Uh-huh, and you just pulled that three point two figure outta your ass, right?

Murder flashed in Barron's eyes and Pilar couldn't stop herself from cringing. "I should've known you were scheming with that nigga when I seen y'all with your empty heads pressed together at the barbeque! You dirty little shitball! You got down on this shit, didn't you? You crossed up your own family just to suck a couple of dollars outta that thug-ass nigga's dick!"

"Well he's sure packin' way more dick than you, you stunted mother—"

Barron hauled off and slapped Pilar so hard her breath was snatched away and she couldn't even scream. She squeezed her eyes closed and hiccupped twice, and before she could catch her breath he grabbed her by the ankle and started dragging her toward the kitchen.

"Get up, you grimy bitch!" Barron snarled as spit gathered in the corners of his mouth and he snatched Pilar up off the floor. By now her breath was back and the color had returned to her cheeks. She opened her mouth and started screaming like a murder was going down.

"Shut the fuck up," Barron barked, not giving a damn how loud she screamed. The Ducane Manor sat on quite a few acres of land, and since his uncle Digger wasn't home there was nobody around to hear Pilar's cries. And trust and believe, if Barron had anything to do with it the bitch was going to cry harder and louder before it was all said and done.

"Pilar, I would tell you that you're a low-down conniving whore, but you already know all that. But what I will tell you is, no, what I will *promise* you is this: I will choke your fucking lights out if you don't tell me where Gutta is holding my sister. You better tell me right here and right fucking now, and even if you do tell me I still might kill you."

Pilar knew she was trapped and there was no doubt in her mind that Barron would do her ass and then get Suge to help him dispose of her body, and right now she was scared to death. Fuck the deal she had made with Gutta. His big ass wasn't here to save her, and judging by the insane look on Barron's face Pilar knew he would fuck her all the way up.

Unless she defended herself.

Without thinking Pilar busted a last-ditch desperate move. She lunged for the silverware drawer hoping she could grab a knife real quick, but she was way too slow. Barron swung on her and connected with a stiff punch straight to her left breast that sent her flying backward and colliding into the refrigerator.

"Where's Mink?" Barron demanded. He jammed his foot down on Pillar's exposed neck and leaned his weight forward as her eyes bulged and she squirmed. "Silly bitch," he breathed down at her. "I can't believe I ever fucked with your sorry ass! You'd better cough up some info right now or I swear to God I'll kill you and bury your ass where won't nobody ever look for you. I'll go to your funeral and cry a whole fucking river. I'll wipe your father's tears and pat him on the back as he mourns you. And then I'll slide enough cash in the right pockets so the police will stop looking for you and you become nothing more than a shitty little memory. Now tell me where the fuck my sister is!"

CHAPTER 32

It had taken him some time, but Barron had finally beaten the truth out of Pilar.

"Okay, okay!" she had finally screamed as he wailed on her ass. "They're in that gated community off highway 87. It's the last house on the last street, and that's all I know.

"How many of them?"

"Two. Gutta and Shy. That's it. Just those two. I swear that's all I know."

Barron gazed down at her as he pulled out his phone to call Suge.

"From now on, your ass is cut off. Done. If you show your face at the mansion again I'll let everybody know exactly what you did and how you tried to get Mink killed."

"You tried to get her ass killed too, remember?" she shot back. "I didn't do a damn thing that you didn't do too!"

Barron nodded as he hit Suge's number on speed dial so he could tell him where to find Gutta and Mink. "Yeah, you're right. My head was all fucked up for a minute too. The difference is, everyone knows the wrong that I did. My shit is all out in the open now and I'm willing to pay my dues and do whatever I gotta do to make it right. But a greedy hater like you will never pay up, Pilar. Snakes like you crawl around on the ground forever. Ask your father how far he's gotten by licking Dominion balls and sucking Ruddman dick! I'm telling you, Pilar. Stay away from my house. Stay away from my family. And when we get her back, you'd damn sure better stay away from my sister."

Barron wasn't the only one who had a phone call to make.

"Get her outta there!" Pilar screamed into the phone after Barron peeled out of her driveway. She had crawled painfully across the floor to get to the phone so she could warn Gutta about what was heading his way.

"Barron made me tell him where you are! He's sending Uncle Suge after you and that nigga will make your black ass disappear!"

Gutta and Shy broke out. They dragged Mink outside to the whip and tossed her screaming and crying into the front passenger seat.

"Gutta, please," Mink begged through swollen lips as that pyscho mothafucka made a mad dash outta the gates of the private community and headed toward the highway. His foot was heavy on the gas pedal as he pushed the small car to capacity and cut in and out of multiple lanes of traffic. Squeezing her knees together to keep from peeing, Mink shifted her ass around on the seat as blood dripped from a gash in her head and every inch of her body screamed in agony. "Where you taking me? Tell me where we going?"

Gutta flinched like he was gonna smash her again and Mink cringed. That nigga had put the hammer on her ass in that little bungalow, but that's not all he had done to her as he brutalized Mink's body and humiliated her mind. He had called her all types of dirty trick-bitches as he swung home runs with his fists and smashed her skull like an egg while digging the toe of his Timbs all up in her ass.

"Lemme go, please," she yelped as he drove with one hand and raised his other one up high like he was about to jack-slap the shit outta her and put her to sleep with the back of his giant hand.

"Shut the fuck up!" he growled, glaring at her with his nostrils flaring.

"But I can get you the money—"

"Fuck your money!" Gutta spit quietly with rage riding on every word. "I don't want your fuckin' cheddar. Ain't no amount of dollars in the world that's gonna save your shiesty life, sweetheart, because I want your muthafuckin' ass, Mink! I want your big, juicy, high-yellow ass!"

"Yo-yo-yo-yo, yo!" Shy piped up from the backseat. "Chill the fuck out, pot-ner! And watch ya fuckin' mouth! Remember the plan, my man! Don't be losing ya fuckin' head, a'ight?"

But Gutta was too far gone to hear that shit. "Gutta, please," Mink went back to begging again.

"Yeah!" Shy blurted out in a panic. "Yeah, nigga, please! Fuck wrong witchu? Don't be telling this bitch we don't want that loot! We *want* that fuckin' money, man! Hell yeah, we came down here to get paid, my nigga! Fuck yo principles, we want that cheesy bread!"

"Fuck that money!" Gutta growled. He reached out and caught Mink by her neck. He gripped her by the throat meat and squeezed hard enough to make her eyeballs pop out. "I'm killing this bitch. I'm deading her. I got one bullet left and when I finish choking this bitch I'ma shoot her in the ass!"

Mink tried to scream but she didn't have so much as a croak in her. Eyes bulging and cheeks puffed out, she jerked away and clawed at Gutta's hand, digging her nails deep into his dark skin as he swerved all over the road, but that nigga held on tight. She fought like a tiger, but Gutta's outstretched arm was harder than a telephone pole as he gripped her neck in a stranglehold. Mink saw stars and heard trumpets and knew she was about to black the hell out.

No, Gutta, no! she screamed silently in her mind as she desperately scratched at him and struggled for a sip of air. Panick-
ing like fuck she started swinging killer blows at the side of his
head, then she raked her nails down his face and tried to dig
out one of his eyeballs. That nigga squinched his mug up nice
and tight, and when Mink dug into the corner of his mouth
and yanked his bottom lip, he opened wide and bit the shit out
of her.

I'm dying! she thought as she snatched her fingers back and
started fading out. Her body spasmed involuntarily and she
arched backward as she kicked out with both feet and tried
not to piss on herself.

This nigga is killing me! He's really fuckin' killing me!

The light was fading from her eyes and suddenly Mink
slumped forward and went limp like a rag doll.

"Yeah, you slimy bitch!" Gutta hollered and chucked her
so hard that her body keeled over and her head slammed hard
into the passenger window.

Mink's forehead busted and her eyes flew open.

I'm alive! I'm alive! she screamed silently as she sucked in a
lungful of sweet air like she was hitting on a crack pipe. Snot
ran from her nose and tears flowed like a river from her eyes as
she tried to play dead and stop her chest from heaving up and
down. Her fake eyelashes fluttered like bird wings as she stole a
peek up at Gutta, and in less than a split second fear and horror jumped right back in her throat and her heart started
pumping Kool-Aid again.

"Bitch, you still breathing?" he barked, surprised to see she
was still alive. That nigga's lips was turned down and he was
foaming at the mouth like he was the one who had gotten
choked out. He drew his arm back and raised his fist to clock
her again but it wasn't his big old crusty knuckles that had
Mink fucked up and her bloodshot eyes all big and wide. Naw,
she thought as she peered over his shoulder at the super-bright
headlights that were coming at them from the side. It was that

huge silver monster truck that had just cut across the median and was racing full speed toward them that got her courage up and made her swell up with pride.

"My nigga's gonna fuck you up," was all Mink had time to moan before the monster truck made a pit stop and t-boned the whip so hard that it tipped over and went up on its side wheels and damn near flipped the hell over. Mink threw her hands up and screamed as she slid over and crashed into the window again. They hovered like that for a quick second, and when the car finally tilted back over it slammed to the ground so hard that Shy went flying straight outta the back window and Gutta, who was still wailing like crazy on Mink's ass, got knocked the fuck out.

Suge's headlights looked like two gigantic moons as they came up outta nowhere and exploded into us. The front end of his truck punched into the driver's door and knocked Gutta over and sent that big nigga slamming right into me. I screamed out loud as every bone in my body felt like it snapped in two places. My head whipped sideways on my neck and my face cracked hard into the window, and that's when time said hold the fuck up Mink, and the whole world went dark.

I opened my eyes and swallowed a mouthful of blood. My jaw was throbbing and all my teeth were aching in my gums. My head was banging like a drum, and for a second all I wanted was my dead mama.

"Owwww," I moaned as I slowly regained consciousness. It felt like I'd been hit by a Mack truck. My head was throbbing and my lips were swollen up like two grapes. I tried to sit up but wouldn't nothing on my body move. Glass was everywhere. In my hair, on my face, and all over my clothes. The smell of gas fumes were going all up my nose.

"Help!" I muttered weakly as everything started coming back to me. I couldn't have been out for more than a couple of seconds because that cray-cray nigga Gutta still had his big ass laying on top of me. "Help!"

"Shut up, bitch." I blinked my eyes and saw blood on his lips and a big-ass noogie on his forehead. That nigga planted his hand in my face and mushed my whole head in as he tried to sit up and crawl away.

"Ouch!" I screeched, and that's when I heard it.

Metal crunched hard on metal as Gutter's dented-up driver's door was yanked open and cool air flew in from outside.

"You punk muthafucka!"

Yes! I screamed as my big bronco-busting boo snatched Gutta's ass outta the crumpled-up whip like that nigga was a toddler! Suge grabbed him by his dreadlocks and dragged that mothafucka back across the seat, swinging killer blows that sounded like gunshots in the night.

Gutta was a slick, street-hard mothafucka who lived in the trenches and had some of the most evil mothafuckas in New York shook down to their drawers. He was legendary on them city streets and he could smash a nigga's dome into silly putty with those big old brick-breaker hands of his.

But that nigga ain't have shit on Big Suge!

Delight surged in my heart as Bae beat the dog shit outta Gutta! My king-sized country boy pounded that Harlem hood-lum into the concrete, landing mug-crushing roundhouses that busted Gutta's grill and sent his head flying and jerking all over the place. It looked like somebody was swinging a black mop as Suge wrung his neck and Gutta's dreads whipped back and forth in the air.

Big Suge Dominion fucked that bitch-ass nigga up! He blackened them eyes and dented that forehead, and cracked that nigga's jaw!

"Get him!" I squeaked as I crawled up on my knees and watched from the driver's window. My head was dripping blood and my hand came down on a sharp piece of glass as I crawled into Gutta's seat to get a better look, but I barely even noticed it.

Suge had that nigga on the ground now, pounding him like he was a tough piece of steak.

"Yeah, get him!" I muttered a little bit louder as my dream man put in heavy work on the ex-nightmare who had tried to take me out. "Fuck him up, Suge! Fuck him up!"

But my excitement turned to dread when I saw Gutta reach down in his pants. I just knew a blicky was about to come out, but when I turned my head to shout out a warning to Suge I saw that my man had already reached for his heat too.

"Suge, watch out! He's got a—"

Pop!

Pop!

Them words froze up right in my mouth as I saw a bright flash of light spit from both their grips. Gutta immediately slumped forward on the ground and Suge went flying backward through the air. Gripping his stomach, he moved in slow motion and he landed hard on his back, bouncing off the pavement twice before rolling over and laying still.

I didn't feel a goddamn thing as I scrambled my ass outta that dented-up whip. No cuts, no bruises, no lumps or sprains, I didn't feel none of that shit as my bare feet hit the ground and I stumbled across the concrete bleeding like crazy and hollering Suge's name every step of the way. I didn't see Shy's broken-up body and I didn't see Gutta neither. There was nothing on my mind except the sound of those bullets, and when I finally made it over to where my man had dropped, I dove on top of Suge's fallen body like a swan, and with a knot of pure fear choking off my breath, I passed the hell out.

CHAPTER 33

Suge's funeral was loud and slamming. Everybody and their mama was crowded into that hot-ass church, and folks were wailing their lungs out left and right. All of his friends and family from Dallas were representing and the crazy Dominion crew from Houston had turned out big-time too. Suge was one of them cats who had never met a stranger. People loved him. They took to him and they wanted to be up under him. And now that he was gone, every damn body was missing him. Especially me.

I was sitting in the front row of the big old church crammed in between Selah and Fallon. The tabernacle choir was belting out "Precious Lord" and the joint was rocking. I had on a long black dress and my whole body heaved as I cried big fat, horrible tears. My man was dead and gone. Wiped out by Gutta's bullet, and no matter which way I looked at it, it was all my fault.

"It's okay, baby," Mama Selah leaned over and whispered as she rubbed my back with sympathy all in her hands. "He's in a better place. God don't make no mistakes."

Just hearing that shit sent a fresh wave of grief surging

through me and I hunched over until my head hit my knees, then pressed my face into my hands and cried real loud and hard, just like a little baby.

The preacher was bringing down the house and the choir was going to town. But all that holy ghost stuff missed me and went right over my head as I sat there crying and snotting into my hands, consumed by the loss of my boo.

"Get up, Mink," Selah said as her and Fallon lifted me by my arms so we could walk up to the casket and say our last good-byes. "Come on, baby. Stand up. We'll help you."

I slow-walked up to that casket crying and shrieking so bad I teetered around in my high heel shoes and almost busted my ass.

"Oooh," one of the church mothers said out loud, "for her to just be his niece she sure is taking it hard."

I ain't his goddamn niece! I wanted to whirl around and scream on her. *I'm his woman! His bae! His boo!*

I pulled away from Selah and Fallon and walked up to his open coffin. Suge was dressed out the ass, just like always. His suit was top-shelf, his white shirt starched, and his sexy moustache was trimmed to perfection. He had on a pair of twenty-thousand-dollar alligator boots, and I knew them babies had been specially made and hand-crafted just for him.

"I luh-luh-lub you, Suge Dominion," I said loudly, blinded by my tears as sticky trails of snot ran outta my nose and down my top lip. "I don't care what n-n-n-no fuckin' body thinks! I'm your *woman*, Suge! You my *man!* And I'ma *always* love you!"

My head was banging and my heart hurt so fucking bad. After all my tricks and ganks and schemes and hustles, I had finally been blessed with the love of a good man, and in an instant our entire future was taken away from us. It wasn't fuckin' fair! I had paid for all my criminal capers and I had suffered enough! Shaking and crying out in grief, I leaned down in that casket and wrapped my arms around my big old handsome man . . . and damn if he didn't sit up and kiss me on my forehead and hug me right back!

"Mink," Suge said, cradling her in his big, strong arms as they sat on the pavement beside his truck. Wake up, baby. C'mon now, sugar. Open your eyes."

Mink's face was swollen and covered with bruises. Fresh blood trickled from a cut in her hairline. Suge found a smooth spot on her forehead, then bent over and kissed her on it. "Wake up, baby. Open your eyes."

"W-w-what?" Mink said as her eyelids fluttered and then opened wide. The wail of an ambulance was sounding in the distance and a look of confusion spread across her battered face. She gazed around. The back lift of Suge's truck was down, and inside the bed she saw Gutta bleeding from his gunshot and hog-tied with his wrists to his ankles with a stone cold look of terror on his face. Shy's body was still on the ground where he had landed when he got ejected from the car. His neck was bent at a funny angle and he was soaking in a pool of blood.

Mink squeezed her eyes tightly closed and trembled. "S-S-Suge?" his name came out in a tortured moan. "How you . . . ? But baby you got . . . ?"

"Don't worry about me, I'm good," he said gruffly as relief flooded his voice. "You a'ight, sweetie? You okay?"

"B-b-but you got *shot*," Mink insisted. Cradling her cut hand to her breast, she ran her good hand all over his chest and down his stomach searching for his bullet wound. "Both of y'all did! I saw that crazy nigga pull the trigger! He shot you and you flew backward and grabbed your stomach. And then you went . . . down . . ."

Suge grinned as he leaned back and yanked up his shirt. Mink's eyes got wide as hell as she stared at the big silver TEXAS belt buckle sitting right below his bulging six-pack.

She frowned at the stupid-expensive piece of solid silver that she had bought him at the mall. There was a big dent in the crosshairs of the letter X where the bullet had struck the belt and ricocheted off, but Suge's muscle-bound chocolate stomach was still smoother than a baby's ass, and other than the sexy trail of curly hair leading from his navel down into his pants, his stomach didn't have a mark on it.

"Y-y-you wore it . . . I left it out on the bed and . . ."

"And I'm good, baby," he reassured her again as her body trembled in his arms. "For real, you saved my life, Mink. You saved me."

Mink tried to grin even though the split that Gutta had put in her lip hurt like hell. "Uh-uh, it was this big old ugly belt," she said, running her grateful fingers over the nick in the letter X.

She turned back to the truck and gave Gutta the stank look.

"That pussy-ass New York nigga must don't know!" she drawled as she reached up and wrapped her arm around Big Suge's neck buried her face in his barrel chest. "Don't mess with Texas!" she muttered. "Don't you mess with fuckin' Texas!"

CHAPTER 34

GiGi Molinex walked into some run-down bar called Last Frontier in some bullshit town just inside Oklahoma. With Barron gone from her clutches she was feeling broke and defeated and she needed a drink to calm her nerves. The whole situation had spiraled out of control before she could get a handle on it, and her strategy had gone to the dogs. She was a far better tactician than what she'd recently shown, but Barron had gotten sensitive over his father being shot, and he'd forced her hand and caused her to fly off the handle.

That stupid bastard, she thought bitterly as she walked past the bar. I had him cross-eyed and pussy strung, but he caught me slipping and fucked up my plans

GiGi sat down at a table near a window. She glanced around the seedy joint and to her surprise she saw a couple of clean-cut-looking men in business suits sitting at the bar throwing back a few brews. They didn't look out of place in the least. In fact, they seemed pretty comfortable as they watched a football game and ate some wings.

Perhaps they were out for a bite after a long workday, GiGi surmised as her eyes roamed over their tailored suits and expensive shoes. They were so well-dressed and groomed that they could have been top execs of a big corporation or maybe even a couple of hot-shot high-powered politicians. GiGi grinned. Either way, they looked like prime targets and she needed to get back on top of her game.

"Hello, ma'am, my name is Brandon," a handsome young man wearing an apron greeted GiGi with a smile. "I'll be your waiter today and I'm happy to serve you. Can I start you off with anything to drink?"

"Yes," GiGi said pleasantly. "I'd like a shot of scotch on the rocks please, Brandon," she said as she stared at the strapping, young All-American-looking boy who was staring down her cleavage and marveled at his deliciousness. She squared her shoulders and let him get a real good peek, but she wasn't impressed. Looks could never satisfy a woman like GiGi. Money was *always* her motivation and her shoes and purse had cost more than what this kid would make slaving in this shitty dump in five years. "Please make sure my glass is sparkling clean. Thank you, Brandon."

"No problem, ma'am," Brandon said with a smile. His eyes came up out of her bosom and lingered on GiGi's beautiful face. He was trying to flirt but she wasn't giving him any play. "Coming right up."

With the handsome young thing off to get her drink, GiGi's mind returned to the slippery fish that she had let get away. Barron Dominion. But just because he had gotten away it didn't mean he was gone forever. GiGi knew what she was working with, and she knew it was potent too. *I'll just have to wait until he drops his guard. Pussy hounds like him always do.*

As GiGi sipped her drink and contemplated her situation she noticed that she had caught the eye of one of the business suits at the bar. They exchanged glances and she played it coy, but she was anxious to see if he had the balls to step to her. And to her glee, after just a little more eyeball tennis he abandoned his barstool and made his way over to her table.

"Good evening, my name is Will Tatum," the attractive blue-eyed man said as he stood over GiGi and offered her his outstretched hand. "I noticed you were drinking alone. Do you mind if I keep you company?"

"My name is GiGi," she said sweetly as she shook his hand and showed Will her irresistible smile. "I'm just having a drink and relaxing. It's been a long couple of days. You can join me if you'd like."

"It's nice to meet you," Will said. "I'm the head marketing director for H and R productions. We just closed a pretty major deal so me and a few of my team members stopped by to watch the game and celebrate a little. This isn't the most up-scale place in town but the wings are pretty good. Would you like something to eat? Or perhaps I can buy you another drink?"

"Oh, no thank you. I'm fine for now," GiGi said. She knew how the big-time boys played. If he thought she was a sucker for alcohol he would be trying to shove drinks down her throat the entire night. "I'm not staying long. I just needed a little something to take the edge off. Congratulations on your big score. It's always good when we get to see our hard work pay off."

"Thank you, I appreciate that," Will said. He signaled to the waiter to bring him another drink. "So, what's a nice girl like you doing in a place like this? Do you work in the area? I'm a great listener if you'd like to talk about what's bothering you."

"That was three tough questions in a row," GiGi laughed easily. "But seriously, I'm an entrepreneur so I work for my-self," she said smoothly, which really wasn't a lie. "Sometimes I do freelance work for a few bigwigs around the country. I set up important meetings between clients and broker deals, that type of stuff. Work isn't really a problem for me, it's just been a long few days of kidnapping people and setting them up for ransom." She flashed him a bright smile. "That kind of thing gets a little wild sometimes, you know what I mean?"

Will nodded. "Oh sure. I do it all the time," he said as they shared a good laugh. "So are you married or involved with anyone, or is that too much of a personal question?"

GiGi shook her head. "No, it's not too personal and no, I'm not married. At least not anymore." She paused and sipped from her glass. "I just kinda got out of a relationship that turned sour pretty quickly. I'm focused on my next move now. When things don't work out you can't wallow in sorrow for too long. You have to stay focused on your happiness no matter what your relationship status is."

As Will kept drinking and GiGi kept talking and filling his head with lies, she could tell how bad he wanted her. GiGi was always looking for the next come up and Will was looking like the perfect mark. Of course he wasn't a Dominion, but a young director in the prime of his career could put her into a pretty comfortable playing field. So GiGi did what she did best. She stroked his ego and complimented him like he was the biggest fish she had ever seen coming up out of the sea. She laughed at all his lame-ass jokes and even had a few slick comebacks of her own. GiGi could do this shit in her sleep. She was a beautiful serpent with a perfectly forked tongue. A stone cold liar in the flesh.

"All right, GiGi. Let's cut to the chase," Will finally said as his happy eyes bounced all over her tits. After four shots of liquor his eyes were wild with lust. "How much do you cost? I mean, whatever your hourly fee is I'll double it. In fact I'd like to rent you for the rest of the night. You're obviously gorgeous and very hot, and best of all you seem to be pretty intelligent as well. But we both know what you are, so how much is this going to set me back?"

"Excuse me?" GiGi said as her eyes flashed at him dangerously. "I don't know what you think this is, but I can't be bought. I'm not some call girl you can rent with a few measly fucking bucks! I'm sorry to disappoint you."

"Oh really?" Will said as he laughed right in GiGi's face. "So you're the high-class fancy type, huh? Come on! Let's not play games. You look a little worn around the edges but I'm sure you'll clean up just fine. Of course you were thinking that you could somehow get to know me long term and get into my pockets, right? Fatten me up for the kill, huh? Listen, darling. Just come outside to my car for fifteen minutes and bob your head and make yourself a quick hundred bucks. That's probably all you're worth anyway."

GiGi sat there frozen for a few seconds, staring at him to see if this was some sort of sick joke. But Will's smug mug was unflinching and his half-drunk eyes were dead-ass serious.

"See there, Will," GiGi spit between her teeth as all the rage from the past forty-eight hours flooded her bloodstream and threatened to consume her. She slid her hand into her purse and clutched her baby .380 pistol and fought to restrain herself. She was dying to blow a clean hole in this bastard's snobbish face so bad that she could already taste his blood. "You obviously don't know who you're fucking with. You picked the wrong whore this time, so I'm going to give you about five seconds to get the fuck out of my sight before you make me redecorate this entire bar with your sorry ass. Please move the fuck along now. I'm finding it so hard not to do something that only one of us will live to regret."

"Yeah, right," Will stood up like he was about to excuse himself from the table. "Used-up chicks like you come a dime a dozen, and I can buy as many of you as I like. I think you need a time out, sweetheart. And maybe a spanking too. Your mouth is filthy."

Chuckling, Will picked up his half-empty glass of liquor and flung it right in GiGi's face, then tossed a couple of dollars on the table before walking away.

His coworkers laughed loudly from the bar as GiGi sat there in total shock. Her face and hair were wet and she smelled like brandy. Murderous thoughts flashed through her mind and she trembled in her seat, not from the embarrassment but from the complete and utter fury that threatened to consume her.

Relax, GiGi, she talked herself down. *Just relax, okay? Take your hand off the gun. If you kill this bastard it will only satisfy you for the moment and you've got much bigger fish to catch. Just get the fuck outta here before you tweak the hell out!*

Moments later she stood up and wiped her face and hair with the small square of a bar napkin, then calmly walked past the hooting men and left the bar without looking back. She was feeling pretty proud of herself as she headed toward her car. She was the resilient sort. Sure, she stumbled a few times and made some mistakes, but she was a professional and setbacks were to be expected in her line of work. GiGi Molinex lived by her own terms and bounced to her own beat, but she knew one thing for sure, and two things for certain: She was damned good at getting her payback, she never forgot a face, and she never forgave a foe. Sooner or later, if God didn't get to him first, GiGi would make Will Tatum pay for that drink he had thrown on her. Pay with his life.

This was the state of darkness and revenge that GiGi's mind was in as she approached her vehicle. She was so hell-bent on future retribution that she failed to pick up on the cues, and when the man came up silently behind her and smiled as he stepped in front of her, she was startled.

"Hello, there," the handsome man dressed in a dark blazer said quietly. "I saw what happened just now in the bar, and I want you to know that I went over and had a few strong words with that guy."

"Oh yeah?" Gigi replied with a shrug as she went to unlock her car door. "Some people are just natural born assholes, but karma is the best cure in the world. Thanks for setting him straight, but what goes around will most definitely come back around."

"You're absolutely right about that," the man said with a smile. "As a matter of fact, Georgia, my friend Larry sent me here to deliver his own batch of karma."

GiGi froze.

"What did you just call me?"

Stark fear pulsated through her from her face to her gut, and GiGi couldn't mask her horror at hearing this stranger call her by her real name. She looked back toward the bar and saw that bastard Will approaching them at a fast, determined clip. By the time she reached for her gun it was too late. She opened her mouth to scream and something came down hard on the back of her head. GiGi crumpled like the life had been knocked out of her and a warm blanket of unconsciousness drifted down covered her up.

"Throw that bitch in the trunk!" she heard Will command, and that was the last damn thing she heard before the light went dark and she passed out cold.

CHAPTER 35

God was good all the time, and Selah was a joyful witness to that.

In desperation she had broken down and called her sister one last time and confessed to what was really down there buried in the ashes of their mother's funeral urn. She had expected Safa to brush her off and give her the cold shoulder again, but instead her sister was merciful and kind to her. She hadn't mailed her back the urn like Selah had asked her to, she had gone even further. She'd flown down to Texas and personally brought it back.

And now, the house was quiet as Selah pulled on a pair of latex hospital gloves and snapped them over her wrists. The last time she had worn such a pair she'd been scrubbing shit off of ol' Wally Su's deathbed, but today she was going in on the plastic for a whole 'nother reason. She opened up the pretty purple vase with the shimmering gold butterflies etched on the surface and grimaced as she peered inside.

"It's your mama, stupid," she muttered, chastising herself under her breath. "It's the body that bore you. The womb that carried you into this world."

Selah frowned. Yeah, the funny-colored pile of dust was all that. That was true. But it was also the key to her future too. A future that depended on her getting right with Viceroy and reclaiming the shattered pieces of her marriage.

Taking a deep breath, she plunged her hand inside and wiggled her fingers around. She couldn't believe that it had come down to this. To her having to sift through the bones of her dead mother in order to save her marriage, but that's exactly what she was doing. She dug down into the corner of the urn and her finger struck something hard. Eagerly, she grasped it and brought it up to the surface, and held it in the air.

"Got it!" she laughed as she shook the ring twice and then blew the dust off of it, scattering tiny particles in the air. "Oops!" Selah giggled some more. "Sorry about that, Mama!"

Replacing the lid on the urn Selah carefully cleaned the ring off with a damp cotton swab, then removed the ring that was on her finger and replaced it with the original gift from her husband.

She stared at her hand critically, admiring the ring with tears in her eyes. Yeah, it had only cost a million bucks back in the day, and it was smaller and less fabulous than the second one that Viceroy had given her, but this one meant much more to her. It meant so much more.

Picking up her cell phone, Selah took a photo of her bejeweled hand and texted it, along with a smiling picture of her and Safa, to her husband. He was coming home today and so was she. She wasn't about to go back out to the pool house and she wasn't leaving her home either. No, sexy Selah Dominion was going to be a real freak in the sheets for her husband tonight. All that neck-cracking, toe-curling sex that Ruddman had laid on her was a thing of the past. There would be no hardcore street-fucking going on in her bed tonight. There'd be time for that later. Nope, tonight was gonna be all about making love. Sweet, sweet love. With the only man that mattered in her life. The only man she had ever really wanted. Her homey. Her lover. Her husband.

"Please, Mr. Dominion," the petite Hispanic nurse pleaded. "Try to relax yourself. Your blood pressure is very elevated and we've given you the maximum amount of medication that we're allowed. If it doesn't come down soon I'll have to call the doctor and ask him to cancel your discharge orders for today. I'm sure you're eager to go home, and I bet if you would just close your eyes and get a little rest your blood pressure would come down on its own."

Viceroy ignored her. He was fully dressed and laying in his hospital bed frowning up at the ceiling with a pulse beating in his temple that just wouldn't stop. His nerves were wrecked and his mind was racing all over the damn place, which was why his blood pressure had shot up sky-high. He was ready to go home, but he knew what he was walking into. A divorce! Selah and Rodney Ruddman. All these years. All these god-damn years! He had been played like a straight-up sucker and there was no denying it. His bullet wound was well-healed but every time he thought about fucking behind the one person he hated above all else in this world, his blood pressure shot even higher and the nurses came running.

And it was all Selah's fault.

She had come up there with her trifling tears and endless lies, swearing on her dead mother's grave that she had never betrayed him, but Viceroy knew better. His lawyer was on the case now, and he didn't care how loud Selah cried or how long she begged, he was through with her ass and that was final.

"Mr. Dominion?" His security guard poked his head through the door. "You have a visitor, sir."

Viceroy scowled and shoo'd him off. "I told you I'm going home today and I don't want no goddamn visitors! Whoever it is, send them away."

"Viceroy!" he heard Selah yell from the hall. "Viceroy,

please! Let me in, dear. I have good news! No, I have *great* news! Come on, honey. Let me come in so I can share it with you."

Viceroy's eyes bugged out as he sat up in the bed and pointed his finger at the guard and snarled, "You get that crazy bitch away from my door and you get her away right goddammit now! How many times I gotta tell your ass the same damn—"

"Viceroy!" Selah pushed past the guard and burst into his room holding her hand in the air and smiling from ear to ear. "Look, baby! My ring! I found my *ring!*"

Viceroy turned his glare on his wife as the million-dollar shine he'd bought her when he was a young pup glinted from her ring finger.

"What?" he sneered with his lip turned down. "You paid somebody to make you another one?"

The smile dropped off Selah's face and her whole mug crumpled. "No!" she wailed. "How could you say such a thing? This is my ring! The ring *you* gave me. The one that you placed on my hand! I found it, Viceroy. I got it back, baby. I got it back!"

"Oh yeah? Where'd you suddenly get it from? A Cracker Jack box?"

"No," said a voice from just beyond the doorway.

The security guard threw his hands up helplessly as yet another beautiful woman pushed her way into Viceroy's room. His mouth fell open and his blood pressure went all the way through the damn roof as his gorgeous sister-in-law Safa walked into the room. That last time he'd seen her he'd been snatching his dick out of her mouth, and all the shame and remorse of that moment washed over him as he choked on his words.

Safa walked over to his bed and stared at him with calm, clear eyes and said, "Hello, Viceroy. Long time no see."

Viceroy's voice was thick with guilt and he could barely look at her as he muttered under his breath, "What in the world are you doing here?"

"I came to give my sister her ring back," Safa said simply.

"She'd left it at my house the night before she caught me and you . . . the day that you and I were in your office and I was . . . the day Sable was kidnapped. I finally worked up the courage and the nerve to face Selah and beg for forgiveness, so I decided to deliver it in person. So, if you were wondering where her ring was all these years, I had it. Her ring was with me."

Dy-Nasty mighta been down but she damn sure wasn't out. She was giving it one more try, but this was gonna be her last damn time fuckin' with these fools and no matter how bad she wanted part of Mink's trust fund she wasn't about to beg that chick too much longer. Mink had hit her up on Facebook talking about how they really were twin sisters and that's why they looked so much alike and had the same DNA. Dy-Nasty had laughed her ass off. She knew who her mama was so she wasn't tryna hear that crazy shit. The only thing she was interested in hearing about was a payday, but even after talking that sister noise Mink still wasn't trying to budge up off a dime.

Saying to hell with Selah's warnings to stay away from the family, Dy-Nasty had busted up in the mansion demanding a share of Mink's inheritance, and now her and the whole damn crew were standing toe-to-toe in the living room going at it hard.

"You need to stop frontin' witcha fake-ass self, Mink! You came down here for the same damn reason I did. To get *paid*! The only reason you standing up here talking that bullshit is because you suckin' from that sweet trust fund pipe! If these mofos hadn't'a paid you your ass would still be stealing from them!"

"Yeah, okay, Dy-Nasty, I guess I gotta believe it that me and you was once bunkies who shared the same womb, but whatever! You might be my twin but you ain't never gonna be no sister to me! And yeah, you right. Both of us came down here to get up on some cash, and I can admit that. But I've *changed*! It don't matter to me no more if I have a dime, I'm happy with my life, boo! The Dominions showed me how a family is supposed to do it, through thick and thin, baybee! They opened their arms and took me in, even knowing full well that I was a hustler and trying to gank them as hard as I could. Even though they knew I was grimy and couldn't be trusted with nothing that wasn't nailed down, they still loved me, get it? And because I'm your sister and me and you got the same DNA, I'm gonna love you too. But I'ma love your trifling ass from the other side of the world, so you can just squeeze your ass on out the door and take your funky-tail right back where you came from!"

Every eye in the joint was aimed at her but Dy-Nasty didn't care. "All y'all fake-ass mothafuckas can go somewhere!"

"Nah, banana-fana," Bunni jumped in and said hotly. "*You* can go on with all that noise! Now scat along on them kick-stand heels of yours, boo-boo! You ain't gotta go back to Philly, but you gotta get them critter-ass feet the hell up outta here!"

Barron stood back quietly while all the drama went down. With Mink and Dy-Nasty posted up nose-to-nose in their battle stances it was easy to see that there was a whole lot alike about them, but when you looked real close it was also easy to see that in the ways that really counted they were nothing alike at all.

"Hey, darling," Peaches called out to Dy-Nasty sweetly as he blew on his lemon-lime fingernails and fanned his hands in the air. "How you getting to the airport, hon? You want me to call you a donkey or a mule? Either way you need to drag them ashy heels on the ground and scrape the crust off them feets!"

Dy-Nasty tooted up her lips and gave him a look so shitty it funked up the whole damn room.

"Who *you* need to call is a fuckin' shrink, you confused mothafucka, you! You got all them titties on your chest and a

dick taped down to your balls! Don't worry about calling nobody for me. I already called Ray and I got my own damn
ride!"

Dy-Nasty gave her twin one last look and said, "I'ma get
your ass back, Mink. We ain't no damn twins, *liar*! Couldn't no
sister of mine be so ugly and so damn dumb! You better watch
your back, *thot*, cause this shit ain't over yet."

And with that, the scraggly Philadelphia con artist whirled
around to leave.

"Don't let the doorknob stab you in the ass on the way
out!" Barron barked.

Dy-Nasty didn't even miss a beat. Instead, she reached back
and grabbed a hefty hunk of her ass cheek and hoisted it toward Barron, letting him know where he could kiss it for her.

With fire in her eyes and her lip poked out, Dy-Nasty
pranced her ass across the threshold and slammed the front
door hard enough to break out all the windows on the first
floor. But her anger disappeared real damn fast when she saw
the whip that was waiting for her in the driveway.

"Oooh!" she squeaked, pushing past the doorman and
running over as the driver got out and held open the back
door. "All this for lil ol' me? This shit is *niiiice*! This shit is real
nice!"

It was a brand-new ebony-shine stretch limo with tinted
windows and rims out the ass. Dy-Nasty got inside and slid
her happy ass into the cool, shaded interior of the whip as the
smell of fresh leather and fine luxury filled her nose.

"You like?"

Dy-Nasty glanced at Ray, who was sitting against the opposite window with a bright smile on his chubby face.

"You damn right, I like! I didn't know you was rolling like
this at work, Ray-Ray!"

The limo took off and Dy-Nasty reached into her bra and
pulled out a spliff. She sparked it up and took a few pulls, then
passed it to Ray so he could get his head right too. They rode

down the streets of Dallas puffing and chilling, chugging liquor and balling hard. Dy-Nasty was so busy getting lifted that she never even noticed where they were going, and minutes later when they pulled into a posh private driveway lined by tall trees and colorful flowers and shrubs, Dy-Nasty bucked her eyes open wide and gave Ray the stupid look.

"What we doing here? I thought we was going back to your crib?"

Ray grinned as the limo pulled into a clearing that revealed a joint so grand and spectacular that if you sat it next to the Dominion Estate they would match up neck and neck.

"*Oooh!*" Dy-Nasty exclaimed as she grinned up at the huge crib and her beady eyes took in all the finery and magnificence. Her mind was clicking like a calculator as she added up the digits on the Porches and Bentleys and whatnot that were parked out front. The driver jumped out and came around back, and Ray helped her from the limo and walked her up to the front entrance, where a chick stood waiting in the doorway with one hand on her narrow hip and a slight smile on her red painted lips. She was wearing a shimmering champagne-colored Vera Wang knee-length shift and her sleek black hair was gathered up in a swirling bun.

"Boss lady, this is the one I told you about," Ray said politely like he was standing in the presence of royalty. "Her name is Dy-Nasty Jenkins and she's the twin sister of Viceroy and Selah's daughter, Mink. I believe the kind of insider information Dy-Nasty has about the Dominion family is going to be instrumental in helping us achieve our success."

The woman smiled with pleasure and a cunning look glinted in Ray's eyes as he completed the introductions.

"And Dy-Nasty Jenkins, this here is my boss. The lovely Miyoko Rose Su."

CHAPTER 36

Ruddman sat in his spacious office nursing a hot cup of coffee and brainstorming on his next move. A pair of detectives had just left his office, pissed off and disappointed that Ruddman still could not remember a single detail about the person who had shot him. They'd warned him that it would remain an open case and tried to make him feel guilty about having a dangerous gunman on the loose, but it was nothing they could say that would make him bite the rat cheese on Zeke Washington. No, he'd take care of that young buck in his own way and in his own time.

Ruddman sipped from his coffee and frowned as he laced his short fingers behind his neck. The morning paper was on his desk and the headlines showed a picture of Viceroy Dominion leaving the hospital with his beautiful wife, Selah, by his side.

Ruddman stared down at the picture with all sorts of thoughts running through his mind. On the surface he should have been living like a king and sitting high on the hog. His oil empire was airtight and he had all the money and fame he could ask for. But something vital was missing in his life and when he looked at the picture on the front page it was obvious what it was.

Selah.

He wanted that bitch Selah. Sure, he could have a chick delivered or pick one up off the street to satisfy his fantasies and fetishes, but those weren't the type of women he wanted. He wanted Viceroy's wife. Selah Ducane Dominion.

The photographer had captured an expression of pure adoration on her face as she walked out of the hospital gazing up at her husband, and Ruddman knew that look all too well. He'd seen it on her face when she looked up from sucking his dick, and after all the intimate moments they'd shared together it enraged him to see her playing her wifely role so well.

"Trifling bitch," he muttered under his breath, staring at the photo of her holding Viceroy's hand and pretending everything was all good for the cameras.

Ruddman snorted. She could fool a lot of people but she couldn't fool him. He knew her. He knew every curve and every mark that she possessed on that pretty little frame of hers. A woman like Selah's rightful place was on a throne beside a true boss. A boss like him. Viceroy was a mere pawn, and Ruddman was going to burn his entire organization to a crisp and walk off with his queen. Sooner or later the whole world would see which black oil man in Texas was the biggest and the strongest. They'd see which one of them had the balls to hunt, kill, and persevere.

Rodney stood up from his desk and penguin-walked his large body as fast as he could toward the door and made his way down to his security office. He had studied the *Art of War* from cover to cover on multiple occasions and it was time to implement some of the same tactics that Sun Tzu had made famous. Because there was no doubt in his mind that he was locked in a vicious battle with Viceroy Dominion, and this shit was far from over.

"Mr. Ruddman!" the startled young secretary dropped a donut she was chewing and stood up abruptly from her desk. It was rare to have the chief CEO pay an unannounced visit, but here he was standing right in front of her.

"Mirinda," Ruddman said curtly as he entered the security office of Ruddman Energy where his chief of cyber networks worked. "Tell Fred Hatcher I'm here."

"Yes sir, Mr. Ruddman," Mirinda answered, scrambling to come out from behind her desk. "I'll get him out here right away, sir. "

Ruddman stepped deeper into the guts of the security operations center and gazed around at all the apparatus. He had some real state-of-the-art shit going on, with the kind of top-tier technology that could make the FBI jealous. Years ago Rodney had taken the advice of one of his geek friends and begun amassing and integrating intelligence into his work systems. He had outfitted his headquarters with rooftop high-tech video cameras that captured everything and everyone that approached Ruddman Energy from a six-block radius. At the time, Ruddman had figured he was too old to be fooling around with computers, but he'd still had the foresight to see the direction the world was moving in and to try to stay ahead of the game.

A few moments later the brain behind Ruddman Energy's security team walked out of a meeting and approached his boss with a smile.

"Good day, sir," he said pleasantly. "Miranda said you wanted to see me?"

"Yes," Ruddman said with a cunning smile. "I need you to find something for me."

Hatcher grinned. He was a tall skinny computer geek who Ruddman paid handsomely for his services and he was worth every dime. He'd been allotted a tremendous operating budget and since the entire video system was Hatcher's baby, he probably knew what was on every inch of tape. "Sure. What are you looking for?"

"Some footage taken right outside of the hotel," Ruddman explained, rubbing his hands together in anticipation. "Footage that was captured several months ago. I know the exact time and the exact date."

"Sure, Mr. Ruddman," Hatcher said as he went to a console and his fingers started flying all over the keyboard. "I'll get right on it."

He got himself dialed in and made sure his software access was on point, and when Ruddman gave him the date and time he pulled up a series of images on a wide screen and began scrolling through them.

"So what exactly are we looking for, by the way?"

"Look for me," Ruddman said coldly. "You're going to see a beautiful woman walk out and then you'll see me following her. We'll pause about halfway down the walk and talk and then you'll see her . . ."

Ruddman's voice trailed off as Hatcher advanced the footage in slow motion.

"There!" Ruddman barked as he saw what he was searching for. "Yes," he chuckled darkly. "Right there."

Hatcher paused the footage and stared at the monitor.

"She slapped you, sir," he said incredulously. "It looks like that woman just slapped you."

The sounds of glee that escaped Ruddman's mouth was enough to make a killer's blood run cold.

"Yes she did," the cunning Texas oil man growled in satisfaction as he pressed rewind and watched the beautiful Selah Dominion slap the living shit out of him for kissing her on her neck. He couldn't wait to send Viceroy this special little gift. "Yes the fuck she did."

Watching the exchange on rewind again, Rodney couldn't even hide the grin that spread over his face from ear to ear. This shit wasn't over yet. In fact, it was far from over. He was going to light a real big fire inside the house that Viceroy had built, and then he'd sit back and see exactly who came running up out of the flames.

Life at the mansion was looking better than it ever had before. A monstrous weight had been lifted from Viceroy's shoulders, and everything around him seemed more colorful and pure. Today he was hiding out in his lavishly padded media room and pigging out in his nice comfy chair. He rarely ever had a chance to kick back and enjoy his favorite foods without being hounded about his health, but he was cramming as much sugar and salt down his throat as he could today.

Dressed in a pair of navy blue Versace pajamas and some matching velvet slippers, Viceroy leaned over a jam-packed serving table in front of his projector screen and stuffed his face like a fat kid at an all-you-can eat buffet. He had sent a private message to the Dominions' chef, who had secretly delivered him some burger sliders, shrimp tacos, caramel popcorn, fried baloney sandwiches, Ritz crackers with jelly, grape quarter waters, and a bunch of other stuff that Viceroy was craving from his childhood in the tough ghettos of Houston.

He was right in the middle of gnawing a chicken bone down to the gristle when the door creaked open and Selah walked in.

"Busted!" she said, her eyes tinkling as she laughed.

"How did you know I was up here, Selah?" Viceroy demanded, anticipating her wrath when she saw the size of his greasy spread. "See now, I came up here to mind my own business and try to relax. I'm like a hungry dog right now, baby, I'ma snap if you take my bowl. I don't wanna eat them pretty little fingers of yours so don't bring them over here."

"I didn't come in here to take your food away, honey," Selah said as she sat down next to him carrying a plate piled high with fried wings, some ranch dressing, and a tall can of Arizona ice tea. "I came to join you."

"What the hell are you over there eating, woman?" Viceroy

said in shock. "Is that chicken from Boscoe's in the hood? I haven't seen you scarf those babies down in years! I know they used to be your favorite. What happened to that strict diet that you so diligently stick to?"

"The hell with all that for now," Selah said as she smiled and stripped a wing down to the bone with no etiquette whatsoever. I've been denying myself the things that I like for far too long. With all the mess that's been going on in our lives lately I think I deserve to get my eat on a little bit. Besides, you only live once, right?"

"Damn right! So why you ain't order me none with ya selfish-ass self?" Viceroy said playfully. "Shit, pass me one of them thangs. I think I just might buy the whole damn restaurant. Why didn't I think of that before?"

"Well, we've been so focused on growing the company that we didn't have time to think about anything else," Selah said as she passed Viceroy a few wings and some sauce. "Sometimes we have to remember the little things, you know? It seems like the stuff that used to bring us joy when we were broke are the things that have given us the best memories."

"You're right about that," Viceroy said as he sipped from Selah's iced tea and pondered what she had just said. "Believe it or not, sometimes I wish I was still hungry and hustling. I mean I hated having light pockets, but I think I appreciated things more." Then he quickly added, "I wouldn't have traded my money away or nothing like that because I didn't want the kids to go through the same things that I did."

"You're only human, baby," Selah responded as she wiped her mouth and grabbed Viceroy by the hand. "You are our provider. Our rock. The king of our kingdom. Being wealthy has its own challenges but it's nothing compared to where we came from and where we could still be today. If we can survive living life at the bottom then we damn sure shouldn't let anything at the top tear us apart."

Viceroy nodded and accepted Selah's embrace. The police

had never found out who it was that had shot him, but after questioning dozens of witnesses they had determined that it definitely wasn't Selah. Viceroy wasn't surprised. Deep in his heart he knew Selah was down for him. She loved him with all her soul, and if all the wealth he had amassed just up and fell apart, Selah would be right there with him to help rebuild his shit penny by penny. And that was the kind of loyalty that a fortune, even one as big as Viceroy's, couldn't buy. He grabbed the remote control and clicked on the projector.

What Selah saw on the screen almost brought her to tears. It was old footage of their family back in the days when they first moved into the mansion. The kids looked so young and happy. They ran around in the front yard like chickens. Viceroy and Selah looked so damn proud and excited that they had arrived.

"Oh my God, Viceroy," Selah gasped. "Where did you find this? I haven't seen these tapes in so long. Look at us! We were so young. This seems like forever ago."

"I know," Viceroy said. "I was going through some boxes and I pulled it out of the stash. Life has been moving so fast for us that it's good to take a step back and revisit some of the beginnings. It puts things in perspective and let's us really see how far we've come."

As they watched their home movie the Dominions held hands and smiled as they enjoyed their trip down memory lane. They laughed together as the kids made funny faces and fell down too hard and cried. It felt good to be able to bond with each other, and both of them were enjoying the healing that was coming down on their marriage. Yes, they were one of the most powerful families in the nation. Yes, they were richer than shit. Yes, they'd given each other good reasons not to trust each other. But right now they were just Viceroy and Selah, captured in a moment together and being reminded of all the reasons they'd fallen in love in the first place.

Viceroy leaned closer to his wife and kissed her on her

temple. "I'm sorry for all the times I hurt you, Selah. I'm sorry I even so much as looked at your sister, let alone touched her. I can't deny that I did it, but I can guarantee you that I've never touched another woman ever since. Can you ever forgive me?"

Selah sighed. "Of course I can. Like I said, you're only human, baby. All of us are. We're born to make mistakes in this world. It's how we recover from them that counts."

Viceroy nodded and waved his hand. "Enough of this! No more Ruddman, no more Safa. I want us to put this whole thing behind us and move forward in our lives, Selah. So I'm going to ask you this one last time, and no matter what you tell me, I swear to God I'll never bring it up again."

"Anything, baby," Selah said solemnly. "You can ask me *anything* you like and I give you my word that I'll tell you nothing but the God's honest truth."

"Did you *ever* sleep with Rodney Ruddman?"

Selah paused for a second, and then she looked her man right in the eye and opened her mouth and said,

Oh Rodney! Yes! Fuck me, baby! Pound me with your long black dick!

She closed her mouth and then opened it once again, and then she did what all good liars do.

"Listen, Viceroy, I want you to know that never in my *life* would I stoop low enough to consort with that atrocious bastard Rodney Ruddman! I've never even been alone in the same room as that asshole or so much as touched him in my life. I mean, look at him! He's hideous! In fact, if I had ever gotten within arm's length of that bastard I wouldn't even slap the shit out of his funny-looking face. So, no!" she said clearly and emphatically. "*Hell*, no. I never, *ever* slept with that troll, I've never touched him, and his little gorilla hands have never touched me either! The answer is no!"

Viceroy sighed with relief as he gathered his woman in his arms and stroked her hair with big-time love in his hands.

"I don't know how I could have ever doubted you, baby. I'm sorry. I'm so damn sorry."

Selah pressed her face into his neck and inhaled his $1,700 cologne and smiled like a cat who had just licked up a whole bowl of cream. How in the world could he ask her some shit like that? Of course she had lied! What the hell did he expect? Selah Dominion was stone cold with her shit, and that's what liars do!

CHAPTER 37

Months had passed since Gutta had kidnapped Mink and damn near killed her, and a whole lot had changed in the Dominion household. For one thing, Mink and Suge had finally come out of the closet with their relationship and they couldn't have been any happier. Today their engagement party festivities were in full swing and Suge couldn't remember the last time he had grinned so goddamn much. He had chartered a bunch of limos to bring his hood family from Houston up to Dallas, and he'd sent the Dominion Diva down to pick up the elders who were too old to ride for long hours cooped up in a car.

Little kids were running around having a great time and good old soul food was being served by uniformed staff from the kitchen. The weed was flowing, the brew was icy, and the weather was picture perfect outside as damn near everybody he loved gathered in the Dominion backyard to give him and Mink their blessings.

Suge was glad as fuck that the cat was finally outta the bag because he wasn't the hiding type and it had been exhausting as hell trying to keep his love life with Mink under wraps. It had taken him a minute to go all out and make that proposal, but after that belt buckle his baby bought him had deflected that bullet and saved his life, Suge had said fuck the world and decided to publicly declare his love for Mink regardless of who didn't like it.

He wasn't surprised to find out where his brother Viceroy was coming from.

"Look, nigga," Viceroy had told him, "Mink is my baby, and for twenty years I couldn't do shit for her. I mean, I didn't know where she was, if she was being taken care of, if she was being mistreated, or if she was even alive. There ain't nobody in this whole goddamn world that I trust more than I trust you, Suge, and if Mink's with you then I know goddamn well she's gonna be straight. I know my baby is gonna be protected, she's gonna be provided for, and she's damn sure gonna be loved. Because that's what Dominion men do. So God bless both of y'all, man. I hope y'all live long and fuck a lot!"

But Selah had come out of a different bag. She thought the relationship was too close for comfort and would be frowned upon by the public, and she wasn't feeling it. She told Viceroy that Mink was vulnerable and Suge was a certified ladies' man, and Viceroy laid it down on her real quick and put it in terms that she could understand.

"Let me ask you something," he said clicking off the remote control. They were laying in bed watching a Netflix show, and instead of paying attention to the damn plot Selah was tossing and turning beside him running her mouth about the upcoming engagement party for Mink and Suge.

"When that oil rig blew up and I was so fucked up that y'all didn't know if I was gonna make it, who was the one person you knew you could turn to and count on without a moment's hesitation?"

Selah frowned but her answer was quick and it was honest. "Suge."

"Damn right. And if I go out here tonight or tomorrow and jump my black ass off a cliff and break my damn neck, who is the one muthafucka you know you can trust to make sure that you and all of these trifling-ass kids of ours will be taken care of even if it costs him his last damn breath?"

"Suge," Selah said. "That would be Suge."

"And if I pulled out my pistol and aimed it at your head right now, which one of Mink's boyfriends would you trust to jump in front of you and take that goddamn bullet?"

The answer was a whisper. "Suge."

Viceroy nodded. "You goddamn right. Hell, I bet you trust my baby brother even more than you trust me. So why in the world wouldn't you want our daughter to have a man like him standing beside her in this crazy world? You think there's some stray nigga out there who can do better for her than he can?"

Selah sighed, feeling silly as fuck. Of course not. There was no other man in the world who was as loyal and fierce as Suge Dominion. Not even his brother Viceroy. Hell, when she thought about it like that then Mink was lucky as hell. She had snagged herself a prize-winning horse and she'd never even stepped foot inside a stable.

"Congratulations, bro," Viceroy said as he walked up behind Suge and clamped a hand down on his brother's massive shoulder. "You got that ring ready, right?"

Suge nodded. He'd picked out a gem that was gonna blow Mink's mind.

"I remember how good it felt when I gave Selah her first ring. It was amazing, and after all these years I'm glad she has it back. Now y'all hurry up and set a wedding date so you can take Mink, Bunni, and that goddamn Peaches up outta my house. I've got love for those New York nutcases but they're your problem now."

Suge and Viceroy shared a laugh as they watched the Dominion family and friends eat, drink, and get real funky and merry. A feeling of joy was in the air, and after everything the family had been through over the last few months they finally had a reason to smile.

"Hey, Daddy," Mink said as she walked up and hugged Viceroy. She was a vision of loveliness in her simple cotton shift dress and designer sandals. "Can I borrow my future husband for a few minutes, please?"

"He's all yours, darling," Viceroy said. "When you're done with him I want you to run your ass over there and tell your uncle Blue to stop drinking up all the goddamn Hennessy! Give that fool some Erk and Jerk and let the rest of the family get a chance to taste the good stuff. Long neck muthafucka!"

Mink and Suge held hands and cracked up as they watched Viceroy head toward a large white tent to join Selah and his aunts.

"That is one solid nigga right there," Suge said as he pulled Mink close in arms and kissed her on the forehead. "You sure you ready for this, girl?"

"Of course I am, baby," Mink said, grinning like crazy as she looked up at her big teddy bear.

"I already told you. It takes a lot to be my woman. The time for little girl games is over. When you step off in this I'm gonna need you to step right, okay? And I promise. I'll be by your side the whole damn way and I'll never let you fall."

Mink melted into him and pressed her cheek against his rocked-up chest. "I'm ready. I swear I am. I'm just glad we don't have to keep all them secrets no more and I'm especially happy that even with all the craziness I've had in my life you still love me and want me in yours. For real, Suge, I've spent so much time tryna figure out ways to beat the game and gank the system that it feels strange not to have to hustle like that anymore. I mean, I did get put up for adoption at birth and then kidnapped by my fake mother and driven into a cold-ass river to drown, so I had some fucked-up luck along the way too, but now I really believe that it's my time to shine."

"Damn right it is," Suge said as he smiled back at his lady. "And I promise you won't nobody ever hurt you again, Mink. I swear on that shit. You got a real man now, so no more hus-

tling, no more pain, nothing but living the fine life and enjoying the best that money can buy every single day. You won't
ever have to watch your back and you'll never be alone. We're
gonna leave the past in the past, and every day we're gonna
wake up to a future that just gets better and better. You just
watch and see."

"Can I have everyone's attention please," said Tevin Mark.
He was a locally known comedian and musician on the rise
who grew up with Suge and was hosting the ceremony. "I'd
like to propose a toast to my main man Suge and his lovely
bride-to-be, Miss Mink LaRue. May God bless you both on
your journey together."

Fluted champagne glasses were lifted in the air, and Peaches
and Bunni jumped up and clinked two beer bottles together
loudly then turned them shits up and guzzled like crazy. A roar
of laughter broke out and rolled over the lawn, but before it
could die down a commotion could be heard coming from inside the house that grabbed everyone's attention.

"You got a warrant?" Journey Haggar, the Dominions'
chief of security barked as him and three armed guards burst
out of the back door surrounded by a crew of heat-packing
Texas Rangers. "We all got guns, bitches! But do y'all muthafuckas got a warrant?"

The Rangers ignored him as they rolled out twelve deep
onto the veranda and started rushing toward the grass.

"Get your hands up!" one of the officers screamed through
a bullhorn. "Everybody get your goddamn hands up!"

The troopers stormed through the crowd, and when they
spotted their target they zeroed in and swarmed on his ass,
converging down on him like a nightmare.

"Superior Dominion!" the lead detective ordered as Suge
stood perfectly still with an expression of calm control on his
face. "I've got a warrant for your arrest! Put your hands behind
your back, Mr. Dominion. We're taking you in."

Flanked by Journey and his boy Blue, Viceroy got up in the detective's face like he was about to rip that shit off.

"Who the fuck are you and what the hell is going on here? You've got the wrong damn house and the wrong damn man! A warrant for his arrest? For what? Signed by who?"

The detective was polite but firm. "The warrant is for first-degree murder and the improper disposal of a corpse. It was signed by the Honorable Judge Anthony G. Matthis."

The entire backyard exploded in complete outrage and the Houston relatives started getting ghetto with it and reaching for their own tools. Mink hollered out loud and then broke down cying as she jumped on Suge and clung to him with her arms wrapped tightly around his neck. Two cops grabbed her gently as three others slapped the cuffs on Suge, and Selah ran over to hold her daughter and lead her away.

"Muthafucka," Viceroy stepped back up on the detective in charge and pointed his finger in dude's face, "If you came up in my house with some bogus shit I will come after your ass and bury you, do you hear me? Suge, don't you say a goddamn word to these bastards and don't you worry about a thing. We'll be rolling out right behind you, trailing these bastards all the way down to the precinct, and we're coming inside to get you."

The high spirits of the backyard party were now angry and hostile. The Houston fam was ready to get stupid and turn shit out, but Big Suge never even flinched. He kept a cool head and cooperated with the officers, even though as a betting man he knew the wins rested with the Dominion posse right now. Ere' last one of the men in his family was strapped, and so were half of the ladies, to include his ninety-two-year-old auntie. If they wanted to get it popping they could spark it off, but for what? He was a pro at this shit. A certified muthafucka whose job it was to sweep dirt away from the Dominion doorstep. He knew exactly what this case was about and he wasn't pressed in the slightest.

He had done his job and done it well. It was no secret that

the dead chick had been in the Dominion poolhouse, but when they got to the heart of it all the threads would unravel and the authorities would be left with exactly what the fuck every last one of them working on this case had started with.

A dead body and nothing else.

But the question was, who was the muscle behind this shit? Who had pushed for it and lit a fire underneath it? Suge didn't know, but he was sure he'd find out. As his family wilded out and got ready to turn the fuck up, he chilled harder than a muthafucka. And as he was allowing the officers to lead him toward the house, Suge turned around and gazed at Mink as she broke down and cried.

That ain't how we do it, Mrs. Dominion.

He didn't have to say a word. He spoke to her using the connection between his eyes and her heart, and he was damned proud when his baby girl read him loud and clear.

Immediately Mink straightened up in Selah's arms and pulled herself together.

Yeah, that's it.

She wiped all them tears away and raised her chin a little bit, and then she stood tall and strong on her own two feet.

Suge grinned a little bit as he winked at her and blew her a kiss, and then he was gone. Whisked in the back door and through the house, and then whisked right out the front door and into a squad car.

They had sent about ten cars to pick him up, and Suge's knees were damn near in his chest as he stuffed himself in the backseat and the lead detective climbed behind the steering wheel. They were pulling into the driveway single file when a black stretch limo came up from behind and pulled up alongside the police vehicle.

Suge stared as the back window went down and he locked eyes with a gorgeous woman with red painted lips and up-swept hair.

Pow! She mouthed as she made a gun out of her hands and aimed it right at Suge.

Pow! Pow! Pow! she jerked her index finger three times, pulling the imaginary trigger.

Peals of laughter exploded from the woman's mouth and the look on her face was one of total elation. Suge held her gaze as she reached out and flipped him the bird, extending her long, manicured middle finger in the air and thrusting it toward the sky in a real obvious manner.

Fuck you, Suge Dominion! Fuck you!

Lil Bit, the name exploded in Suge's mind. *Miyoko Rose Sue.*

She laughed again and her lying eyes were hard as stone. And colder than hell.

Well ain't this some shit, Suge thought as Miyoko grinned and rolled up the window on her sparkling stretch whip. *This bitch done set me up. She done set me up real good!*

To be continued . . .

STONE COLD LIAR

Noire

About This Guide

The suggested questions that follow are included
to enhance your group's reading of this book.

Discussion Questions

1. Life is one great big misadventure in *Stone Cold Liar* as the Dominion family evolves to accept its new members and their roles. How do you think Mink is adjusting to life as a member of a filthy-rich fam? Has anything about her changed?

2. Once again Barron Dominion allowed his little head to think for his big head. What's behind his fatal attraction to GiGi Molinex, and what do you think he should have done when she pulled that gun on him?

3. Big Suge is the family closer. How do you think his loving Mink and wanting to have a relationship with her has affected his ability to do his job?

4. Gutta was a greedy killer who warned Mink not to cross him. Since Mink really did do all the foul things to him that he said she did, was it only right that he came to Texas to take a big bite outta her ass?

5. Pilar might have been raised in the suburbs, but she is just as dirty or even dirtier than Mink and Bunni. What do you think about the way she got her ass out of a jam and got Mink into one? Do you think she really believed she was putting Mink in danger?

6. Pilar's ex-boyfriend Ray ended up on the shiesty end of the stick. Did you see that one coming? Who do you think he was working for, and do you think he has the heart to get dirty and nasty with the Dominions and to try to take them down to the mat?

7. Dy-Nasty is still not feeling all that twin-sister shit Mink is talking. She doesn't believe it, not one bit. Since their mother and father are both dead and they missed out on being raised together, do you think her and Mink should try to start over from scratch and build a sisterly relationship?

8. Selah Dominion is a scandalous liar down to her bones. Could you have dug your hand down in that urn to get *anything* back?

9. Viceroy blamed Selah for shooting him. Do you think his instincts are right not to trust her? He's pretty loud about accusing her of messing around with Ruddman, but what do you think Selah should have done when she caught him messing around with her sister?

10. Safa Ducane paid a visit to Texas to see her sister Selah and to help get her out of a jam. Could you have forgiven a close family member who did what Safa did, or is it unforgiveable to cross some lines?

Noire's

Misadventures of Mink LaRue series

Available wherever books and ebooks are sold.

Natural Born Liar

What happens when beautiful, twenty-year-old petty thief and ex-stripper Mink LaRue finds out she's a dead ringer for the age-progressed photo of the missing oil heiress Sable Dominion?

Harlem-born Mink LaRue makes a beeline to Dallas, Texas, pretending to be the Dominions' long-lost daughter, Sable. But it's not long before Mink's newfound siblings grow suspicious of the ghetto princess, who has a rap sheet a mile long. If Mink is to worm her way into their pockets and get her hands on their dough, then she must tell enough lies to convince everyone that she really is the precious daughter who was stolen from their fold. But with a DNA test standing between her and a hefty inheritance, how long can Mink's bag of lies keep her rolling in the Dominions' riches?

Sexy Little Liar

She seduced Texas's richest oil family out of a fortune. But now petty thief and ex-stripper Mink LaRue has a rival for the ultimate temptation . . .

Dirty Rotten Liar

When con-mami Mink LaRue joins forces with her slick-tongued look-alike Dy-Nasty Jenkins to run a hustle on the super-rich Dominion oil family, what can possibly go wrong?

Red Hot Liar

She's an heiress to a mega-fortune. But expert con-mami Mink LaRue will have to go beyond the top of her game to win the biggest hustle of all . . .

Coming in December 2015

Games Women Play
by Zaire Crown

In this fast-moving, gritty debut novel, one woman learns that even the strictest rules are made to be broken . . .

The Bounce House was not one of those inflatable castles parents rent for children's parties. It was a small gentlemen's club set in a strip mall on 7 Mile with a beauty supply store, a rib joint, an outlet that sold men's clothing, and an unleased space that changed hands every few years. In no way was The Bounce House on the same level as some of the more elite clubs in Detroit; with a maximum capacity of two hundred and fifty and limited parking, it would never be a threat to The Coliseum, Cheetah's, or any of the big dogs. It wasn't big, but it was comfortable and well-managed, plus the owner was very selective in choosing the girls, so this had earned it a small but loyal patronage.

The owner, Tuesday Knight, knew that Mr. Scott, her neighbor and owner of Bo's BBQ, would be waiting in the door of his shop the moment her white CTS hit the lot. The old man had a crush on her and always made it his business to be on hand to greet her whenever she pulled in to work.

She frowned when she saw that someone had parked in her spot right in front of The Bounce House. The canary Camaro with the black racing stripes belonged to Brianna, and

she was definitely going to check that bitch because she had
been warned about that before.

Since all the other slots outside The Bounce, Bo's BBQ,
and KiKi's Beauty Supply were taken, she had to park way
down in front of the vacant property, and she speculated about
which business would spring up there next. In the past five
years it had been an ice cream parlor, a cell phone shop, and an
occult bookstore. She wished its next incarnation would be as
a lady's shoe outlet that sold Louboutins at a discount.

She shrugged the Louis Vuitton bag onto her shoulder
then slid out of the Cadillac.

Up ahead on the promenade, Mr. Scott was standing in
front of his carry-out spot pretending to sweep the walk but
really waiting for her. This was practically a daily ritual for
them.

"Hi, Mr. Scott," she said, beaming a smile.

He did an old-school nod and tip of the hat. "Hey, Miss
Tuesday, you sho lookin' mighty fine today." He always called
her Miss Tuesday even though it was her first name.

"Thank you, Mr. Scott. You lookin' handsome as always."

He removed his straw Dobbs hat and was fanning himself
with it even though the afternoon was mild. "Girl, if I was
thirty years younger, I'd show you somethin'!"

"I know you would, Daddy! You have a nice day now,
okay?"

She strutted by him, and since her jeans were particularly
tight today, she threw a little something extra into her walk
and made the old man howl: "Lord, have mercy!" Mr. Scott
was seventy years old and had always been respectful of her
and all the dancers, so she didn't mind putting on for him. Plus
the harmless flirting made his day and got her free rib dinners.
When Tuesday reached the door of the club, she turned back
to give him another smile and coquettish wave.

What The Bounce House lacked in size it attempted to
make up for in taste. There was nothing cheap about the place

even though it was a small independent establishment. The design wasn't unique: a fifteen-foot bar ran against the far right wall, a large horseshoe-shaped stage dominated the center with twenty or so small circular tables surrounding it, booths were lined against the left wall and wrapped around the front, the entrance was where that front wall and the right one intersected, and the deejay booth was next to it.

Before Tuesday had taken over, the entire place was done in a tacky red because the previous owner thought that it was a sexual color. The bar was a bright red Formica that was peeling, the stools and booths were done in cheap red leatherette, the floor was covered in pink and red checkered tile, and the tables wore these hideous black and red tablecloths with tassels that made the place look like a whorehouse from the '70s. Tuesday had brought the place into the new millennium with brushed suede booths, a bar with a granite top, more understated flooring, and mirrored walls that gave the illusion of more space. She even gave it a touch of class and masculinity by adding dark woods, brass, and a touch of plant life.

When she came through the door, the first thing that jumped out at her was that the fifth booth hadn't been bused. There were half a dozen double-shot glasses on the table, an ashtray filled with butts and cigar filters, and a white Styrofoam food container that had most likely come from Bo's. She knew that it was her OCD that caused her to immediately zero in on this, but before she could start bitching, one of the servers was already headed to clean it up. Everyone who worked there knew their boss had a thing for neatness, so she shot the girl a look that said: *Bitch, you know better!*

Things were slow even for a Monday afternoon. There were only three customers at the bar, with eleven more scattered throughout the tables and booths. Most of them were entranced by a dancer named Cupcake, who was on stage rolling her hips to a Gucci Mane cut. Two more girls were on the floor giving table dances.

Whenever Tuesday came in, on any shift, her first priority was always to check on the bar. The bartender on duty was a brown-skinned cutie named Ebony who had started out as a dancer then learned she had a knack for pouring drinks. She took a couple classes, became a mixologist, and had been working at The Bounce since back in the day when Tuesday was just a dancer.

Ebony called out: "Boss Lady!" when she saw her slip behind the bar.

Tuesday pulled her close so she wouldn't have to compete with the music. "Eb, how we lookin' for the week?"

From the pocket of her apron Ebony whipped out a small notepad she used for keeping up with the liquor inventory. "What we don't got out here we got in the back. We pretty much straight on everythang, at least as far as makin' it through the week, except we down to our last case of Goose."

Tuesday made a mental note to send Tushie to the distributor.

Ebony asked, "How dat nigga A.D. doin'?"

"He all right. Reading every muthafuckin' thang and workin' out. That nigga arms damn near big as Tushie's legs."

"When was the last time you holla'ed at em?"

Tuesday scanned the bar, quietly admiring how neat Ebony kept her workstation. "Nigga called the other day on some horny shit. Talkin' 'bout, 'What kinda panties you got on? What color is they?'" she did a comical impersonation of a man's deep voice. "Nigga kept me on the phone for a hour wantin' me to talk dirty to 'em."

Ebony poured a customer another shot of Silver Patron. "No he didn't!" she said, smiling at Tuesday.

"So I'm tellin' him I'm in a bathtub playin' with my pussy, thinkin' bout his big dick. The whole time I'm out at Somerset Mall in Nordstrom's lookin' for a new fit."

"T.K., you still crazy!" Ebony was laughing so hard that she fell into her. "The funny part is, he probably knew you was lying and just didn't care."

"Hell yeah he knew I was lying, A.D. ain't stupid. But when I know that's the type of shit he wanna hear, I always tell 'em somethin' good."

"That nigga been gone for a minute. When he comin' home?"

Tuesday's smile faded a bit. She hated when people asked that question, especially when most of them were already familiar with his situation. A.D. was doing life, and a lot of times people asked her when he was coming home just for the sake of gauging her faith and commitment to him. If she said "Soon" she looked stupid when the years stretched on and he didn't show, but if she said "Never!" it looked as if she'd just wrote the nigga off. Her and Ebony had been cool for a long time, and she didn't think that the girl was trying to play some type of mind game, but the question still bothered her.

As much as she hated being asked about A.D., it happened so often that over the years she had come to patent this perfect response: "He still fighting, but that appeal shit takes time." This way she doesn't commit herself to any specific date while still appearing to be optimistic.

Ebony nodded thoughtfully. "Well, next time you holla at 'em, tell that nigga I said keep his head up."

Tuesday left from behind the bar agreeing to relay that message.

She was crossing the room by weaving her way through the maze of tables on the floor when suddenly: *whack!* Somebody smacked her on the ass so hard that it made her flinch.

At first Tuesday thought it was some new customer who didn't yet know who she was, and just as she turned around ready to go H.A.M., she realized that it was her big bouncer DelRay.

DelRay was six foot seven and close to four hundred pounds.

He was heavy but didn't look sloppy because it was stretched out by his height. He also knew how to handle himself, possessing a grace and speed rarely seen in men his size. DelRay could be very intimidating when the job required it but by nature was a goof ball. While he had the skills to deal with unruly customers physically, he had the game to get most of them out the door without making a scene. This was what Tuesday liked most about him.

She said, "Nigga, I was about to flip!"

"We at four!" he yelled over the music. Lil' Wayne was playing then.

She shook her head. "Hell naw, nigga, we at five!"

He used his thick sausage-like fingers to count. "Two Saturday night, one Sunday before you got in your car and one just now." He grinned and rubbed his hands together like a little kid eager for a gift. "I get to smack that fat muthafucka six more times!"

"Fuck you!" she said but with a smile. Actually she knew it was only four.

He teased her. "Don't be mad at me, you should be mad at yo boy Lebron! When it get down to crunch-time he always choke."

Tuesday was a diehard Miami Heat fan who swore that she was going to suck Dwayne Wade like a pacifier if she ever met him in person. At the time Miami had the second-best record in the Eastern Conference, so when they came to Auburn Hills to play a struggling Pistons' team, dropping a hundred on them seemed like a safe bet. After the Heat lost in overtime, the bouncer asked his boss if he could trade that bill she owed him for the right to smack her on that juicy ass ten times. Tuesday had no interest in fucking DelRay, but they were cool like that so she agreed.

"That's all right though," she fired back. "I still like Miami to win it all. Yo weak-ass Pistons ain't even gone make the playoffs."

"Give us two more years to draft, we gone be back on top again!"

Changing the subject, she asked, "I saw Bree's car out front, but is the rest of 'em here?"

DelRay nodded. "Everybody but Tush. Jaye in the locker room skinnin' them bitches on the Poker. Bree and Doll in there with her."

"Tush will be here in a minute, I already holla'ed at her. But go tell the rest of them bitches I'm in my office."

"I got you, Boss Lady."

Just as she turned to walk away: *whack!*

She whipped around trying to mug him, but DelRay's fat face made one of those goofy looks that always melted her ice grill. "I'm sorry, Boss Lady, I couldn't help it. You shouldn't have wore that True Religion shit today. You in them mutha-fuckin' jeans!"

She jerked her fist like she was going to punch him. "Now we at five!"

"You wanna bet back on Miami and Orlando?"

"You ain't said shit, nigga, I ride or die with D.Wade! But if you win this time, goddammit, I'm just gone pay yo heavy-handed ass."

DelRay lumbered off toward an entryway at the left of the stage and parted the beaded curtain that hung over it. That hall had three doors: One was for a storage room where all the extra booze and miscellaneous supplies for the bar were kept; the second was the locker room, where the dancers changed clothes and spent their downtime in between sets; the third, the door at which the hall terminated, was a fire exit that led to the alley behind the strip mall. DelRay went to the second door, knocked three times, then waited for permission to enter.

An identical hall ran along the opposite side of the stage, only this one did not terminate in a fire door. It was where the restrooms were located, and just beyond them was a door stenciled with the words: Boss Lady.

Her office was a modest but tidy space that was only fifteen feet wide by twenty feet long. It had a single window with only a view of a garbage-strewn alley. There was a cheap walnut-veneered desk holding a lamp and a computer, a small two-drawer file cabinet, two plastic chairs that fronted the desk, and an imitation suede love seat given to her by a friend. The most expensive thing in the office was her chair: a genuine leather high-back office chair ergonomically designed for perfect lumbar support; it cost over fourteen hundred dollars, more than she had spent on her computer. The office also came with a wall safe that Tuesday never kept any cash in. Other than the above-mentioned items, there was nothing else in the way of furniture or décor. Tuesday didn't have anything hanging on the walls, and no framed photos were propped on her desk to give it a personal touch. She stepped into her spartan little space and closed the door.

Tuesday had spent twenty-one years at The Bounce House—ten as a dancer, four as a manager, and seven more as owner—but whenever she walked into the office her mind always flashed back to that first time she had stepped into it. She was sixteen years old, expelled from all Detroit public schools, a runaway crashing at a different friend's house every night, and desperate for money. She had an older cousin named Shameeka who danced there, but at the time the place was called Smokin' Joe's. Because Tuesday was light-skinned, pretty with green eyes, and a banging body, Shameeka swore she could earn enough money for her own car and crib in no time. So led by her favorite cousin, a young and naïve Tuesday was brought in and walked to the door of this office. Shameeka handed her a condom then pushed her inside like a human sacrifice to a sixty-two-year-old bony Polish guy whose name, ironically, wasn't Joe. There was an eight-minute pound session in which he bent her over the very same desk she still had, then fifteen minutes after that Tuesday's new name was X-Stacy and she was on the floor giving out lap dances for ten dollars a pop. The old man never asked her age, or anything else for that matter.

She dropped her bag on the desk and sank into her favorite chair. She thought about what his place had given her, but mostly all that it had taken away.

She was snapped from her reverie when the door swung open. Jaye came in, followed by Brianna, and Tuesday immediately cut into her: "Bitch, how many times I got to tell you to stay out my spot?"

Brianna responded with an impudent smirk. "It wasn't like you was using it. Shit, we didn't even know when you was gone get here."

"The point of havin' my own parking space is so that I'll have a place to park *whenever* I pull up at the club. I don't give a fuck if I'm gone three weeks, when I roll through here that spot right in front of the door is me! Every bitch who work here know that shit, even the customers know it."

Brianna took a drag off the Newport she was smoking then flopped down on the love seat. "Well you need to put up a sign or somethin'."

"I don't need to put up shit!" Tuesday barked. "The next time I come through and you in my shit I'm a bust every muthafuckin' window you got on that lil weak-ass Camaro!"

Brianna shrugged nonchalantly and blew out a trail of gray smoke. "And it ain't gone cost me shit if you do. 'Cause like a good neighbor State Farm will be there . . . with some brand-new windows."

Tuesday pointed a finger at her. "Keep talkin' shit and see if State Farm be there with a new set of teeth!"

Jaye quietly witnessed the exchange with a smile on her face. She took one of the plastic chairs that fronted the desk.

Just then Tushie came in rubbing her ass with a sour look on her face.

Tuesday laughed. "DelRay got you too, huh? Was it that Miami game?"

She poured herself into the second chair. "Naw, you know fucks wit dat sexy-ass Carmelo Anthony," she said with her heavy southern drawl. "New York let da Celtics blow dem out by twenty."

Tuesday asked, "How many he got left?"

Tushie thought back. "He done got me twice already, he only got three left."

"You only gave that nigga five, he got me for ten! How my shit only worth ten dollars a smack and yours worth twenty?"

Laughing, Jaye said. "Maybe because she got twice as much ass!"

Tuesday shot back at her. "And I still got three times more than you!"

After sharing a laugh she then said, "We can settle up soon as Doll bring her ass on." Tuesday looked to Brianna. "I thought she was with y'all. Where the fuck she at?"

"How the fuck should I know!" Brianna snapped back at her. "Just because the bitch little don't mean I keep her in my pocket!"

Baby Doll came in as if on cue and closed the door. She snatched the cigarette out of Brianna's mouth, dropped onto the love seat next to her, and began to smoke it.

Brianna said, "Ughh, bitch. I could've just got finished suckin' some dick!"

Baby Doll continued to drag the Newport unfazed. "Knowin' yo stankin' ass, you probably did. Besides, my lips done been in way worse places than yours."

Baby Doll took a few more puffs then tried to offer it back to Brianna who rolled her eyes and looked away. "Bitch, I wish I would."

Tuesday handed her an ashtray. "Well now that everybody *finally* here, we can take care of this business."

This was the crew: Tuesday, Brianna, Jaye, Tushie, and Baby Doll. Five hustling-ass dime pieces with top-notch game who was out for the bread. Individually they were good but together they were dangerous. These were the girls who played the players.

Tuesday looked at Baby Doll. "You get yo shit up outta there?"

She butted what was left of the Newport and blew the last of the smoke from her nostrils. "The little bit I had being moved today. I only brought *what* I needed for the lick—just enough to make it look like home. It ain't like him and Simone spent a lot of time chillin' at her crib anyway. We either went out or was chillin' at his loft."

Code name: Baby Doll. She was only four feet eleven inches tall, with hips and ass that stood out more because of her short stature. Her buttermilk skin always looked soft even without touching it. Delicate doll-like features had earned her her name and made her age hard to place: if Doll told a nigga she was thirteen or thirty, he would believe either one. The type of men who typically went for Doll had low self-esteem and loved the ego boost she gave them; her small size and the helplessness they wrongly perceived in her made them feel bigger and stronger while that child-like naïveté she faked so well made them feel smarter. Baby Doll's greatest asset was her bright hazel eyes because she could project an innocence with them that made men want to protect and possess her. It was because of this that, of the five, Baby Doll was second only to Tuesday in having the most niggas propose marriage to her.

Tuesday asked, "What about Tank?"

"He don't think nothin' up," said Doll. "He done spent the last two days blowin' up that phone and leaving texts for Simone. Of course he thinking that lil situation done scared her off. Same shit every time."

Tuesday nodded. "Good. Text his ass back and break it off. Tell him you thought you could deal with his lifestyle but after what happened you can't see being with him—"

She cut her off. "T.K., I know the routine! I ain't new to this shit."

"Make sure you lose that phone too," Tuesday reminded her. "How did he feel about that loss he took?"

Doll shrugged. "He wasn't really trippin' bout the money and he say he got insurance on the truck so he gone get back right off that. He was just so happy that ain't nothin' happen to me."

"That's 'cause you his Tiny Angel!" Jaye said, teasing her. "'All right, I'll open the safe. Just don't hurt my Tiny Angel.'" She did a spot-on impression of Tank's pathetic voice that made them all laugh.

Code name: Jaye. She was five foot nine with a medium build. She wasn't that strapped, but her face was pretty as hell; she had dark brown eyes, a cocoa complexion, and big full juicy lips that promised pleasure. Jaye was not the stuck-up dime, she was the ultimate fuck buddy. She was that fine-ass homegirl you could hit and still be cool with. Staying laced in Gucci and Prada heels, Jaye was a girly girl but had some special tomboy quality about her that made a nigga want to blow a blunt or chill with her at a Lion's game. She was cool, she was funny, and could easily make a mark feel at ease with her sense of humor. Her best asset was her personality but Jaye's secret weapon was her amazing neckgame. She sucked dick like a pornstar and the same big lips that got her teased in school were now her sexiest feature. Not too many niggas could resist a bad bitch who kept them laughing all day then at night gave them the best head they ever had.

"I know the type of nigga Tank is," said Tuesday. "He gone be suckerstroking real hard about you." She looked at Baby Doll. "Lay low for a while and you might wanna do something different to yo hair. Trust me, this nigga gone be stalkin' you for a minute."

While they spoke Brianna just quietly shook her head with a look of disgust on her face. "I know having to get next to some off-brand niggas is part of the game, but god damn, Doll, you a better bitch than me. That fat, black, greasy-ass nigga with them big bug eyes—I don't think I could've pulled this one off." She jerked forward pretending to dry-heave, then put a hand over her mouth. "How could you look that nigga in the eye and say you love him with a straight face? Just thinkin' about that nigga kissing and touching on me got me ready to throw up."

Doll looked at her sideways. "Bitch, like you said, it's part of the game, that's what we do. I'm playin' his muthafuckin' ass the same way you done had to play niggas and every other bitch in this room. I don't give a fuck what a mark look like, I'm about my paper!"

"Church, bitch!" Tushie leaned over so her and Doll could dap each other.

Brianna leaned back on the love seat and inspected her freshly polished nails. "Well, I guess I just got higher standards than you bitches."

Code name: Brianna. She was six foot one with the long slender build of a runway model except for her huge 36DDs. Bree had that exotic look that came when you mixed black with some sort of Asian. Like the singer Amerie, she had our peanut butter complexion and thick lips but had inherited their distinctive eyes. Nobody really knew what Brianna was mixed with—Tuesday didn't even think she knew—but whatever she was, the girl was gorgeous. The type of men who were attracted to her were typically looking for a trophy. They liked rare and beautiful things and had no problem with paying for them. Brianna played the high-maintenance girlfriend so well because acting snotty and spoiled wasn't really a stretch.

Tuesday told the girls that they needed to work on their

choreography. She felt that it didn't look real enough the other night when Brianna pretended to hit Baby Doll with the gun. "Y'all timing was off. Bree, you looked like you was just tryin' to give her a love tap. And Doll, you looked like you knew it was comin, you was already going down before she could hit you."

Brianna responded the way she typically did to criticism. "Why is you trippin'? The shit was good enough to fool him."

"I'm trippin', bitch, because we can't afford to make mistakes like that. Small shit like that is what could get us knocked."

"Watch this." Tuesday stood up and came from behind her desk. Tushie rose from her seat knowing that she had a role in the demonstration.

The girls squared off then pretended that they were two hoodrats in the middle of a heated argument: they rolled their necks, put fingers in each other's faces and Tushie improvised some dialogue about Tuesday fucking her man. They pushed each other back and forth then Tushie gave Tuesday a loud smack that whipped her head around. She held her cheek, looking stunned for a second, then came back with a hard right that dropped Tushie back into her chair.

She fell limp with her head dropped against her chest unconscious but two seconds later she opened her eyes and smiled. "See, bitches, that's how it's done."

Code name: Tushie. This Louisiana stallion was five foot seven, and while she only had mosquito bites for breasts, her tiny twenty-four-inch waist and fifty-six-inch hips meant she was thicker than Serena Williams on steroids. "Tushie" was the only name that had ever fit her because by thirteen the girl was already so donked up that all her pants had to be tailor-made; by fifteen she was causing so many car accidents from just walking down the street that the police in her small town actually labeled her a danger to the community. Her Hershey bar skin and black Barbie doll features made her a dime even without being ridiculously strapped. Despite having an ass like two beach balls, Tushie's best asset was really her mind. Many people had been fooled by her deep southern accent but she only talked slow. Tushie knew how to play on those who thought she was just a dumb country bammer and rocked them to sleep. Any nigga thinking she was all booty and no brains would find out the hard way that southerners ain't slow.

Jaye was impressed by the girls' little fight scene. The moves and timing were so perfect that it looked as if they had spent time training with actual Hollywood stunt men. Jaye was only a foot away from the action, and even though she knew it was fake, she still thought that their blows had made contact. "Wait a minute," she said curious. "I know she ain't really just slap you but I swear I heard that shit."

"What you heard was this." Tuesday clapped her hand against her meaty thigh. She explained: "Because I'm the one gettin' hit you lookin' at my face and her hand. You ain't watching my hands! Me and Tush just got this shit down because we been at it longer than y'all."

"Well, I ain't gone go through all that," Brianna said, standing up to stretch. "Next time I'm just gone bust a bitch head for real!

"And now can we wrap up this little meeting so I can get paid and get the fuck outta here? I got shit to do."

Tuesday went into her Louie bag and pulled out a brick of cash. She carefully counted it out into five separate stacks then began to pass out the dividends. As the girls took their individual shares, Tuesday could see the disappointment on their faces. They were expecting more and she was too.

She passed two stacks to Doll, who took one then handed the other to Brianna. Bree made a quick count of the cash then dropped the sixty-five hundred onto the love seat as if it were nothing. "What the fuck is this?"

Tuesday sighed because she knew this was coming and knew it would be from her. "Look, I know it's kinda short. Shit fucked up all the way around. I got twenty for the truck, seventeen for the work, and my mans said I was lucky to get that."

After doing two months of surveillance on Tank, Tuesday had put Baby Doll on him. It took another seven weeks of Doll's sweet manipulation to get everything they needed for the lick: personal information, alarm codes, copies of his house keys, the location of his stash, and a head so far gone that he wouldn't risk Doll's life to protect it. The girls had hoped for a big score but found out that Tank was not the hustler they thought he was. The scouting report said that he was heavy in the brick game and the team targeted him expecting at least a six-figure payoff, but when they opened fat boy's safe all he had was forty-two thousand in cash and twenty-four packaged-up ounces of hard. Disappointed, the girls took his Denali even though it wasn't originally part of the plan. They split the cash that night but it was Tuesday's job to slang the truck and dope; now the girls didn't even get what they hoped for that. Minus what was due to their sixth silent partner, almost four months of work had only grossed them a little over thirteen racks apiece—if you factored in the expenses of renting a temporary place for Doll's alter ego Simone and the Pontiac G6 she drove, they actually netted a lot less. The team typically went after bigger fish, and while they only did about five or six of these jobs a year (and sometimes had a few going on at once), they were used to making twenty-five to thirty stacks each, so a lick that only pulled seventy-nine total was a bust.

Tuesday leaned back against her desk. "Look, ladies, I know shit ain't really come through how we wanted on this one. That's my bad but I promise we gone eat right on the next one." She took the blame because as leader of the group the responsibility always fell on her.

Code name: Tuesday, aka Boss Lady. Tuesday was light-skinned, five foot nine, and thick. She didn't have junk like Tushie but her booty was bigger than average and had been turning heads since puberty. Aside from a pretty face and juicy lips, she had cat eyes that shifted from green to gray according to her mood. Tuesday had put this team together and was the brains behind it. She realized when she was just a dancer that clapping her ass all night for a few dollars in tips wouldn't cut it for a bitch who had bills and wanted nice shit. At nineteen she started hitting licks with A.D., and after he went away, she continued on her own. Over time she recruited Tushie, then slowly pulled in the others. Each of these girls had come to The Bounce just as broke and desperate as she had been, and Tuesday saw something in each of them that made her think they would be a good fit for the team. Tuesday's best asset was her experience. She had years on every other girl in the group and none of them could crawl inside a mark's head better than she could. She gave them all their game and therefore had each of their skills. She knew how to make a read on a nigga and adapt to the type of girl it took to get him. She could play the innocent square better than Doll, the cool homegirl better than Jaye, and the high-maintenance trophy bitch better than Brianna. She could play one role to a tee or blend a few of them together if it was necessary. Her strength was that she was not one-dimensional like the others. Tuesday's secret weapon was actually her secret weakness. None of the girls knew she suffered from obsessive compulsive disorder. Her illness caused her to reorganize things over and over until they were perfect. Her nature, which was to obsess over every little detail, did make her a neat freak, but also the ultimate strategist. Tuesday had a way of seeing all the moves ahead of time and putting together airtight plans that accounted for every problem that might arise.

"He only gave you twenty for the truck, rims and all?" Bree asked with some skepticism in her voice that everybody heard.

Tuesday nodded. "He said he couldn't do no better than that."

"You know that was the new Denali right? That's at least a fifty-thousand-dollar whip."

Tuesday frowned. "It's a fifty-thousand-dollar whip that's *stolen!* You thank he gone give me sticker price for it?"

Brianna shrugged and studied her nails again. "I don't know. Just seem like you got worked to me. Either that or somethin' wrong with yo math!"

That made Tuesday stand up straight. Every other woman in that room felt the sudden shift in the vibe as her eyes quickly changed from lime-green to icy gray. "Bitch, is you tryin' to say somethin'?"

Bree didn't retreat from her stare. "All I'm sayin' is that we done put in a lot of time for a punk-ass thirteen Gs! If you figure it all out we basically got a little over three thousand a month. A bitch can get a job and do better than that!"

"The lick wasn't what I thought it was and I apologized for that." Tuesday inched closer to her. "But when you got to talkin' all this bullshit about my math, I thought you was tryin' to hint at somethin' else. So if you got anythang you wanna get off yo double Ds about that, feel free to speak up!"

Jaye and Doll just sat there silent because they both knew what Brianna had tried to insinuate and knew that Tuesday had peeped it.

Tushie was quiet too but she was more alert. She knew Tuesday better than anybody and she knew if Brianna said the wrong thing that Tuesday was going to beat her ass. The girl was just tits on a stick and Tushie figured Tuesday could handle that skinny hoe alone, but Doll and Bree were tight. Jaye fucked with Brianna too even though Tushie didn't know how cool they were. She was getting ready just in case she needed to have Tuesday's back.

The tension that swelled in the room seemed to have distorted time, so after a second that felt much longer Brianna tucked her tail by looking away. She snatched up the money and threw the straps to her Fendi bag on her shoulder. "Well if we ain't got no more business then I'm out." She pushed off the love seat and started for the door. "Doll, if you wanna ride you betta come on!"

Just as Baby Doll got up to follow, Tuesday called out to Brianna. She paused to look back just as she grabbed the knob.

"You done got you a lil' Camaro, a couple purses, and some shoes and let that shit go to yo head. You the same broke bitch who pulled up in a busted ass V-Dub Beetle three years ago beggin' for a job, the same bony bitch who used to be out there on the floor looking all stiff and scared, barely making enough to tip out. I pulled you in, gave you the game, and got you together. Bree, don't forget that you came up fuckin' with me, you ain't make me better."

To that all Brianna could do was roll her eyes.

"But if you ever decide you don't like what we doin' in here, that door swing both ways." Tuesday looked around, making eye contact with each of them except Tushie then added, "And that go for everybody!"

"Is you finished?" Brianna tried to redeem herself from getting hoed out earlier by trying her best to look hard again.

Tuesday just waved her off. "Bitch, beat it."

Bree left out the office with Doll right on her heels. Jaye got up too but threw Tuesday a *we're still cool* nod before she dipped.

When Tushie got up and went to the door it was only to close it behind them. She smiled, "I thought you wuz bout to whup dat bitch."

"I was. She did the right thang!" Tuesday went behind her desk and fell back into her chair. "I don't know where this bitch done got all this mouth from lately but she startin' to talk real reckless. If she keep it up, what almost happened today is definitely gone happen soon."

Tuesday dug into the inside pocket of her bag and pulled out a quarter ounce of Kush that was tied in a sandwich bag. She passed the weed to Tushie along with a cigar because her girl rolled tighter than she did.

Of the team, Tushie had been down with her the longest and been through the most shit. Even though she was five years younger they were tight, and if Tuesday were ever asked to name her best friend, there was no one else more deserving of the title.

Back in the early part of '05 that ass had already made Tushie a legend in the New Orleans strip clubs. Magazines like *King* and *BlackMen* were calling her the new "It girl," and for a while rappers all over the south were clamoring to have her pop that fifty-six-inch donk in their videos. She had milked that little bit of fame into a brand-new house and a S550 Benz until Katrina came along and washed it all away.

Then she found herself living in Detroit and having to start from scratch. Tushie featured in a few clubs and because she still had a strong buzz, she was the most sought-after free agent since LeBron James. All the big gentlemen's clubs were shooting for her and as bad as Tuesday wanted her, she didn't think she had a chance. She quickly learned that this country girl had a sharp business mind because Tushie agreed to come dance at the struggling little spot that Tuesday had just bought, but only if she made her a partner.

Tuesday was leery at first but it turned out to be the best decision she ever made. When Tuesday took over The Bounce House it was losing money faster than she could earn it but when Tushie the Tease became a regular featured dancer all that turned around. She was like a carnival attraction as niggas from as far as New York came to see if she could really walk across the stage with two champagne bottles on her ass and not spill a drop or clap it louder than a .22 pistol. The club was packed like sardines whenever she performed and within months The Bounce House was turning a decent profit. Tushie kept the place jumping for five years, until she finally hung up her thong and retired from the stage.

Single-handedly saving the club made her a good business partner, but years of loyalty and her down-ass ways made

Tushie a good friend. Tuesday trusted her so much that she put her up on how they could make some real money together: by robbing niggas who couldn't report the losses.

Tushie finished rolling the blunt, lit it, and took her first three hits. She was passing it across the desk to Tuesday when she spoke in a voice strained from the smoke in her lungs: "I already know you gone talk to Dres 'bout dis shit."

Tuesday accepted the weed with a nod. "Hell yeah," she said in between puffs. "I'm on my way to do that soon as I leave here. I'm damn sure 'bout to find out why he sent us on this dummy mission."